THE SILENT STREAM

THE SILENT STREAM

NIGEL DUCK

Chalk Stream Books

1

The Question of a Chance Encounter

I opened the book at random and read:

Can you accept
the part of you
that doesn't accept
yourself?

The words were in dark green ink in a style of calligraphy suggestive of a medieval manuscript. They were framed by an intricate pattern in shades of orange and green. I glanced up at Aldo, then read the question again.

* * *

It was the summer of 1998. The school in Athens where I taught English had closed for the holidays and I was travelling around the Greek islands on my own, trying to come to terms with the latest twist in my life story: my girlfriend had broken up with me. The idea had just been to spend a few weeks apart in the hope that it would help us understand why the enthusiasm seemed to be fading from our relationship, but during this time she had met someone else. I had found out at the end of July when I had gone to see her on Santorini, where she was working for the summer. I had left on the first boat to anywhere, and by late August I had made my way to Amorgos, one of the quieter, lesser-known islands of the Aegean.

Since I was getting low on money, I was sleeping on a beach about half an hour's walk from the port. I didn't have a tent, so I was glad to have found a spot under a stooping tamarisk tree – one of several that had somehow taken root in the sand just a stone's throw from the water's edge. Only a few other people were camping there, and once the last of the daily visitors had left on the little shuttle boat, we had the place to ourselves.

Most of the tents were pitched alongside the stone wall which separated the beach from the surrounding olive groves, but one had been set up at the far end – in the ample shade afforded by the larger of the two rocky hills that flanked the cove. Here, the only approach to the beach was by way of a steep path which was barely visible amongst the mass of bushes overrunning the hillside.

In the late afternoon of my first full day on the island, I set off in that direction to see what lay beyond the hill. I was about three quarters of the way along the beach when it occurred to me that I should have put my trainers on. I thought about going back for them but carried on, hoping I would be able to negotiate the path in my bare feet.

When I came within a few metres of the solitary tent, I caught sight of a young man near the rocks on the other side of it. He was sitting cross-legged on a straw mat with his head bent over a guitar. His hunched shoulders and lean torso were almost the same colour as the faded maroon trousers he was wearing. The tune he was playing sounded like something you would hear on a sitar. I stood still to listen.

The lapping of the waves, the murmuring of the breeze and the tinkling of distant goat bells blended with the notes on the guitar to drown out all the thoughts in my head. I can't be sure how long the moment lasted; it was probably no more than a few minutes, but in my memory it lives on in another dimension.

The steady pulse of nature became more distinct. The guitar playing had stopped. I continued on my way past the tent. The young man looked up and smiled, so I quickly thought of something to say.

'Do you know where that path leads to?' I asked, pointing towards the hill.

He shook his head. 'Anyway, it might be more interesting not knowing.'

I was about to tell him it had been my intention to see for myself where the path went, but as this would contradict my asking about it, I just nodded in agreement. By now I had seen that I wouldn't be able to climb the hill in my bare feet.

'I liked that tune you were playing,' I said. 'It was a bit like Indian music.'

'It's just something I wrote when I was in India a couple of years ago.'

Since I had been to India too, we got into a conversation about our respective travels, and before long I had sat down.

With a seemingly permanent half-smile slightly raising his ruddy cheeks, his face reflected the eagerness of youth, though his words echoed the voice of experience. It was therefore hard to tell how old he was. I guessed he was a few years younger than me. His dark, close-cropped hair highlighted his clear blue eyes, which lit up while he was speaking, as if the events he was relating were taking place in front of us. There was a hint of an accent in his perfect English, but I couldn't place it.

We must have been talking for nearly an hour before we got round to introducing ourselves:

'My name's Jake, by the way.'

'Oh yeah – I'd forgotten about names. I'm Aldo.'

I was going to shake hands, but the moment had passed.

'Do you write lyrics as well?' I asked, seeing a notebook by his feet.

'Sometimes.'

'Do you keep them in that book?'

'No, that's something else.' He averted his gaze.

'I take a notebook with me as well when I'm travelling. I like to keep a record of anything interesting that happens. Or sometimes I just write down what I'm thinking about.'

Aldo offered a nod of approval before sinking back into his thoughts.

'Actually, this isn't mine,' he said, picking up the book. 'Well, in a way it is, since it was given to me ... but it's probably more accurate to say it was lent to me, even though I don't have to give it back to anyone.'

I tried to figure out what he meant.

'Have a look – you might find it interesting,' he said, and handed me the notebook.

It had a brown leather cover and was bound with orange-and-green string. The string extended from a knot on the middle of the spine so it could be wound around the cover. On the front there was a pattern in the form of a question mark. Inside the question mark, the words 'Possibilities Abound' had been inscribed. On the back was a similar design, containing the phrase 'The Mystery of Serendipity'.

I opened it at random.

Can you accept
the part of you
that doesn't accept
yourself?

'What does it say?' asked Aldo.

I read the question to him, but he just looked at me, as if he was trying to gauge my reaction to it.

'Am I supposed to give an answer?' I said.

'Not necessarily. Maybe it's a message for you.'

I glanced at the opposite page.

If you didn't find it so hard
to do nothing,
would you have done anything
you lived to regret?

I flicked through the rough-textured pages. They all had questions on them – each one written in dark green ink in the same style of calligraphy.

'It's quite original, but I'm not sure how interesting it'll be if it's full of questions,' I said, handing the book back to him.

'Would you say the same about your life?'

'It depends how many answers I get.'

'Don't you think the questions you ask can be interesting as well?'

'In what way?'

'Maybe they can give you some clues about who you are.'

'Isn't that something I already know?'

'I don't know,' said Aldo. 'What do *you* think?'

'That I've got to know myself pretty well over the last thirty-three years.'

'And how have you done that?'

'By seeing the way I behave in different situations.'

'Haven't some of those situations involved asking questions?'

I changed my position to relieve the stiffness in my legs. The setting sun was approaching the final stage of its descent and the sea had taken on a darker hue, except for the glittering path of gold stretching out to reach us on the shore. The water was stirred into a flurry of activity; then, once again, it was calm.

'Have you ever tried to go through a day without asking any questions?' said Aldo as he pulled on a T-shirt.

'Why would I want to do that?'

'To see how many you really need to ask.'

I wondered how many questions I had asked in my life that maybe I shouldn't have, and I recalled more than one occasion when my frustration at not getting an answer from someone had blinded me to the fact that they might have been feeling equally frustrated at not knowing the answer themselves.

The lapping of the waves was the only sound as the twilight crept up on our shadows and they sank into the sand. In an instant the sun had slipped out of sight, leaving a trail of glowing embers that gradually dissolved in the encroaching shades of dusk. As the light grew dimmer, the stars began to show themselves, growing steadily bolder in the knowledge they could no longer be outshone by the sun. Before long it was so dark that Aldo's figure was almost indistinguishable from the rocks behind him. I imagined I, too, was merging with the surroundings, so that the waves were now breaking on the shore of my mind.

My thoughts returned to Aldo's book of questions. Could it really contain a message for me? Looking up at the vast expanse of stars, I got a taste of that timeless silence in which all the mysteries of the universe are suspended.

2

Echoes of India

The next morning I woke up at dawn. There was no sign of activity on the beach, just the stirring of the branches above me in the breeze. But the sky was a canvas coming to life: as pale blue soaked through and grew into azure, wisps of cloud took on tinges of rose. The silence of the morning felt different to that of the previous night, when I had been gazing at the stars. Could there really be more than one kind of silence? I drifted back to sleep.

When I woke up again, the picture of daybreak had faded. But I was glad of the extra rest as I had spent most of the night talking to Aldo. We had arranged to go to some ancient ruins later, and since I had plenty of time until then, I decided to walk to the port and get something to eat. I could take the dirt track that led off the beach and weaved its way through the olive groves, rising steadily until it joined an asphalt road which looped inland to enter the port from behind, or I could follow the more scenic but more difficult route along the hilly shoreline. I opted for the less taxing way and set off towards the dirt track, which met the beach about halfway between my spot under the tree and the end where Aldo's tent was.

Passing through the olive groves, I was surrounded by the sporadic chirping of birds. I tried to imagine what they were saying, and wondered if they enjoyed listening to themselves as much as people liked hearing them.

I recalled my conversation with Aldo. I had told him about the break-up of my relationship, and when he had asked how I felt about it, I had taken the opportunity to give voice to some of the thoughts that had been occupying my mind for the last month. But our dialogue had ended up being more of a monologue. I would make sure I let him do most of the talking when we met again. Perhaps I could ask him about his experience of spending his childhood in two different countries: he had told me that he was born in England but had lived in Italy – where his mother was from – since the age of nine, and was now studying psychology in Bologna as a mature student.

I reached the port just after a ship had come in. Smoke billowed out of the funnel, its engines idling impatiently as it waited to set sail again. I sat on a bench in the little square near the harbour to watch the activity. A tanned port policeman in dark glasses was blowing his whistle and directing cars up the ramp while the foot passengers shuffled along the gangways on either side of it.

Most of the new arrivals were waylaid by the group of locals armed with 'Rooms for Rent' signs who had congregated on the quayside. One of the few to escape the clutches of this welcoming party was a fairly tall man of around my age, who came striding towards the square with a hefty rucksack, not quite looking the part in his cut-off jeans and crisp white shirt.

I recognized him from somewhere: the mop of light brown hair, the strong jaw and prominent nose – and that semi-frown of his which made it look as though he was struggling to puzzle something out yet relishing the challenge. Where had I seen him before? As I sat there with my mind on hold, I was gripped by that strangely enjoyable sensation of 'knowing but not knowing' and found myself wanting to delay the moment of recall for as long as possible …

My memory produced a picture of him with a broad grin on his face, sitting opposite me at the breakfast table in a guest house on the island of Diu, in India. That was where I had met him, in January of the previous year. I hadn't got to know him very well because I had been travelling with my girlfriend and my attention had been focused on her, though we had bumped into him several times – the most memorable of them being the day we had rented a motorbike and gone to a deserted beach, only to find he was there too.

He walked through the square and stopped near a phone box to get his bearings. His name came back to me. I got off the bench and approached him.

'Do you want the campsite?' I said.

'I was looking for a room, actually. Do you know where I can find a good cheap one?'

'I'm sure there'll be one here in the port. It won't be as cheap as India, though, Dan.'

'I *thought* I'd seen you somewhere before.'

'I thought you might still be there.'

'That was the plan, but when I'd got through all the diseases in the guidebook I decided it was time to leave,' he said with a chuckle. 'Thanks for letting me have it, by the way – eventually.'

'Have what?'

'The guidebook you were in such a hurry to get your hands on.'

I was embarrassed to be reminded of the incident: one morning at the guest house on Diu I had spotted a guidebook of India on the bookcase and pushed in front of him to get it before he did. I had then kept it in my room for several days without reading it.

While we were talking, a local man in flip-flops pulled up on a scooter. He said he had a vacant room at a good price. Dan was interested in seeing it, so he hopped onto the back of the scooter, leaving his rucksack with me, and was whisked away down a narrow street leading into the cluster of whitewashed buildings that formed the main residential area of the port.

I sat on the kerbside to wait. A bougainvillea flowed over the wall of a nearby garden: splashes of purple leaping out of the surrounding white, their shadows below them creating patches of dappled light.

Within a few minutes they had returned. Dan was happy with the room and wanted to get settled in, so we agreed to meet that evening at a nearby taverna. When he had gone, my stomach gave me a gentle reminder of my intention to have something to eat. I followed the scent of freshly made bread to a bakery down a side street and bought a loaf, then got some bananas and water from a grocery and walked back to the square near the harbour, where I sat down on the same bench as before.

The bench on the opposite side of the square was occupied by three elderly men. While two of them carried on an animated discussion, the other one stared into space, his hands clasped over the walking stick he was leaning on. Between us, a handful of children were playing together, letting out squeals of laughter as they chased each other around. At a nearby café, a young couple were engrossed in a game of backgammon; beneath their table a cat lay curled up asleep.

After I had finished eating, I lingered for a while in this little haven, while all my cares lingered elsewhere …

Walking back to the beach, I was accompanied by a host of images from the time I had spent in India with Efrosyni, my ex-girlfriend: our auto-rickshaw driver using his feet to steer through chaotic traffic on the streets of New Delhi as he turned round to shake hands and wish us Happy New Year; a gaggle of barefooted children in ragged clothes, smiling and giggling as they followed us through the backstreets of Udaipur; a myriad of colourful kites fluttering above the skyline of Jaipur; solitary monkeys skipping across the rooftops at sunset in the holy city of Varanasi; an elegantly dressed man in an orange turban riding an elephant along a beach lined with palm trees in Goa; open countryside as far as the eye could see flashing past the window on a train bursting at the seams with hopeful souls on their way to seek their fortunes in Calcutta; and the gleaming peaks of the Himalayas rising through the clouds in the distance as we stood on the roof terrace of our guest house in Darjeeling after the week-long mists had begun to clear.

Interspersed with these scenes were snapshots of Efrosyni: sitting opposite me on a train with that distant look in her dark brown eyes; lost in thought on the back seat of a crowded bus; gazing out of the window of our room in Darjeeling, trying to will the setting sun to rise; far away from me on a beach in Goa, searching for shells amongst the rocks, her luxuriant curls straying across her face in the breeze.

* * *

Later that morning, my thoughts turned to the book of questions which Aldo had shown me the day before. Although I had found it interesting, I hadn't admitted this to him. It had irritated me that, as far as I could see, his main concern had been to create intrigue around the book: he had said it had been given to him but it wasn't his; then he had said it was more accurate to say it had been lent to him, though there was no one he had to give it back to.

At first I had imagined it must have belonged to a friend of his who had died after lending it to him – in which case it would have been this person's death that had effectively given it to him. Or perhaps it had been the person's family, in that they had let him keep it in memory of his friend. Since I had assumed the book's content to be personal, I had respected his reluctance to volunteer any more information about it. It had then occurred to me that if my idea was right, it was strange that he hadn't dropped the subject when he had had the chance to. I had therefore thought there might be another explanation as to its origin. And when he had suggested I take a look at it, I had figured that was probably the case. But this had made me wonder why he had been so vague about it. Why couldn't he have just told me what it was?

After reading the two questions and flicking through the pages, I had come to the conclusion that the reticence on the part of Aldo had been a ploy to build up my curiosity about his book in order to maximize the effect when its unusual content was revealed – at which point he had no doubt been expecting me to be further intrigued so that this guessing game of his could continue. In the course of our conversation, however, it had become apparent that he had a genuine reason for wanting to share it with me. And later on, when my desire to appear unimpressed had subsided, I had asked him where he had got it from. But once again he had seemed reluctant to give me any details, saying it was a long story and he would tell me some other time. On this occasion I had put his reticence down to my previous show of indifference, and, feeling embarrassed about that initial reaction of mine, I had steered clear of the subject for the rest of the evening.

3

Does a Cloud Have a Home?

In the late afternoon I went to see Aldo. He was sitting on his mat, strumming his guitar. His eyebrows were furrowed in concentration as his fingers embraced the frets. I noticed he had the book of questions beside him. I stood near his tent and waited for him to finish the tune he was playing, then sauntered up to him.

'I'm in no hurry to visit the ruins if you want to play a bit longer,' I said, sitting down on the sand.

'Do you still want to go?'

'Maybe we could leave it for another day.'

'OK, if that's what you prefer.' He put down his guitar.

'What have you been up to today?'

'Not much – playing guitar mainly. How about you?'

'Not much either – apart from thinking.'

'What about?'

'Everything: the past, the present, the future – and your book.'

I waited for Aldo to say something, but he just glanced down at the book.

'I'd be interested to know where you got it from, if you feel like telling me.'

He hesitated. 'Only a few people know about it, so if I tell you, I'd prefer it if you didn't tell the whole world.'

'Don't worry, I'm pretty good at keeping secrets.'

'OK then. As I said, it's a long story, so make yourself comfortable …

'When I was in India, I spent over a week in Calcutta. I was staying at a hotel outside the centre, and one afternoon I went to a restaurant in another part of town. I sat at a table by the window and put my bag on the seat next to me. I was carrying my money, passport and plane ticket in my money belt, and in the bag I had my camera, a map of the city and a book I was reading.'

'Not a book of questions, by any chance?'

'No – it made me ask a few, though, since it was a mystery story … Anyway, after a few minutes a boy brought a jug of water along with the menu. I said he could take the jug back because I was going to have bottled water, but he didn't seem to understand. Another boy was working with him, and he came to take my order. They were both in shabby clothes and can't have been more than ten years old.

'After I'd finished eating, one of the boys came to clear the table. As he reached in front of me, he knocked over the jug of water. I jumped up and stepped back to avoid getting wet, and then the second boy arrived with a cloth so I let him finish mopping up before I sat down again. I stayed for about ten more minutes, watching all the activity on the street, then decided to leave because the restaurant was getting full and I was taking up four places. I was about to go when I remembered my bag. I pulled out the chair next to me, but it wasn't there. I couldn't believe someone had taken it.

'An older boy was now serving the tables. I asked him where I could find the manager and he pointed to a man behind a counter in the corner. When I told the manager what had happened, he said if I was sure my bag had been stolen, I should report it to the police. Up to that point I'd been thinking another customer had stolen it, but now I realized the two boys must have taken it, and they'd spilt the water deliberately to distract me. So I went into the kitchen to find them.'

'And he just let you?'

'Yeah. I was so angry I didn't think about it at the time, but I imagine he didn't want to make a scene … The kitchen was enormous, though, and there were so many people working in it that I didn't know where to start. A few faces looked up at me but no one seemed willing to help, and I began to think they might all be in it together.

'Then I noticed some steps to an upper level. I was extra careful as I went up them because they were wet and there were no handrails. At the top it was so dark I could hardly make anything out except for some silent figures crouching in the shadows. They were probably just some of the kitchen workers taking a break, but they all seemed to be staring at me and I started to feel uneasy. So I turned round and set off down the steps … and the next thing I knew I was waking up in a strange bed.

'It was daytime and I was in a little room with bare walls and hardly any furniture. I could feel a bump on the back of my head but I had no recollection of how I'd hurt myself. My first thought was that I'd been kidnapped, then I figured if that was the case, I wasn't likely to be in a bed.

'I threw back the sheet and sat up – and realized I wasn't wearing my money belt. Then the door opened. I jumped to my feet and thought about trying to make it to the window, but before I could take a step, a middle-aged man with greyish hair was standing in front of me. He was wearing a white kurta and had a calm expression on his face. He was quite tall but didn't seem very muscular – which made me feel a lot braver.

'I demanded to know who he was and why he was keeping me there. Before he could answer, I asked him where my money belt was. He told me to open the drawer of the bedside cabinet, and I found it inside. After I'd made sure all my money was still there, he told me his name was Darshan and I was in his house. He said I was free to leave whenever I wanted, though he advised me to stay and rest another day. When I asked if he was a doctor, he smiled and said, "Not usually."

'He told me he'd been on his way up the steps in the kitchen as I'd started to come down. I'd slipped at the top, fallen backwards and hit my head. The blow had knocked me out, and when I'd come round, he'd helped me down the steps and tried to find out where I was staying. He hadn't been able to get much sense out of me, so he'd taken me to his home in a taxi.

'Before leaving the restaurant, he'd called a friend of his who was a doctor and asked him to come to his house to examine me. The doctor had said there were no signs of any serious damage but it was best for me to stay where I was so he could come and see me again the next day. Apparently, I'd then asked how much I should pay him and taken a hundred-rupee note out of my money belt. As I'd done so, the card with the name of my hotel on had fallen out. Not only had the doctor refused the money, but he'd also offered to call the hotel and tell them where I was.'

'And you didn't remember *any* of that?'

'Not at first. After Darshan had told me what had happened, a few things came back to me, but most of it was a blur. He said the doctor had left around half past seven and I'd fallen asleep soon after. When I woke up, it was the next morning.'

'So had Darshan left you on your own that night and gone back to the restaurant to finish his shift?'

'It turned out he didn't work there. He told me he'd been having a walk in his neighbourhood when two boys had come rushing out of an alleyway and bumped into him. One of them dropped a bag but they ran off without picking it up. He opened it to find out whose it was and noticed an address written on the map that was inside. It was the address of the restaurant, which I'd made a note of before leaving the hotel. Since the place was nearby, he went there to see if he could trace the owner of the bag. When he arrived, he had a word with the manager and then went into the kitchen to find me.'

Aldo paused. 'I expect you're wondering what all this has to do with the book.'

'Now that you mention it, I suppose I am. But I was actually wondering why the manager let Darshan go into the kitchen instead of going himself.'

'I agree it was a bit strange. Maybe he wanted to make it look as though what had happened had nothing to do with him.

'Anyway, after Darshan had explained everything, he opened the door of the bedside cabinet, took out my bag and said: "Can you think of any reason why it might have been right for you to lose this?" I asked him what he meant, but he just repeated the question. He said I could think about it while he made some tea. When he came back, I still hadn't thought of anything. He told me to think about the things I had in the bag and went off again to prepare some food.

'If you remember, I was carrying three things in the bag. The map was just a cheap one I'd picked up from the station and the book was an old second-hand one, but the camera was a good one I bought a few years ago.

I never got round to using it much, though, and ended up swapping it for a friend's guitar. But before leaving for India, I began to wish I'd held on to it. I didn't have much money to spare and I didn't want to buy another camera just for the trip, so I persuaded my friend to let me have it back for the time I was going to be away.'

'So it can't have been right for you to lose the bag.'

'That's what I thought. Darshan saw it differently, though. He came back in with a big bowl of rice and insisted I eat it all before he heard what I had to say. After I'd told him about the camera, he asked if I'd learned anything from nearly losing it. I said something about taking more care of things I borrowed. He didn't seem satisfied, so I tried to think of something else.

'Then I started feeling bad about getting my friend to lend me the camera. I knew she'd be missing it, and I'd only taken around a dozen photos in over two months. So I told Darshan I shouldn't have got the camera back from my friend, and that's why I'd nearly lost it. He nodded and said I now had another chance to give it away, but this time I had to let go of it completely. He said it didn't matter who I gave it to, and I could even give it to the two boys if I wanted. I told him I couldn't give the camera to anyone else since it belonged to my friend now, but he said I could always buy her a new one.'

'So what did you do?'

'I hung on to it. When I went to give it back to my friend, though, she told me to keep it in case I needed it for any more trips. She felt sure another one would come her way sooner or later. But since I now knew I definitely didn't need a camera, I insisted on giving her it. Then, on my way home, it struck me that I hadn't really given her anything – I'd just got rid of something I didn't want. But she'd been willing to give up something she did want. She'd been able to do what Darshan had said I should do: give without feeling any resistance inside. And she'd ended up getting back what she'd let go of.

'This got me thinking about some of the other things Darshan had talked about. He told me that life has no desire to harm anyone, and situations which seem difficult are often there to help us in some way. He said if we can remember what our thoughts were before the situation came about, we might be able to see the part we played in creating it.

'Before meeting Darshan, it had never occurred to me that there wasn't necessarily anything to worry about when something was unclear or wasn't going the way I wanted. It was impossible for me to stay calm and trust something good would come out of it. I was either trying hard to make things happen or driving myself crazy with questions I couldn't answer.'

'I know the feeling.'

'That's why I'm telling you all this: you remind me a bit of what I used to be like.'

'So you're saying you're a different person now?'

'Not exactly, but at least when things seem to be going wrong I remember what Darshan said about life not wanting to harm us.'

'And that was enough to make you change?'

'It certainly gave me the idea I might be able to see things differently. But it was the book that helped me put the idea into practice. Darshan gave it to me before I left his house to go back to my hotel.'

'I thought you said it had been lent to you.'

'I was just getting to that bit … He said it would only be mine until I found the right person to pass it on to – which couldn't be anyone I already knew. I asked him what he meant by "the right person", and he said I'd know when I met them. He told me that the next person to have it should also pass it on to someone they met after receiving it, and this had to be the case whenever the book was passed on. He said this was "the will of the book".'

'The will of the book?!'

'That's what he said.'

'Had someone given it to *him*?'

'No. Someone had given him the idea for it, though.'

'Was he a writer, then?'

'When I asked him that, he said: "Not any more – this was my last book." I asked him how many he'd written, and he said, "One."

'He told me we could meet again one day if I wanted, but I would have to give the book away first. I didn't know if I'd ever come back to India, but he said I wouldn't need to because there was another place we'd be able to meet. He claimed the book was magic and would lead me there when the time was right. He said it could also be useful in situations that were unclear or didn't seem to be working out: if I found myself going over the same question in my mind without getting anywhere, all I had to do was open the book and I'd get some help. I told him I sometimes did the same thing with my own books when I needed an answer to a question that was bothering me, but he said although opening a book at random was a well-known way of getting an answer to a problem, I wouldn't find any answers in his book. So I asked him what the point of opening it was. He told me it was to find "the question behind the question", and that I should ask this to myself without trying to give an answer straight away, then notice the feelings that came up.

'He said if I ever felt I wanted to see him again, I'd have to study the book from cover to cover to discover where and when we could meet. I remember him repeating "cover to cover to discover", as if he liked the way the words sounded. He told me I might need someone to help me, and if that was the case, this person would be the one I should give the book to – as long as it was someone I'd met after receiving it …

'Maybe this "someone" is you.'

'What makes you say that?'

'One or two coincidences … Yesterday I spent about two hours studying the book to see if I could work out how to find Darshan. I didn't come up with any ideas, so I picked up my guitar and began to play a tune I'd written when I was in India. After a while, you appeared and we got talking – about India. This afternoon I read through the questions another time, but I still couldn't think of anything. I started playing my guitar again, and after a few minutes I looked up to see you – just like before. And then you asked me about the book.'

'So if I managed to help you, you'd give it to me?'

'I'd have to.'

'You could always hang on to it and just *say* you'd passed it on.'

'I couldn't imagine lying to Darshan. Anyway, he made it clear it wasn't mine to keep.'

'Why is it so important for you to see him again? Is there something you want to talk to him about?'

'Nothing specific.'

'You must have some reason for wanting to see him.'

'What reason did you have for coming to Amorgos?'

'I'd heard it was worth visiting.'

'That doesn't sound very specific. Wasn't there anything else?'

'I just had a feeling it was the right place to go.'

'And I've got the feeling it's right for me to see Darshan again. Who knows, it could be that the real reason for you coming here was to help me with the book, and it was this that your feeling was guiding you towards, even though you didn't know it at the time. So maybe I'll discover my reason for wanting to see Darshan again when I meet him – if I manage to find him, that is.'

'Haven't you got his number?'

'He didn't have a phone, as far as I know.'

'Didn't you say the doctor who came to his house had called your hotel to tell them where you were?'

'Yes – but he must have done it later from his own house.'

'What about his address? Didn't you make a note of it?'

'I did, actually.'

'So why don't you write to him and ask where you can meet?'

'For one thing, he obviously wanted me to figure it out myself, and for another, I wouldn't know where to send the letter …

'On my last day in Calcutta, I went to say goodbye and thank him again for helping me, but he wasn't at home. Some of his neighbours were sitting outside and I asked them if they knew where he was. They just said, "Not here, not here." I wasn't sure whether it was because they didn't speak English very well or because they didn't want to tell me for some reason.

'I went to get something to eat and called back later. By now it was dark and there was a light on inside. But it wasn't Darshan who opened the door – it was a young man. I assumed he was a relative of Darshan, but he said there was no one with that name living there. He'd only just moved in, and all he knew about the previous tenant was that they'd moved out two days before. I thought Darshan might have left a forwarding address with the landlord, so I got the young man to give me his number.

'I found one of those public phone places and rang the landlord, but he didn't have Darshan's new address. So I went to the restaurant to see if anyone there knew anything. The manager looked uncomfortable when he saw me. He apologized for what had happened before and told me he'd got rid of the two boys. I was sorry they'd lost their jobs, since it was obvious they were poor – though it crossed my mind he could be lying: maybe it didn't happen to be their shift at that moment.

'When I asked him if he knew the man who'd helped me the other day, he said it was the first time he'd seen him in the restaurant. I was half thinking about going into the kitchen to ask some of the workers, then I remembered the doctor. He was bound to know where Darshan was. I didn't know his name, but I imagined he'd given it when he phoned my hotel to tell them about me. I went back to the telephone place and rang the hotel. The man on reception said he remembered a doctor had phoned a few days earlier and he'd made a note of his address. He told me to hold on while he found it – and then gave me *Darshan's* address.'

'So Darshan was a doctor after all?'

Aldo gave me a quizzical look. 'Don't you see what had happened? Since it was Darshan's house where I was staying, that was obviously the address the doctor would have given the receptionist.'

I struggled to mask my embarrassment at not having made such an elementary deduction and my irritation at the way Aldo had pointed it out to me.

'So you know what Darshan's job is, then?' I said.

'He told me he ran a bookshop … Anyway, in the end I decided that since I'd already thanked him and said goodbye, there was no real need to see him again – apart from the need to satisfy my curiosity about where he'd gone.'

'So what makes you think you'll be able to find him now if you couldn't while you were still in India?'

'I don't know. It's just that the more I read the book, the more I feel it could be possible.'

'Have you followed his advice about how to use it?'

'Yeah – not in the beginning, though. I opened it from time to time and read some of the questions, but not in the way Darshan had told me to. Then, a few months after coming back from India, I started to feel a bit disillusioned with life in Europe. I wasn't sure I wanted to live here any more, but I didn't think I'd be able to live in India, either, and I wondered if there was any place where I'd feel I fitted in. I remembered what Darshan had said about getting help from his book, and I opened it at random. This was the question I saw …' Aldo opened the book near the middle and turned over a few pages. 'The one on the right,' he said as he passed it to me.

Doesn't a cloud have a home
anywhere
in the sky?

'After asking that to myself a few times, I began to feel better about everything.'

'I'm surprised you didn't feel worse.'

'I might have if I hadn't remembered what Darshan had told me about not trying to answer the questions straight away.'

I read the question again.

'I see what you mean,' I said, though I wasn't sure that I did.

'Anyway,' he continued, 'as time went on, I used the book more and more in the way Darshan had said I should. And I have to say it's helped me a lot.'

I looked at the words on the opposite page.

Does a bird doubt
that it can sing?

Does a lion ask
if it may roar?

Do wild horses know
where they are running to?

'So how do you think *I'm* going to help you?' I asked.

'I don't know – maybe you'll notice something I've missed, like a clue of some sort in one of the questions. But even if I end up figuring it out on my own, I'll still give the book to you – if you're sure you're interested in it. I think it could help you too.'

'Well, if that's how you feel, thanks a lot. I'd be very happy to have it … How many more days are you going to be around?'

'I'm not sure, but not that many – so why don't you have a look through it now while I practise some songs on the guitar?'

4

Turning the Page

I opened the book at the beginning.

The first question is: What is the first question?

*The second question is: How many questions
are there to answer?*

The third question is: What is the last question?

As I was trying to work out the meaning of the riddle, my eyes wandered to the artwork around the border of the page. The different shades of orange and green resembled falling leaves, twisting and turning in the wind. I flicked through a few more pages. The pattern was similar in each case.

I had a look at the final page.

'I thought it was a book of questions,' I said.

'It is,' said Aldo, continuing to strum his guitar.

'What about the last page?'

'That's the only one without a question.'

I decided to go through the pages in order, making a note of the questions and any ideas that came to me. I borrowed a pen and notepad from Aldo and turned back to the beginning.

Although the three questions were straightforward in the way they were phrased, there was clearly some ambiguity regarding the context in which they were to be answered. Maybe that was the point: questions which appeared simple could be complex. Or maybe they really were simple and it was I who was making them complicated by trying too hard to find a hidden meaning.

I looked at the next two pages.

Do you want
to want,
or do you dare
to love?

*

Can you love
in fear
of not being loved?

My relationship with Efrosyni came to mind. Had my fear of losing her prevented me from really loving her? Had my desire for us to be together ended up being stronger than my desire for her happiness?

Since these thoughts weren't relevant to the task in hand, I chose not to dwell on them for the time being.

I turned the page.

Is it wise
to bear desires
that turn to lies
the day you find
what you wanted
and what you want
live separate lives?

*

Will you have
when all there is
cannot be had,
and not to have
is not to lose
what is no one's
and part of you?

I realized that my wanting Efrosyni to want to be with me and my reluctance to accept that this wasn't the case had been the main cause of my inner resistance to our break-up, rather than any conviction that it was right for us to stay together. Once I had begun to feel her heart wasn't in it, I had known deep down that it would be best for us to separate, and I had gradually resigned myself to the fact during the time we had spent apart at the beginning of the summer. But when I had learned she was interested in someone else, I had felt a resurgence of resistance to ending our relationship.

It was now clear to me that if I had really desired her happiness, I wouldn't have found it so difficult to let her go. I hadn't even acted in the interests of my own happiness – unless it made me happy to remain in a relationship with someone who was having doubts about continuing it. It was also clear that my fear of losing her had stemmed from the idea that she belonged to me, since, as the question on the fifth page pointed out, you could only lose something you had in the first place. But it was never possible to have a person … which meant it was never possible to lose someone … So I had nothing to fear.

And I had nothing to lose by loving someone.

A surge of energy rose through me, lifting the chains of emptiness that had been weighing me down for the last month.

'Maybe this really is a magic book!'

'What have you found?' asked Aldo, breaking off from his guitar playing.

'The questions on the second and third pages made me ask some of my own. Then the ones on the next two pages helped me find the answers to them.'

'That's what I was hoping for: a different way of seeing how it's all been put together.'

I would have preferred to stay until I had read all the questions, but I had arranged to meet Dan at eight o'clock. Wishing I hadn't made the arrangement, I handed the book back to Aldo. When I suggested meeting early the next day, he said he wanted to have some time to continue looking through the questions on his own. I reluctantly agreed to meet at five o'clock, then set off for the port.

I had said I was going to see a friend I had bumped into earlier, but I hadn't told him it was someone I had met in India.

5

Expanding the Present

Dan was already there when I arrived at the taverna. He was reading the menu on display outside the door and had his back to me, but there was no mistaking his mass of curly hair. We sat at an outside table near the quayside, where the smell of sea air mingled with intermittent wafts of grilled fish. I tried to catch the attention of the waiter – a swarthy young man with a ponytail, dressed in jeans and a T-shirt – who was gliding back and forth between the kitchen and the half a dozen other tables that were occupied. Eventually he came over, spread a paper tablecloth and took our order, after which Dan began to study the simplified map of the island that was printed on the tablecloth.

By now the horizon had faded and darkness enveloped the array of boats in the harbour, which were rocking gently in the soft breeze. Each one bore a name. I looked for 'Efrosyni' amongst them, telling myself this would be a sign of some sort. But all the names were the more common ones, such as 'Eleni' and 'Maria' – the latter of which was emblazoned across the stern of an elegant yacht moored directly in front of where we were sitting.

I turned to look at Dan. 'Have you figured out where we are, then?'

'Well, according to my calculations … somewhere not far from here.'

'I didn't realize map reading was one of your talents.'

'Neither did I.'

Dan proceeded to scrutinize the map of the island in an exaggerated fashion.

'I never got round to asking you what you do,' I said.

'Now's your chance, then.' He looked at me and waited.

'So what do you do?'

'I eat, drink, sleep … and do lots of breathing.'

I tried to think of a good response.

'How much do you get paid for doing all that?' I said.

'They're more like hobbies, really.'

'Do they leave you any time for work?'

'I'm working pretty hard these days as well, actually – though I'm not getting paid for that, either.'

'Voluntary work, you mean?'

'You could say that.'

'Who for?'

'Me.'

'Hmm. And what does it involve?'

'Putting distance between my past and my future.'

'Sounds interesting – though I've no idea what you're on about.'

'I suppose you could say I'm expanding my present,' said Dan. 'That's what I'm trying to do, anyway.'

'And how are you doing that?'

'By doing as little as possible.'

'I thought you said you were working hard.'

'You think it's easy? Tell me how long *you* can sit on your own without doing anything.'

'I don't know exactly, but I must have done it loads of times,' I said.

'Without thinking?'

'I didn't mean that.'

'I said without doing anything.'

'Not even breathing?'

'OK, breathing's allowed – but nothing else,' he said.

'So you're saying it's possible not to think?'

'I am.'

'To have no thoughts at all in your mind?'

'That's right – as if it was an empty room, with the windows wide open so the wind can blow right through it.'

'Very poetic! But what would be the point of that? Aren't we supposed to use our mind for thinking?'

'So people keep telling me,' said Dan. 'But if you can empty it – even for a moment – you'll see that you're not who you think you are.'

'It can never be completely empty, though. Even if it felt like that, there'd still be the thought that you weren't having any thoughts.'

'That's what I'd have said – before I went to India … When I was in Varanasi, I met a Belgian girl in the guest house where I was staying. One day I went with her to the home of an Indian friend of hers. After I'd finished telling him where I'd been and where I was planning to go next, he asked me if I wanted to practise doing nothing for a while. I laughed and said I didn't need any practice at doing nothing. Then he asked how long I could sit still without having any thoughts. When I told him I didn't think that was possible, he said: "It looks like you do need some practice."

'He told me that doing nothing was one of his favourite activities and he did it every day. I didn't think he was being serious, but then he said it was time for him to go and practise and we could join him if we wanted. Isabelle, the Belgian girl, said she'd like to and suggested I give it a try. I didn't fancy sitting there on my own, so I agreed.

'We followed him into a smaller room, where we all sat on some cushions on a rug in the middle of the floor. There was a little window high up in the wall, and a shaft of sunlight was shining through it onto the rug. He said I should sit with my back straight and chest relaxed, and let the air move my belly in and out as if breathing was something that was happening to me rather than something I was doing myself. He put on this really soothing flute music, but he told me not to listen to it since that would count as doing something. He said: "Just close your eyes and let the sound waves wash over you."

'After a couple of minutes I opened my eyes and spent a few moments watching the specks of dust floating around in the sunlight. But it soon became clear we were going to stay like that for quite a while. Since there wasn't much else I could do, I closed my eyes again and began to feel more relaxed.'

'In other words, you had a lesson in meditation.'

'I don't know about that – it felt more like a game than a lesson in anything. All I know is that while we were sitting there quietly with the music playing, there was a moment when it felt as if my mind wasn't inside my head any more – a bit like how you feel when you're floating on your back in the sea, when it's all calm and you're just suspended there, between sky and earth. And it seemed that everything had stopped – including my thoughts.'

I remembered the moment of stillness I had experienced on the beach the previous day.

'I think I've felt something like that too,' I said. 'I'm not sure what I did; it just happened.'

Dan furrowed his brow. 'Maybe that's why I haven't had much success in finding that feeling since I came back from India: I've been trying too hard.'

'So that's how you've been spending your time: trying hard to do nothing?'

'That's right.'

'You haven't stopped travelling, though.'

'I don't really count that as doing something. All you do is sit down, and the ship or plane does the rest.'

'There's a bit more to it than that! You can't say travelling's the same as doing nothing.'

'It depends how you look at it,' he said with a shrug.

'What about eating and sleeping and the other "hobbies" you mentioned before? Don't they count as doing something?'

'In some ways they do, though you could also say they're a bit like travelling.'

'How do you mean?'

'You just sit down – or lie down – and the body does the rest. Come to think of it, we don't even do the sitting or lying down; we just decide to and the body carries out our order without a second thought. And think of what happens to the food we eat after it's been swallowed. We can hardly claim to be doing all that.' Dan's face lit up. 'So I'm doing even less than I thought I was!' He raised his arms triumphantly and nearly hit the waiter behind him, who managed to make a swift side-step before depositing our bread and wine on the table and making his retreat.

'So why do you want to put distance between your past and your future?' I asked as Dan poured the wine.

'I want to change my life.'

'Why don't you just do something different?'

'It's like wanting to put new furniture in your house: you've got to get rid of the old stuff first or there won't be enough space.'

'You could always keep it down in the cellar.'

'In case you might need it again, you mean? That's what I did at first – but it stopped me from making a clean break.'

'From what? You seemed happy enough when you were in India.'

'Exactly: I *seemed* happy,' said Dan. 'But it was just a role I'd got used to playing.'

'You played it pretty well, though.'

'That's why I played it for so long.'

'So you're going to try and be yourself from now on?' I said.

'That's impossible, I'm afraid.'

'Why?'

'Because you can't do both.'

'Both what?'

'Try to be yourself, and be yourself.'

'OK, so you're just going to *be* yourself, then.'

'I thought I was doing that before,' he said. 'Maybe I could try out some other roles instead.'

'You mean pretend to be someone you're not?'

'I wouldn't call it pretending – more like experimenting. If we're all actors on the world's stage – as I once said …'

'As Shakespeare said, you mean.'

'Shakespeare as well, eh? Anyway, as I was saying: if the world's the stage and we're the actors, why not play different roles from time to time? At least it would make life more interesting.'

'Or more confusing.'

'Not if you know it's only a role you're playing. Then you can enjoy it – instead of getting stressed about it.'

'It all sounds a bit insincere to me.'

'Maybe, but do you know anyone who's completely natural all the time?'

'I can't think of anyone right now.'

Dan took a few sips of wine, and I did the same.

'So you're going to spend your life playing different roles?' I said.

'Only until I feel I don't need to any more.'

'Then what?'

'I'll live happily ever after with who I am.'

'Are you sure there'll be enough room?'

'For what?'

'You and who you are.'

Dan frowned and stroked his chin theatrically. 'There will be if I end up *becoming* who I am,' he said, and beamed with satisfaction.

'Just make sure one of you doesn't get left down in the cellar.'

The waiter arrived and placed a huge bowl of Greek salad between us, having approached our table side-on this time. We took a few forkfuls each and ate them in silence.

'So every time you find yourself not enjoying a role, you'll give it up and try a different one?' I said.

'Not necessarily. Maybe there'll be something I can do to make it better. The real problem will come if I start taking it too seriously. That's when it might be a good idea to leave it and not do anything for a while.'

'What if *that* becomes a role you take too seriously?'

'Then it'll be time to do something again.'

Dan loaded his fork with a piece of feta and managed to get it into his mouth before I could ask him anything else.

'What's wrong with taking a role seriously, anyway? Surely it's right to do that if you're a parent?' I said as soon as he had swallowed the feta.

'I said you shouldn't take it *too* seriously. When parents start behaving as if their children belonged to them, it means they've forgotten they didn't create them themselves – all they did was play their part in nature's programme.'

'So if you were a father and got too serious about it, you'd go away and leave your kids?'

'I think the wine's gone to your ears! I said it *might* be a good idea to give up a role. Of course I wouldn't do that if I was a parent – at least I hope not. I hope I'd be able to give up some of my control, though, by remembering we're all children of something greater.'

'You mean Mother Nature? Or are you talking about God?'

The waiter arrived with the rest of our food. As he was setting the dishes down, I thought about how different Dan was from the way I remembered him. In India our exchanges had consisted of little more than amusing comments and anecdotes.

'It doesn't matter what you call it. The main thing is to recognize it,' he said after the waiter had gone.

'Uh?'

'The answer to your question.'

While Dan tucked into his moussaka, I took the opportunity to get a decent share of the chips we were sharing. It didn't take us long to eat all the food on the table.

'So what were you doing before you started doing nothing?' I asked.

'Stand-up comedy.'

'You're joking?'

'Not any more.'

'Hmm, so I see … Did you make a living from it?'

'Not exactly. I had to do various other jobs as well to keep me going.'

'It can't be easy standing up in front of a load of people who expect you to make them laugh.'

'That's why I packed it in: I started having anxiety dreams about telling jokes to an audience that just sat there staring at me. In the end it was all stress and no fun.'

'When did you stop?'

'November 96. I remember my last show went so well I even thought about going back on my decision. But I knew I'd only enjoyed it because I'd told myself I wasn't going to do another one. So the week after, I set off for India with no regrets.

'Since I was travelling alone, I had a lot of time to myself. At first I spent most of it trying to figure out what I was going to do with my life. But I was still carrying my old role with me. I'd always felt a sort of duty to make people laugh, and I struggled with the urge to say something funny whenever I got half a chance. Then I realized the point shouldn't be to try to live without humour, but just to stop making it the main focus of my life – since it wasn't leaving much space for anything else.'

'So now you've got space to do nothing.'

'Exactly.'

'And it looks like you've managed to keep your sense of humour as well.'

'I reckon what I really did was find my sense of humour. I don't feel any pressure to make others laugh now, so I can pay more attention to what I find funny. And it's helped me enjoy my own company a lot more than I used to.'

'Don't tell me you're one of those people who sit alone on park benches laughing out loud!'

'Not just on park benches.'

'So it's now your duty to make *yourself* laugh?'

'I don't know about duty, but it's certainly a challenge – since I've heard all my best jokes before.'

* * *

Later that night, as I lay in my sleeping bag under the gaze of the Milky Way, I thought about the more serious side to Dan's character which had emerged since I had last seen him. It crossed my mind that it might have been one of those roles he had been talking about, and I wondered if I would see yet another 'side' to his character when he came to meet me on the beach the following morning.

6

Into … and out of … the Blue

I hadn't mentioned anything to Dan about Aldo and the book of questions for two reasons. Firstly, it seemed Aldo would rather I didn't; and secondly, I wasn't sure I wanted to myself. I was looking forward to reading the rest of it and trying to help him work out how to find Darshan, and I didn't want anything, such as Dan's curiosity, to get in the way of this. That was also the reason I hadn't told Aldo how I had originally met Dan: no doubt they would be interested to hear about each other's experiences in India, and if they ended up having a long conversation, it wouldn't leave much time for Aldo and I to discuss the book.

I went for my morning swim in the glassy blue water, the gentle lapping of which had provided a soundtrack for my sleep. As I waded in, my mind played host to a succession of images from a dream – each one like a silvery fish emerging from the depths, only to dart away the instant I grasped at it.

I dived in and found myself immersed in blue. But shades of the night lingered inside. Scenes from the dream began to filter through. By the time I resurfaced to take a breath, I was feeling the need to capture these shadows before they melted into the day. I returned to my place under the tree and took out my pen and notebook:

I was sitting on a bench in a deserted park. I had Aldo's book in my hand and was waiting to meet Darshan. I heard some movement in the trees behind me and turned round. Dan was approaching with an amused look on his face. I tried to hide the book but wasn't quick enough. He asked me what I was doing. When I said I was waiting for someone, he laughed. I was hoping he would go away, but he sat down next to me. He told me he had arranged to meet Aldo in the park and Aldo was going to give him the book of questions. I looked down at what I was holding. It was a stone with question marks engraved on it. The question marks started to move off and float upwards. I tried to grab them, but they crumbled to dust and the scene faded away.

I hadn't arranged to meet Aldo until much later, but I wanted to ask him what he thought I should do if he happened to pass by when I was with Dan. Would he agree that it was better if I didn't introduce them so we could continue our search through the book without interruption?

I walked along the beach to his tent. The flaps were down with the zips closed. 'Aldo? Are you there?' I said.

There was no sound from inside. Maybe he had gone for a walk over the hill. I decided to climb it to see if I could spot him from the top. And even if I couldn't, at least I would find out what was on the other side.

As I made my way up the steep slope, I tried to steer clear of the thorns on the bushes and took care not to lose my footing on the loose stones which formed the surface of the winding path. But with my sights set on reaching the top, I was soon moving fairly quickly. A gecko shot out in front of me. I adjusted my step and dislodged a rock from under my foot, nearly losing my balance. After that I went at a slower pace. About halfway up I paused to take in the view: an endless expanse of blue beneath the hue of a cloudless sky, with distant islands like lilac mountains emerging in between.

I resumed my steady climb and didn't stop again until I got to the top. The final stretch wasn't that steep, and I couldn't resist almost running these last few metres. Down below was a pristine beach of shingle curving gently around a bay of sapphire water. Beyond that was another rocky hill forming part of the untamed coastline that stretched out before me, rising defiantly from the depths of the ocean.

But there was no sign of Aldo.

I sat on a rock to think about my next move. The warmth of the rock rose through me. I closed my eyes and let the humming of bees and the subtle scent of thyme fill my mind ...

The descent to the bay looked even steeper than my ascent had been, and the path I had been following had lost itself amongst the prickly shrubs that carpeted the terrain, which was no doubt why the beach was deserted. It wasn't inaccessible, though. I wondered if Aldo had made his way down the slope and continued over the next hill. That was what I would have done had I had more time. Once again, I wished I hadn't arranged to meet Dan.

Someone was coming over the hill in the distance. I strained my eyes to see if it was Aldo, even though the colourful headband they were wearing told me this was unlikely – as did the flowing white top and pink shorts. It was a young woman.

I turned my gaze towards the open sea, checking her progress out of the corner of my eye. If she stopped at the beach for a swim, I would leave; but if she continued, I might be tempted to wait. If only I had brought my pen and notebook with me. It would have been the perfect prop to make it appear that I was minding my own business until she happened to pass by.

She reached the foot of the hill and started walking along the beach. The closer she came, the more uneasy I felt. Although part of me wanted to orchestrate a chance encounter, I knew I would only end up acting unnaturally. I stood up to leave, but I couldn't resist glancing down one more time. At the same moment, she raised her arm and waved. I assumed she was making an ironic gesture to show that she knew I had been watching her, so I pretended to be admiring the view. Then, as casually as I could, I turned round and headed back down the hill.

By now my keenness to find Aldo had reduced itself to a vague feeling that there was something I had been intending to do. All I was concerned about was what the young woman would think of my behaviour – and whether she would recognize me if she saw me again.

No sooner had I returned to my place under the tree than I spotted her following the path down the hillside. I was surprised by how quickly she was moving. I figured she must be rushing to catch up with me to tell me she didn't appreciate being spied on. This time there was no escape: I couldn't leave because Dan would be arriving any minute. I did consider heading for the port to try and meet him before he got to the beach; the only problem was that I didn't know which way he would be coming. So I chose to stay put and face the music. At least I now had something to occupy myself with: I would read the notes I had made the previous day when I had been looking through Aldo's book of questions and copy them into my notebook ...

But with one eye on the lookout for the young woman, I didn't get very far with this.

She had stopped about a third of the way along the beach and was standing at the water's edge, holding her sandals in her hands and letting the waves caress her feet. She had also removed her headband, freeing her wavy chestnut hair to play with the breeze.

'So that's why you're sleeping here: so you can spend all your time looking at the girls!'

I turned my head. Dan was walking towards me. He had a red beach towel draped around his shoulders and was wearing an enormous pair of bright green shorts.

'Nice shorts! I could use those as a tent.'

'Don't change the subject!' he said, passing behind the tree and plonking himself down next to me.

'What took you so long, anyway? I was starting to think you might be lost.'

'I thought the same about you when I saw how you were looking at that woman.'

'What if I said I was looking at her in the way you'd admire a sunset?'

Dan gave me a quizzical look and began to unlace his trainers.

'You don't think I'm being serious?' I said.

'I'm just wondering if *you* think you are.'

'At least the idea can help me not to get too carried away.'

'How's that, then?'

'A sunset can only be admired from a distance.'

'Don't tell me you've become a monk!'

'Not exactly. It's just that I know it doesn't do me any good to see a nice woman and start wishing she was mine.'

'So you've fallen in love with the sunset instead?'

'You know what I'm trying to say.'

'I'm not sure I do, to be honest.'

'Remember what you said last night about some parents behaving as if their kids belonged to them? Don't we make the same mistake in our relationships sometimes?'

'Mm, I suppose we do.'

'But we don't make that mistake with the sunset, no matter how much we like it.'

'That's because it wouldn't make a very good girlfriend.'

'Come on, Dan – let me finish! ... So the way we feel about a sunset shows we're perfectly capable of appreciating something beautiful without any thought of wanting to have it.'

'We are if we know it's not possible to have it anyway.'

'I *told* you you knew what I was trying to say.'

'Uh?'

'Isn't it the same with a person? It's just that it's not so obvious, so we tend to forget ... So when I see a nice woman, if I think of how I feel about a sunset, it'll help me remember that it's not possible to have a person, either, and it's therefore pretty pointless to start wanting someone in the first place.'

'Mmm, interesting idea.' Dan fixed his gaze on me. He seemed to be suppressing a smile. 'So you expect me to believe you were feeling no desire for that slim, athletic, suntanned young lady coming this way?'

I looked to my right. The young woman was almost level with us. As she passed by, she cast a glance towards where we were sitting and I caught a glimpse of her shining eyes and smooth features.

Dan smiled to himself.

'What are you looking so smug about?' I said.

'I can always tell when someone's impressed with my shorts.'

Whether or not Dan's shorts had diverted the young woman's attention, I felt confident that she hadn't recognized me. I now began toying with the idea of going to talk to her. Despite my growing desire to make a move, my feet remained rooted to the ground. As I sank deeper into indecision, she moved further away. When she got to the end of the beach, she started to make her way up the rocky hill that formed the headland. I continued to watch her until she reached the top and disappeared from sight.

'Did you enjoy the sunset?' said Dan.

'I thought you'd given up being a comedian.'

'And I thought you'd given up fleshly desires.'

I struggled to come up with a response.

'I think the time has come,' he announced, and stood up.

'For what?'

He gave a daft grin, then raced down the narrow stretch of sand towards the sea. When he got to the water, he stopped abruptly, took something out of his pocket, turned on his heel and ran back to where I was sitting.

'Now I'm sure the time has come,' he said, and tossed his room key onto his towel.

He charged back down to the sea and hurled himself in, vanishing in a flurry of foam.

I ended up smiling to myself about Dan's comments regarding my theory on how to see an attractive woman in a different light. But I was disappointed that the conclusions I had reached about the different attitudes of having and loving had not led to a real change in my behaviour: although I had resisted the urge to try and get to know the young woman, I knew this wasn't due to a new way of seeing things; it was because I was afraid of recreating the tension I had felt in my last relationship ...

I still had vivid memories of my visits to the little café on Santorini where Efrosyni had been working in the summer of 1996. Every morning I would sit at the table outside the door, spinning out my breakfast as I waited for a lull in the stream of customers, which would give me the chance to nip inside and exchange a few words with her. Eventually I had persuaded her to come for a walk to the beach one afternoon. Due to my persistence, our relationship had developed from there. But I had often felt that my desire for us to be together was stronger than hers, and I had never been able to stop wondering how things might have progressed had I allowed them to do so in their own time.

7

A Butterfly

When Dan came back from his swim, I shared my thoughts with him as he stood with his towel round his shoulders and water dripping off his shorts onto the sand near my feet.

'That's pretty deep,' he said. 'You'll end up drowning if you're not careful.'

'Aren't we supposed to ask ourselves from time to time whether the way we're living is right for us – then try to change if it isn't? Isn't that what you did when you gave up being a comedian?'

'I was sure I wanted to change, though. And even then, I didn't manage to shake off my old role until I'd become clearer about the type of person I wanted to be. But in your case, it seems you still haven't made up your mind to leave your old role behind, despite the fact you're obviously not happy with the way you are.'

'It looks to me as though you haven't left your old role behind either.'

'I agree it might seem like it's trying to make a comeback every now and then. But as I said last night, the difference is I'm not so bothered about making anyone else laugh now. I don't feel that tension inside any more.'

'I dread to think what you were like before.'

'So do I,' said Dan, pretending to look concerned.

'Hmm … So anyway, what do you think I should do?'

'I'm not qualified to say.'

'Why not?'

'Because I'm not you.'

'You could at least tell me what you'd do if you were.'

'I wouldn't ask me, for a start.'

'Thanks for the advice!'

He thought for a few seconds. 'The only thing I would say is that while you're still not sure you want to change, there's not much point in trying to. And the moment you're ready to change, there'll be no need to try because you'll already be different.'

'You're sure it's that simple?'

'It was for my dad when he gave up smoking. He was on thirty a day until he read about how bad it was for you. I'd just been born, so he stopped straight away – and he's never smoked since.'

'It's certainly pretty impressive what your dad did, but giving up smoking isn't exactly the same as changing the way you think about relationships.'

'You're right – it's probably a lot harder.'

Dan stroked his chin and gave a slight frown.

'You don't look very convinced,' I said.

'Uh? No, I'm just trying to figure out what to do. I want to lie down but my towel's all wet.'

'It'll soon dry out.'

'It'll get messed up, though.'

'You won't need it if you lie in the shade. Or are you worried about getting sand on your nice shorts as well?'

'No, I'm going to go for another swim later. It's just that I wanted to get a bit of sun. But I suppose I can wait till my towel's dry.'

He hung his towel over a branch; then, using his trainers as a makeshift pillow, he stretched out under the tree and closed his eyes.

The change in Dan's father appeared to have come from an insight into the way in which his need to satisfy a desire was harming others as well as himself. He must have had the sensation that his 'old role' had simply been left behind – as an actor might feel after walking off stage – as against feeling it had been given up following a struggle.

So what about the insight which I had had? I had seen that my sadness at losing Efrosyni was a consequence of my belief in the fallacy that it was possible to have someone, and, by wanting her to be mine, I had been feeding this illusion rather than thinking about what it meant to really love her. Yet my desire had not dissolved; it had merely been submerged – only to re-emerge and attach itself to someone else …

'You're not asleep, are you, Dan?'

'Uh?'

'I just wanted to ask you something.'

'What?'

'You know when your dad gave up smoking – he didn't start drinking or anything, did he?'

'He didn't have time.'

'Why not?'

'He was too busy helping my mum look after me.'

'And he never smoked again?'

'Didn't I tell you that before?'

'I was just checking.'

'Can I go back to sleep now?'

'Yeah, sorry.'

'Will you do me a favour, though?'

'What's that?'

'Wake me up when my towel's dry.'

It seemed I had not had a flash of insight after all, since, unlike Dan's father, I hadn't managed to rid myself of my old desire. I found it hard to believe I would continue behaving in the same way if I really had become aware of the negative effect it was having on myself and others. But I couldn't deny the sense of liberation I had experienced when it had occurred to me that love had nothing to do with the idea of having. Maybe it needed time for this new perspective to sink in because of resistance from my 'old role' – and because I still didn't have a clear idea of what love was.

I had never heard anyone give a definition of love; it was apparently taken for granted that we knew what it was. It was also commonly accepted that there were different kinds of love, which made me wonder if it ever could be clearly defined. I thought about 'romantic love', which was often accompanied by feelings of jealousy and possessiveness, had a tendency to fade rapidly, and sometimes degenerated into hatred. But what kind of love could turn to hate? Could love be such a fickle friend?

A butterfly had settled on Dan's towel. Its yellow-and-black wings quivered in the breeze. As I admired the intricacy of its markings, it took off and fluttered up into the tree, where it rested awhile before flying away, leaving me alone with the whispering of the breeze through the feathery branches … then silence – the silence that had been there all along.

From this silence came an idea: love was not a butterfly flitting through life in search of the next bright flower on which to alight … but a silent stream flowing from the source of life itself.

As we were all connected with the source of life, it must be accessible within. And if the source was inside me, it must be possible for this stream to flow through me.

But how could I make this happen?

Maybe Dan would be able to give me some answers.

'Dan?'

'Uh? What?'

'I think your towel's nearly dry.'

'Nearly?'

'Near enough.'

'Pity it couldn't have taken a bit longer,' he said with half-closed eyes. 'I was having a great dream.'

'What about?'

'I don't know. All I remember is that I was laughing.'

'That doesn't surprise me.'

'It surprises me: I've never laughed in a dream before.'

He got up and took his towel off the branch, then spread it out in the sun and lay down.

'You're not going to go to sleep again, are you?' I said.

'I never have a fixed plan as far as sleep goes. I just close my eyes and it tends to show up. But I wouldn't mind getting back into that dream I was having – maybe I'll find out what I was laughing about … On second thoughts, it's probably better to keep my eyes open, because if I'm going to have another swim, I'll have to do it soon to give my shorts time to dry out before I go back.'

I had a vision of us sitting under the tree as the sun went down, waiting for Dan's enormous shorts to dry so he would leave and I could go and meet Aldo.

'Have you got time to answer a question before you go for your swim?' I said.

'Go on, then.'

'Actually, maybe we should save it till after.'

'Why's that?'

'It might lead to a big discussion.'

'Another one?'

'If you can handle it.'

'In that case, you'd better ask me now so I can prepare my answer while I'm in the sea.'

'OK – though it's not the sort of question you'd usually ask someone you don't know that well.'

'Don't tell me you're going to ask me to marry you!'

'Of course not – I know you're in love with your towel.'

'You could be right there.'

'How long have you been together?'

'Since I was in India … Remember I told you that when I was in Varanasi a Belgian girl took me to the home of a friend of hers? On the way back, I passed through a market and saw an old woman selling towels. I wanted to help her out, so I bought the biggest one she had – which happened to be the same colour as the rug in the house I'd just been to. So now it always reminds me of that day, and it takes me back to that moment I told you about, when it felt as though my mind was empty – like I was floating – and I realized I wasn't who I thought I was.'

'Sounds like the towel could be a magic carpet.'

'Maybe. Sometimes all I have to do is look at it and it's as if I'm there in that little room again, with the flute music playing and the sun coming in through the window – and it makes me remember I don't need much to enjoy being alive.'

'You usually need a bit more than that, though.'

'You're right: I forgot to mention food and water.'

'Come on – I don't believe that's all you really want from life.'

'Maybe not, but I'm beginning to see that a lot of other things I've wanted were just ways of trying to make me feel something I could have felt without having to do anything in particular.'

'Are you counting your towel as one of those things?'

'How do you mean?'

'It's not as if you need it in order to remember what happened in Varanasi.'

'I know – but it helps me remember more often.'

'I'm surprised you need reminding so much, considering it was such a unique experience.'

'I'm surprised too. I thought it was going to change me forever, but I soon slipped back into my old way of behaving: looking for things to make me happy instead of just being happy to be here … So maybe what the towel's really reminding me of is that I'm not able to live in that state of mind from day to day.'

'You mean you'd like your mind to be empty all the time?!'

'Not all the time – I might end up floating away! Once a day would be enough. But the point isn't necessarily to have no thoughts at all, just to have some quiet moments when I'm neither thinking about the good times I've had in the past nor about the things I want to do in the future – and I'm quite content in that space in between.'

A gust of wind stirred up some sand and sprinkled it onto my rucksack, which was beside me under the tree. Although I was travelling light, I had still given myself a sizeable load to carry. What would it be like to travel through life with nothing except for the minimum of clothing, as the fakirs in India did? Could they have discovered how to experience love in their day-to-day existence?

'By the way, what was that question you wanted to ask?' said Dan.

'It doesn't matter, I think you more or less answered it.'

'So now I can answer questions without knowing what they are. It must be the magic carpet,' he said, and patted his towel.

'I've got another one for you, though. I was meaning to ask you the other night, but we got talking about something else and I forgot.'

'It'll have to be quick – it's nearly time for my swim,' he said, sitting up.

'I just wanted to ask you about that man whose house you went to in Varanasi.'

'OK, fire away.'

'Who was he? Was he a Yogi? And what was his name? … And did you see him again?'

'Aargh! I've been shot!' yelled Dan, and started writhing around on the ground.

'I'm not laughing.'

'Neither am I after that bombardment!' he said as he sat up again.

'So are you going to tell me who he was? Or is it a big secret?'

'It is a bit of a secret, actually.'

I waited for him to continue.

'Maybe I should have my swim first.'

'Look, if you don't want to tell me, fair enough.'

'There's nothing much to tell, really.'

'It's taking you long enough to tell it!'

'The fact is I know very little about him. After he'd introduced himself, I forgot his name, and I was too embarrassed to ask him to repeat it.'

'Hmm.'

'That's what happened – honestly.'

'The Belgian girl obviously knew what it was, though. Didn't you ask her after you left?'

'We didn't leave together. It was her last day in Varanasi and she wanted to spend it with her friend, so I left on my own after a couple of hours. She must have come back late, because I didn't see her at the guest house that night. Then she checked out first thing in the morning.'

'Didn't you keep in touch?'

'I was meaning to get her address but I never got round to it.'

'How well did you know her?'

'Not that well, really.'

'So how come you ended up going to her friend's house?'

'We often sat together for breakfast, and one morning we got into a conversation about happiness. She told me that her idea of what it meant had changed since she'd been in India, and it was partly because of someone she'd met in Varanasi. I imagined she'd fallen in love or something, but she said it was nothing like that. Then she said she was going to see this person that afternoon and I could come along if I wanted.'

'You don't know if he was a Yogi, then?'

'No. When I asked him what he did, he said: "As little as possible and as much as possible – at the same time." I assumed he preferred not to tell me, so I didn't ask him again.'

'How old was he, would you say?'

'Around fifty, I imagine.'

'What did he look like?'

'Like a man of around fifty.'

'Come on, Dan! Did he have dark hair or was it grey, for example?'

'Quite dark – with a few grey bits. But don't ask me how many!'

'What about his build?'

'I can't be sure about that because of his loose-fitting clothes – though it's safe to say he wasn't into bodybuilding.'

'How tall would you say he was?'

'I didn't notice, I'm afraid. He rode off in a stolen rickshaw before I could get a good look at him.'

'What?!'

'I feel like I'm in the witness box!'

'Sorry, but I'm just curious to know what he was like, since he obviously made an impression on you.'

'To tell you the truth, it was more the situation than anything in particular about him. And I can't remember him saying anything especially deep. In fact I don't remember him saying much at all.'

'What did you do for two hours, then?'

'That's the whole point: we didn't really do anything. It was enough for me just to be there – with these two virtual strangers who'd made me feel so welcome.'

I wished I had had a similar experience during my travels in India.

Dan stood up abruptly and cleared his throat. 'I think the time has come.'

'I know – for your swim.'

'No – to find the key.'

'The key to happiness?'

'Just for my room, I'm afraid.'

'Are you being serious now?'

'More than I'd like to be – I completely forgot I'd left it on my towel.'

8

The Sea of Desires

While we were groping around in the sand for Dan's key, I noticed a shadow to my right. Aldo was standing there with a bag of groceries in his hand, watching us with amusement.

'Searching for buried treasure?' he said.

Dan looked up. 'Just my room key, I'm afraid.'

Aldo glanced at Dan, then looked at me.

'This is Dan … and this is Aldo – he's camping here on the beach as well,' I said.

'I might be joining you at this rate,' said Dan, standing up to shake hands with Aldo. 'You don't fancy giving us a hand, do you?'

'There's not much point, really. I'm pretty sure you're not going to find it.'

'What makes you say that?' I asked.

'Just a feeling … in the sole … of my right foot.' Aldo lifted his foot to reveal a key half buried in the sand.

'That's it!' said Dan, and bent down to pick it up. 'Well done!'

'I'm pretty good at finding things I'm not looking for. I'm sorry I spoilt your fun, though.'

'It wasn't exactly fun,' I said, though it was true that I had been absorbed in what I was doing – and had been hoping I would be the one to find the key.

Aldo appeared to hesitate. 'I'm going to head back to my tent with this stuff. No doubt I'll see you around, Dan.'

'Yeah. I'm in no hurry to go anywhere. It's like paradise here.'

I hoped Dan was referring to the island and not the beach: it might be awkward if he was still around when the time came for me to meet Aldo.

'Where's he from?' he asked when Aldo had gone.

'Italy – and England.'

'How did he manage that?'

'Italian mum, English dad.'

'Don't bilingual people usually speak both languages without an accent?'

'You can hardly say he has a foreign accent.'

'OK, I agree it's not very noticeable – but you can tell he's not completely English, if you know what I mean.'

'I suppose you're right,' I said.

'But if he grew up speaking two languages, shouldn't they both sound like his mother tongue?'

'He only lived in England till he was nine.'

'That wouldn't have stopped his dad speaking English to him in Italy – unless he stayed behind in England.'

'You're beginning to sound like a private detective. Is that your latest role?'

'Maybe,' said Dan. 'I like trying to guess things about other people. I reckon everyone's got something to hide.'

'Including yourself?'

'Of course.'

'What are you hiding, then?'

'I haven't found out yet.'

I wondered if Dan could be right about Aldo's father. I had just assumed he had moved to Italy with Aldo and his mother … and that he was English.

'By the way, are you doing anything tonight?' asked Dan.

'Why?'

'I'm going to meet a couple of girls and I thought you might like to come along.'

'Who are they?'

'I'm not sure. There was a note on my door this morning saying: "How about dinner tonight around 6?" It was signed "The French girls".'

'You mean you've been invited out by some women you don't even know?!'

'Not exactly – it's just that I said hello to two pairs of girls yesterday. They both passed by the kitchen area when I was making a cup of tea.'

'So you don't mind which two they turn out to be?'

'No – they all seemed nice. And it's not every day I get the chance to go out with two women.'

'It sounds like you'd prefer to go on your own.'

'I admit I'm tempted, but I reckon it'd be more of a laugh if you came as well.'

'They might not want a complete stranger there.'

'Another one, you mean? Anyway, it's up to you. Why don't you think about it while I'm having a swim?'

He put his room key in one of his trainers and strolled off towards the sea.

I forgot how much I had been looking forward to my meeting with Aldo and began thinking about what I would miss out on if I didn't take Dan up on his invitation ... Something from the book of questions came back to me:

Is it wise
to bear desires
that turn to lies
the day you find
what you wanted
and what you want
live separate lives?

I got the feeling that trying to satisfy my desires was like chasing breaking waves up and down the beach. But, like different levels of the sea, there were other desires beneath the surface: ones that ran deeper and were more constant; and below those, the deepest of all – which dwelt in silence and stillness, secure in the knowledge that they would be fulfilled if this was the will of the ocean.

I closed my eyes and immersed myself in the sea of my desires. I pictured Dan and the two mystery women enjoying a night out; I relived my moment on the hilltop, watching the young woman approaching; I thought of Efrosyni and how much I had wanted to be with her; I felt my eagerness to read Aldo's book of questions and be the one who helped him figure out how to find Darshan. All these desires were clinging on to me, pulling me to and fro. But as I went deeper, one by one they let go and floated to the surface, leaving me to descend unhindered …

I became aware of the breeze on my face and the warmth of the sand on the soles of my feet. I had no desire to go anywhere or do anything. The moment was my home and there was nothing lacking in it.

'Have you made up your mind, then?'

I opened my eyes. Dan was standing in front of me, dripping water all over the sand.

'I think I'm going to give it a miss,' I said. 'Thanks all the same.'

'Fair enough.' He wrapped his towel around his waist before wriggling out of his shorts, which he hung over a branch on the tree. 'I'm surprised you're passing up the chance to go out with two nice women, though.'

I hesitated. 'The truth is I'm meeting Aldo later.'

'That's no problem – he can come as well.'

'I'm not sure he'll want to. He likes to keep himself to himself most of the time.'

'Maybe he's just a bit shy. Why don't I go and ask him? I can say it's a way of paying him back for finding my key.'

'The thing is … we were going to look through this book he's got with him, and it'll probably take us most of the evening.'

'Why didn't you say so before?'

'Because Aldo isn't too keen on people knowing about it. It's something personal.'

'I see.'

Dan made sure his towel was wrapped firmly around his waist, then set off in the direction of Aldo's tent.

'Where are you going?'

He glanced back at me. 'For a walk – to pass the time until my shorts are dry.'

'Isn't this a good chance for you to practise doing nothing?'

'I'm not very good at doing nothing when I'm waiting for something,' he said, and continued on his way.

Though I felt the urge to go after him, I knew I would feel ridiculous doing this, so I went for a swim instead – which would allow me to keep an eye on him without making it look obvious. I waded in and swam out a few metres, turned round and began treading water. It wasn't difficult to spot him in his big red towel, which nearly reached his ankles. Aldo was in his usual place near the rocks, playing his guitar. He might not be too pleased to learn I had mentioned his book to someone else. But what bothered me more was the possibility that he wouldn't mind showing it to Dan, and then Dan might end up figuring out how to find Darshan – in which case he would be the one who got to keep it.

It seemed that life was enjoying a joke at my expense … Or was it testing me? Could I still say the moment was my home and there was nothing lacking in it?

I remembered what Darshan had said to Aldo about life not wishing to harm us. Nothing but my own desires had caused me to feel this way. Yet what made me so sure it was right for me to have the book of questions? What if the only person who could help Aldo with it was Dan – and my role was simply to enable them to meet so this could happen?

I floated on my back and tried to forget about what was happening on the beach. Directly above me was a single cloud. I recalled something else from the book of questions:

Doesn't a cloud have a home
anywhere
in the sky?

I had originally assumed the answer to be no, but perhaps it was yes … The point of the question dawned on me: wherever we went, we could feel a sense of belonging, since the world was our home.

But I wasn't ready to feel a sense of belonging while drifting out to sea. I swam back towards the shore and stopped when the water was shallow enough to touch the bottom. Aldo was still playing his guitar, but there was no sign of Dan. I remembered my comment about his towel being like a magic carpet. As I amused myself with the image of him flying away on it, I glimpsed something red out of the corner of my eye. He was on his way up the hill. I couldn't believe he was climbing it in his bare feet.

I left the sea and walked back to my place under the tree. After drying off, I sat down and took out my notebook, in which I had written some of the questions from Aldo's book. I wanted to have another look at the ones on the first page:

The first question is: What is the first question?

The second question is: How many questions are there to answer?

The third question is: What is the last question?

There appeared to be three contexts in which the questions could be answered: the book, the page, or life. If they referred to the book, getting the answers would be straightforward. If they referred to the page, then presumably the answer to the first question would be 'What is the first question?', the answer to the second one would be 'Three', and the answer to the third would be 'What is the last question?' (though I had no idea what the meaning of such a riddle could be).

But if the questions referred to life, answering them would not be so simple. What was the first question we asked in life? Was it the same for all of us? And what was the last question a person asked before they died? Again, could it be the same for everyone?

I thought about the wording of the second question: 'How many questions are there to answer?' as against 'How many questions are there?'. Perhaps it was to make us think about how many questions in life we needed to find answers to. And the same could apply to the questions in the book: although the main point of asking them was to see what feelings they evoked, there might be certain ones which needed to be answered – and maybe these answers would be clues to where Darshan was.

Dan had reached the top of the hill and was sitting on a rock, taking in the view. He was supposed to be meeting the two women at six o'clock, but the shuttle boat didn't leave until six thirty so he was obviously intending to return on foot. As it was now nearly twenty past four, he would probably be setting off within the next half hour – which meant, with any luck, there wouldn't be time for him to become involved in a conversation with Aldo. But I wanted to be there just in case.

9

The Last Question

As I started to walk along the beach, Dan began to descend the hill. By the time I got to Aldo's tent, he was nearly halfway down. Aldo was strumming his guitar and singing to himself:

> 'You don't need to run barefoot
> to feel you're free
> when you find the shoes
> to fit your feet.'

When he noticed me, he stopped.

'Sorry if I'm a bit early,' I said. 'I'm not disturbing you, am I?'

'No, it's fine. I was going to suggest meeting earlier when I got back from the port, but since you were with Dan, I didn't say anything.'

'Was that because you'd have felt you had to invite him too?' I asked, sitting down.

'No, it just didn't look like you were going to be free to come earlier. Now that you mention it, though, I suppose it could have been a bit awkward if we'd arranged to meet without asking him if he wanted to come as well.'

'And then if he'd ended up coming, we wouldn't have been able to talk about the book.'

'Probably not.'

'You don't sound so sure. I thought it was something you weren't that keen to share with people.'

'It's true that I don't want to share it with someone who isn't genuinely interested in it. I've already done that once. A friend of a friend came to my flat one day for a guitar session and saw the book on my bookcase. He asked what it was, so I showed it to him and ended up telling him all about it. But later I found out he'd told my friend that we hadn't done much guitar playing because I'd insisted on telling him a long story I'd probably made up just to impress him. So since then I haven't been in such a hurry to tell people about it.'

'I mentioned it to Dan, I'm afraid. I didn't tell him what it was exactly; I just said we were going to have a look at a book of yours, and that's why we couldn't join him tonight – he's off for a meal with some people from the place where he's staying. You wouldn't have fancied it, would you?'

'Maybe some other time. I don't really feel like going all the way to the port again. Anyway, I thought we could have something to eat here.'

'That'd be great – I've hardly eaten anything all day. I've been too busy thinking.'

'What about?'

'Whether you'd mind if Dan knew about the book, for one thing.'

'Don't worry about that. He seems like someone you can trust. Was he that friend you went out with last night?'

'Yeah, that's right.'

'Does he live in Greece as well?'

'No – England.'

'And you just bumped into him here?'

'Yeah. I couldn't believe it.'

'When was the last time you'd seen each other?'

'Over a year ago … So he didn't say anything about the book when he went past?'

'No.'

By now Dan had reached the foot of the hill. As he came closer, I noticed he was wearing sandals.

'Great view from the top. Thanks a lot,' he said, taking off the sandals and handing them to Aldo. 'Now I owe you two favours.'

'You've already done me one, actually.'

'What was that?'

'You gave me an idea for a song.'

'Let's hear it, then,' said Dan.

'I've only got a couple of lines, so it's not much of a song yet.'

'It doesn't matter – I'm proud to have inspired even that much.'

'You might be disappointed. It's pretty simple.'

'Don't worry, I'll take responsibility for that.'

'OK. I'm not going to sing it, though.'

Aldo recited the words he had been singing when I arrived.

'You could be right, there,' said Dan. 'I was glad your sandals fitted me, anyway.'

Aldo smiled at his comment.

I looked at Dan. 'Didn't you say you were meeting some people at six?'

'Why, what time is it?'

'Just gone quarter to five.'

'I suppose I'd better be getting back, then.'

When Dan had gone, I told Aldo my idea that there might be some questions in the book which needed answering and maybe these answers would provide clues as to how Darshan could be found.

'The only problem is that all the questions seem to be rhetorical,' he said. 'And even when an answer can be given, it's usually just yes or no.'

'You don't think it's worth checking?'

'It won't do any harm, I suppose.'

Aldo crawled inside his tent and re-emerged with the book in his hand.

'Do you want to eat straight away?' he said as he passed it to me.

'I wouldn't mind.'

'I was just going to do some rice with tomatoes, peppers and olives. Is that all right?'

'Sounds great. I wasn't expecting anything so elaborate.'

Aldo took a saucepan and a gas ring out of his tent and set them down on a piece of wood near the rocks. He filled the pan with water from a bottle and lit the gas, then disappeared inside his tent again and came out with the tomatoes and peppers, some plastic plates and forks, and a Swiss army knife.

'Do you fancy some wine?' he said.

'I think I'll wait and have it with the food if that's all right – I'll be dizzy enough as it is looking through all these questions. How many pages are there altogether?' I asked, remembering they weren't numbered.

'I don't know exactly.'

I opened the book and counted the pages.

'Twenty-six.'

'That's not too many, is it?' said Aldo.

'That's without counting both sides, don't forget. And are there any other pages like the first one, with more than one question?'

'At least a dozen, I think.'

'So that's well over sixty questions in total.'

'You'd better get started, then.'

I began opening the book at random to see if I could find any questions (apart from the three on the first page) which required a fixed answer. Aldo was kneeling on the sand, cutting up the tomatoes on a plate he had placed on a flattish rock.

'Do you want a bit of bread to keep you going until the rice is done?' he said.

'Yeah – thanks.'

He went over to his tent and came back with a loaf of bread and a packet of rice. He handed me the bread, then knelt down to chop the peppers.

'Actually, maybe it's not a bad idea to have a drop of wine after all – now that I've got some bread to go with it,' I said.

'It's just inside the tent if you want to go and get it, and there should be some plastic cups there as well.'

I fetched the wine and poured some out for both of us before resuming my search through the book. This time I opened it at the following page:

What is it that keeps the heart beating
as we rest to keep pace
with forms that race
against the backdrop of closed eyes?

And who are the players that appear
with different faces in different scenes
then disappear without trace
in the morning light?

Is it they who orchestrate
those random remarks of the day
that assure them of life
beyond the night?

'There are two questions here that can't be answered yes or no,' I said. 'And I wouldn't say they're rhetorical.'

I read the first one to Aldo.

'What's the answer to that, then?' he asked as he got up to put the rice in the saucepan.

'I thought it was obvious.'

'What is it, then?'

'Oxygen!'

'There's a bit more to it than that.' He sat down and took a sip of wine.

'Maybe we should say "Our breathing", then.'

'What makes us breathe, though?'

'Our desire to, for one thing.'

'Even when we're asleep – or unconscious?'

'All right, so it's the automatic nervous system.'

'You mean "autonomic",' he said.

'OK, whatever it's called.'

'And how does that work?'

'It's controlled by the brain, isn't it?'

'And where does the programming for the brain come from?'

'Our DNA, I imagine … OK, I know what you're going to say next. What about the second question?' I said, and read it out to him.

'You're the one with the answers.' He took another sip of wine.

I remembered something I had read in a book on dream interpretation. 'I reckon the "players" could be the various parts of ourselves that are represented by images of different people in our dreams.'

'True, but if we want to answer the question more precisely, we need to recognize what those parts are – and that isn't always easy.'

I had to admit that the answers to the two questions were not as clear-cut as I had believed.

I abandoned the idea of opening the book at random and returned to where I had left off the previous day. On the sixth page was the following question:

> *If a colour knew*
> *it wasn't pleasing to you,*
> *what would it do?*

'What about this one?' I read out the question. 'Isn't the answer "Nothing"?'

'That's what I thought at first. But if a colour knew that someone didn't like it, it would mean it had consciousness – in which case we couldn't be sure it would do nothing.'

'You mean it might try to change itself?!'

'That's what people sometimes do,' said Aldo.

'We can hardly compare colours to people.'

'Is that because every colour's unique – or because every person is?'

I couldn't think of a response.

'Anyway,' he said, 'even if the answer *was* "Nothing", it would hardly be a clue to where Darshan is.'

I looked at the question on the opposite page.

*What would become
of the moon and the sun
if they stayed side by side
never ceding the sky?*

Although it also seemed to be of the type I was looking for, I found there was no definite answer to this one either.

'What about the three on the first page?' I said. 'What do you think they refer to?'

'How do you mean?'

'Is it the page, the book, or life?'

'Maybe all of those – or none of them.'

'What else could they refer to?'

'Whatever you happen to be thinking about when you open the book at that page. So, in my case, the answer to *What is the first question?* would be "How do I find Darshan?"'

'And the answer to that?'

'By studying the book.'

'What about the second question? *How many questions are there to answer?*'

'Well, since I'm thinking about the ones in the book and how they can lead me to Darshan, and since I've come to the conclusion that they're all basically rhetorical, then, assuming the question means "How many questions need to be answered?", the answer would have to be "None".'

'So why do you think Darshan told you to look in the book to figure out how to find him?'

Aldo frowned, then his eyes lit up. 'That's it!'

'What?'

'The answer to *What is the last question?*: Why did Darshan tell me to look in the book to discover how to find him if the answers to the questions aren't going to help me?'

'And what's the answer to that, then?'

'It must be that the point is to focus on the questions themselves, not the answers.'

'That's what you've been doing, isn't it?'

'Maybe not enough. Even though I haven't been looking for specific answers to the questions, I've still been focusing on the meaning behind them, and if you think about it, that's more or less the same as trying to answer them.'

'What else could you do, though?'

'Maybe I've got to forget about the content altogether and look for some sort of hidden code.'

'Like what?'

'I don't know … Maybe the first letters of all the questions can be put together to spell out a sentence.'

'That's an idea. Why don't you get your pen and notepad so you can write them down as I read them out?'

While Aldo went to his tent, I checked the first letters of the questions on the first page: W, H, W. The next seven pages each had one question on them. The first letters were: D, C, I, W, I, W, D.

'It doesn't look too hopeful,' I said when he returned.

I read out the letters to him.

'I see what you mean.' He thought for a moment. 'Maybe we can form a sentence by taking the first letter from each *line* of every question. We'll have to leave out the first page, but we can regard that as a kind of introduction.'

Starting from the second page, I read out the first letters of each line as Aldo noted them down:

'D, T, O, T, C, I, O ...'

'OK, I reckon that's enough,' he said.

'Any more ideas?'

'Not really. How about you?'

'I hate to say it, Aldo, but maybe Darshan never intended you to find him in the first place, and the reason he said studying the book could help you track him down was that he wanted to make sure you'd spend enough time thinking about the questions – so the meaning behind them would sink in and you might start seeing life in a different way.'

A change came over Aldo's face, like the shadow of a cloud creeping across a hilltop on a breezy day.

He got up to see if the rice was ready, then turned off the gas ring and took the saucepan over to the rock where he had left the chopped peppers and tomatoes. He had covered them with a couple of plastic plates but one of these had blown off.

'I hope you don't mind a few grains of sand mixed in with the tomatoes,' he said solemnly.

'Is that a traditional Italian recipe?'

I tried to catch his eye, but he just gave a half-smile before adding the tomatoes and peppers to the rice.

He went inside his tent and came out with a little jar of olives, which he emptied into the pan. I poured myself some more wine and observed him as he served out the food. Perhaps he was regretting having told me about the book. I hadn't been much help with it so far, and now I had probably made him think he had been wasting his time reading through the questions in search of a clue that didn't exist.

10

A Door to the Past

When Aldo had finished eating, he put his plate down and drank the remainder of his wine.

'Maybe you're right,' he said. 'Maybe Darshan did play a trick on me. It's true that reading through the questions again has made me appreciate them more. I doubt I'd have spent so much time on them if I hadn't been looking for a hidden clue. And I don't think I'd have been so intrigued by the book in the first place if he hadn't told me it was magic and would lead me back to him. So I guess I shouldn't be so disappointed. It's just that he'd seemed so sincere about the whole thing.'

'Best not to dwell on that. Why don't you just look on it as a clever way of getting you to do something that was good for you?'

'That's no doubt how my mum would see it. The only way she could get me to go to bed when I was little was by saying the magical world of dreams was waiting for me.'

'What about your dad? Did *he* have to use tricks to get you to do what he wanted?'

'I can't remember that much about my dad. He died when I was still a kid.'

'That must have been hard for you … How old were you?'

'Nine.'

'Wasn't that when you went to live in Italy?'

'That's right.'

'Was your father English, then?'

'Yes.'

Aldo avoided my gaze and looked towards the sea.

'Sorry, I shouldn't be asking so many questions.'

'It's all right,' he said, glancing back at me. 'It's almost as if it's someone else's father I'm talking about. Even though my mum's told me a lot about him, it's never been enough to make me feel I really knew him. But I can clearly remember the last time I saw him. It was in the summer holidays, which was when my mum and I used to go to Italy for a month to stay with her parents in Trieste. She worked as a freelance translator so she had plenty of time off, but my father could only usually join us for the last week. He would always hug me when he saw us off at the airport, but that day he gave me a bigger hug than usual. Then he told me to look out for his postcards, because while we were in Italy he'd be going abroad.

'After we'd been in Trieste for about two weeks, he phoned to say he was going to be away longer and wouldn't be coming to join us after all … Can you guess where he'd gone?'

'Where?'

'India.'

'India? What was his job?'

'He worked with his brother – my uncle John – who has a shop in London selling craftwork. He'd originally been a teacher, but after ten years he'd started to find it stressful and he saw the opportunity to try something different when my uncle's wife was pregnant. At the time, she was helping to run the business, so the idea was for my father to take her place when she had the baby.

'About a week after we'd got back from Italy, the police came to tell us he'd been killed in an accident. It must have been awful for my mum: as well as having to deal with her grief, she had to go to India to identify the body and make the arrangements for it to be brought home.'

'Who looked after you while she was away?'

'My grandparents on the Isle of Wight.'

'Did your mum go alone, then?'

'No, my uncle went with her … A few months after the funeral, she sold our house in London and we went to live in Italy – close to her parents' home in Trieste.'

'Did you ever go back to England?'

'Yeah, we used to go and stay with my grandparents in the school holidays, and we often saw my uncle and his family as well.'

'Are your father's parents still alive?'

'Yes. They're getting on a bit now but they're both in good health.'

'Do you see them much?'

'Not as often as I used to, but I try to get over to England once a year.'

'That's how often I go as well – every Christmas.'

'Actually, I haven't been for the last two years. I haven't found the time.'

Aldo gave a half-smile, then looked away. He picked up a stone and tossed it into the sea.

'How old was your father when he died?' I asked.

'Thirty-four.'

'And you said he died in an accident?'

'Yes – he was hit by a bus as he was crossing the road.'

'At least he wouldn't have known much about it.'

'I'm not sure that's such a good thing,' said Aldo.

'How do you mean?'

'To be totally unprepared for death – to have no chance to reflect on your life before you leave it behind.'

'It's better than feeling a lot of pain, though, isn't it?'

'I don't know. Obviously, I wouldn't want to die a long, painful death, but I'd like to have some time to prepare myself for whatever comes next.'

'How can you prepare for the unknown?'

'Maybe the answer to that becomes clearer the longer you live.'

I wondered if I would live long enough to be able to say I felt prepared for death.

'Whereabouts in India do you think my father was when he died?' said Aldo.

'I've no idea … Varanasi?'

'No – Calcutta.'

'Isn't that where you met Darshan?'

'Yeah. It's a pretty strange coincidence, isn't it?'

'Did you tell him your father had died there?'

'No, it didn't really seem appropriate.'

'I suppose not … So was it mainly because of your father that you went to India?'

'Probably, though I don't think I was so aware of it at the time. When I was younger, it was the last place I could have imagined going. Then, when I was twenty-seven, I met some people who'd been there, and after hearing about their adventures I wanted to go myself. My mum wasn't too pleased when I told her, but she knew there was nothing she could do to stop me.

'I dug out the old postcards my father had sent, and while I was looking through them, I had the idea of following the route he'd taken. He went from Mumbai to Goa, then down to Cochin and right to Kanyakumari on the southernmost tip before making his way back up to Madras and finally Calcutta – all in the space of about a month. In his last postcard, which he sent from Calcutta, he said he'd be flying back from Delhi and his final stop on the way there was going to be Varanasi. The postcard arrived more than two weeks after the police had called to tell us he'd died. I remember it being pretty hard for me to understand that at the time.

'Before I went, I also wanted to have a look in the rucksack he'd had with him to see if there was anything that could be useful to me. My mum had brought it back with her, but I didn't know about it till I was seventeen …

'It was the summer holidays and I'd gone to stay with my grandparents on the Isle of Wight. One day we were talking about my father, and my gran said she'd always regretted not going to India with my mother, even though she knew she wouldn't have been much help, since for one thing, she wouldn't have been able to carry my father's rucksack, as my uncle John had done. I phoned my uncle to find out if he had the rucksack, but he said my mother had kept it.

'When I got back home, I asked her where it was. She told me she'd thrown it out because it had made her too sad to have it in the house. I felt she wasn't telling the truth, though, and I wondered if she'd hidden it away somewhere.

'That night, I crept out of my bedroom onto the landing and stood on a chair to reach the hatch to the loft. But it was locked. The next morning I asked my mum where the key was. She said she couldn't remember where she'd put it. I looked everywhere but I couldn't find it, so I told her I was going to break open the hatch. I didn't mean it – I just wanted to see how she'd react. And then she admitted the rucksack was in the loft. When I asked why she'd hidden it, she said it should be left in the past where it belonged. Then she started crying, so I dropped the subject.

'Not long after, I went to live on my own in Bologna, and the whole issue became something we never talked about.

'Then, a couple of years ago, after booking my flight to India, I went to ask her if there was anything in my father's rucksack I might be able to use. One thing I had in mind was a camera, because, if you remember, I'd given mine to a friend. But she told me my father had had his camera on him when the bus hit him, and it had got smashed. The next thing I asked about was a guidebook. She hesitated, then said even if there was one, a lot of the information would be out of date. I asked whether she'd mind if I went into the loft to have a look, but she said she'd rather I didn't. I told her my father would have wanted me to make use of his things, but she refused to give me the key. So I went upstairs with a hammer. When she saw I wasn't bluffing, she showed me where the key was. It turned out to be the one in her bedroom door – which was no doubt why the door was never locked!

'So anyway, I went into the loft and found the rucksack – in a corner under a pile of empty boxes.'

'What was in it?'

'Mainly clothes – all washed and neatly folded. There were also a few pieces of craftwork my father had brought back with him … as well as a guidebook. It felt strange touching the clothes and imagining my father wearing them, and I had to take them all out to get to the guidebook, which was right at the bottom – together with a book of poems. I also found two of those little plastic containers you keep film in for your camera. One was empty and the other had an unused roll inside, and it crossed my mind that there might have been some used films as well but my mum had removed them.

'I took out the guidebook and went downstairs, where my mum was waiting, drying the tears from her eyes. I asked her about the films, but she said there hadn't been any more and it had been impossible to develop the one in the camera. This time I believed her – maybe because it suited me to think my father had been like me when it came to taking photos.'

'So was the guidebook any good?'

'Yeah, there was some useful stuff in it.'

'Did you really need it, though?'

'How do you mean?'

'Don't you think travelling's more of an adventure without one? And it makes your rucksack lighter, too.'

'Actually, I didn't take it with me to India – I just copied down a few things and gave it back to my mum.'

'How come?'

'That was how she wanted it.'

'Why?'

Aldo hesitated. 'It wasn't the guidebook she was bothered about – it was something that had been written in it.'

I waited for him to continue.

'As I was about to leave my mum's that day, she told me to look inside the back cover. There was a poem – a love poem – in my father's handwriting.'

'To your mother?'

'That's what I thought, but she said it had probably been written for another woman. Then she told me to sit down because she was going to tell me the truth about my father …

'About six months before going to India, he'd begun to have contact with an ex-girlfriend. They weren't having an affair, though he'd confessed to my mum that he couldn't get her off his mind. The situation was beginning to affect his work as well as their marriage, so he decided he needed some time alone to sort himself out.

'He'd recently become interested in Indian philosophy, and he convinced himself that going to India would help him discover what he really wanted in life. He was also hoping to find some craftsmen there who he might be able to do business with. Even though my mum wasn't happy with the idea, she more or less accepted it in the end, because at least it meant he'd be away from the other woman.

'He'd only intended to go for three weeks – during the time my mum and I would be in Italy – but then he changed his flight to stay longer. All the time he was away, my mum was hoping he'd begin to see things clearly and forget about his ex so they could make a fresh start. And she could have at least held on to that idea after his death if it hadn't been for the poem.'

'How come she thought it was for the other woman? Because it wasn't in Italian?'

'No, that wasn't the reason – my father could hardly speak Italian, let alone write a poem in it. It was just that he'd never written anything like that before, so my mum figured he must have been inspired by his ex, because the book of poems in his rucksack was a present from her.'

'That doesn't necessarily mean he wrote the poem for her.'

'That's what I said. But my mum said some of the lines suggested he did – though I imagine the reason she didn't get rid of it was that she could never be completely sure it was for the other woman.'

I was tempted to ask about the content of the poem, but I managed to resist.

'What stuff did you note down from the guidebook?'

'Names of hotels and restaurants, mainly. My father had written comments next to the ones he'd been to, and I liked the idea that I might end up going to the same places. That was the reason I stayed at the hotel in Calcutta and went to the restaurant there – and I was especially curious about those places since they'd been added in my father's handwriting.'

'So, in a way, your father was responsible for you meeting Darshan.'

'Yeah – though I didn't give it much thought till I got back from India. That's when I realized my trip had really been about trying to feel a connection with my father.

I know it might seem obvious to everyone else, but I hadn't admitted it to myself until then – probably because I'd been feeling resentful after finding out he'd gone off like that when I was so young. He often used to travel because of his work and I'd always accepted this, but after my mum had told me the real reason he'd gone to India, I'd begun to wonder if he'd been planning to leave us, and I'd become aware of some bitterness mixed in with the sadness I'd always felt.

'After returning from India, though, I started to see things differently. Meeting Darshan and reading the questions in his book had made me realize how little I knew myself – and that I didn't really have any answers to the problems in my life. And I thought about my father, who wasn't much older than I am now when he died. When I was a kid, I expected him to know everything, but now I can see that in some ways he was still a kid himself.'

'So what about Darshan? Do you think you see him as a substitute father?'

'That's no doubt what a psychologist would say. And I suppose I can't deny it – though, again, it didn't occur to me till after I'd returned from India ... which was when I started my psychology course, by the way.'

It was now clear why Aldo had seemed so disappointed when I had mentioned the possibility of there being no way of finding Darshan. I wished I had said something more encouraging.

The last of the day's sunlight was flickering on the waves. Before long we would be sitting in darkness. If we were going to have a final look through the book of questions without having to use a torch, now was the time. But I had no idea what to suggest. I felt we had exhausted all the possibilities – just as Aldo must have felt after searching all over the house for the key …

'I was just thinking about the key to your mum's loft,' I said. 'What if it's the same with Darshan's book and the solution's been staring us in the face all along?'

'What have you got in mind?'

I thought for a few moments. 'Why don't you ask the book?'

11

A Falling Leaf

I handed the book to Aldo and he opened it straight away.

'What does it say?'

He passed the book back to me. 'The page on the left.'

Could the sun
cease to shine
except to set
at the end of time?

Should a river
continue to flow
if just one drop
resisted so?

I read the words a couple of times.

'What do you think?' I asked.

'It's funny – I've thought about that second question a lot over the last few days, but it never occurred to me that I might not be completely sure about wanting to figure out how to find Darshan.'

'How do you mean?'

'Even though I feel I'd like to see him again, I don't know if I'm ready to give up the book yet. It's as if part of me wants to solve the riddle but another part doesn't. So maybe subconsciously I've been making it a lot more difficult than it is in order to delay things for as long as possible. And I reckon it was a similar thing with my father's rucksack: if I'd really wanted to, I could have broken into the loft straight away. The truth is I probably wasn't ready.'

'For what?'

'I think deep down I was still waiting for him to come home, hanging on to that last memory I had of him – and to that last postcard, which had given me hope that he might not have died after all and it had somehow been a case of mistaken identity.'

'OK, I can understand you not wanting to accept the truth about your father, but I'm not sure I see the connection with how you feel about Darshan and the book. What is it you don't want to face now?'

'My reluctance to let go of things, for a start. But also the possibility that the reality of the situation will be harder to deal with than the mystery I've created around it in my mind. Maybe it's like you said and there never really was a way to find Darshan. But while I still have the book and believe there's a riddle to solve, I can hang on to the idea that I might be able to see him again.'

'All right, but suppose there definitely was a way to find him. Forgetting about the book for a minute, would you say you felt ready to meet him again?'

'Yes, I'm pretty sure about that.'

'And did he say you weren't to make a copy of the questions?'

'No, he didn't.'

'So what is it you don't want to let go of?'

'It's not just the questions, it's the book itself. I don't think I've ever had anything so unique. What if I give it away and then discover my solution to the riddle was wrong?'

'But if I'm the one you've given it to, you can just get in touch and I'll give it back to you.'

'I'm not sure that would be right.'

'Come on, Aldo – you don't have to take it all so seriously.'

I picked up his pen and notepad and wrote down my address and phone number for him.

'Anyway, whatever happens, we can still keep in touch,' I said. 'For one thing, I'm curious to know what Darshan will say to you. No doubt you'll find out why he set you this riddle in the first place instead of just telling you where you could meet him.'

'You seem to be forgetting something.'

'What?'

'We haven't solved it yet.'

'I get the feeling we're going to, though.'

'Have the questions about the sun and the river given you an idea?' asked Aldo.

'No, but the ones on the other page have.'

I showed him the questions.

Can you remember
the last time
a falling leaf
landed
at your feet?

Will you remember
the next time
you push your way
through the day?

'Don't they confirm what I was saying before about the solution to the riddle?' I said. 'Sometimes we don't notice things that are right in front of us. We're so busy rushing around trying to get what we want that we end up losing touch with the present moment – and with nature. You can't fully appreciate nature if you've got your mind on something else.'

'Mm, that's true … But we're still no closer to finding what it is that's right in front of us.'

'Maybe we are. What did you say the last question was?'

'The last one in the book?'

'No, your answer to *What is the last question?* – the third one on the first page. Remember?'

'Yes. It was: "Why did Darshan tell me to look in the book to discover how to find him if the answers to the questions aren't going to help me?"'

'And you said the answer to that was because he wanted you to focus on the questions, not the answers.'

'That's right. So?'

'What if he didn't want you to focus on the questions, either?'

'How do you mean?'

'What about the designs on the pages?'

'What about them?'

'Don't they look like leaves?'

'I suppose they do. But that doesn't seem like much of a clue.'

I thought for a moment. 'Didn't you say Darshan told you to study the book from cover to cover to discover where and when you could meet him?'

'Yes, that's right.'

'Are you sure he said "study", and not "read"?'

'Yes, because I remember it made me think the book must have some pretty serious stuff in it.'

'So that suggests the clue could have something to do with the designs.'

'Why's that?'

'Because "study" can also mean "look at carefully".'

'I'd never thought of that.'

'And did he definitely say you had to study it from cover to cover?'

'Yes, he made a point of repeating those words.'

'All the pages must be important, then.'

I had a closer look at the designs, which consisted of leaf-like shapes made up of smaller ones entwined around the border of each page.

'Have you noticed how many leaves there are on the pages?' I said.

'Yes – too many to count!'

'I don't mean every single one, just the bigger ones.'

'I haven't counted those, either. Anyway, they all seem to merge into each other.'

'It's still possible to make out several main parts to the pattern.'

I handed him the book.

'Mm, you're right,' he said. 'It looks like there are seven on this page.'

'And there were seven on the others I looked at. Don't you think that could be significant?'

'Maybe – if there are seven on all the pages.'

Aldo passed the book back to me and I checked every page.

'That's strange,' I said. 'All the pages have seven leaves on them apart from the last one.'

'How many has that got on it?'

'Eight.'

'Are you sure none of the others have eight?'

'Yeah, I'm pretty sure.'

'But it makes sense, I suppose, since the last page is the only one that doesn't have a question on it ... What do you make of it, by the way?'

While you learned
what you thought you were learning,
what you needed to know
was being taught.

'I'm not even sure what I *think* I'm learning,' I said.

'I'm beginning to feel like that too.'

The sun was hovering over the horizon, preparing to make its exit from the day. We sat in silence as it melted into the sea and the evening wind began to blow.

'Pass me the book a minute, will you?' said Aldo.

I did as he asked, then turned my gaze back to the horizon, which was slowly fading as sky and sea merged beneath the creeping shadow of dusk.

When I looked at Aldo again, he was smiling to himself.

'You were right,' he said. 'Just like the key to the loft: right in front of us all the time.'

'What was?'

'The leaves on the pages.'

I waited for him to explain.

'Think about it,' he said. 'Why seven?'

'I don't know ... Maybe it refers to the Seven Wonders of the World, and they can give us some clues about where to find Darshan.'

'It's a lot simpler than that.'

I thought for a few seconds. 'Well, there are seven days in a week, of course.'

'That's it.'

'How do you mean?'

'How many pages are there in the book?'

'Twenty-six – unless I miscounted.'

'You didn't. I just counted them myself. And what did you say after you'd counted them and I said twenty-six wasn't that many?'

'I don't know. What did I say?'

'That that was without counting both sides.'

'Oh yeah, that's right,' I said.

'So how many pages are there altogether?'

'Fifty-two. Of course! So each page represents a week of the year … Wait a minute – what about the last one?'

'I'm sure you'll work it out.'

'I already have: the extra leaf stands for the extra day in a leap year.'

'No, that's not it. Just do some simple maths and you'll get it. You can use my pen and notepad if necessary,' he said with a grin.

'That's OK, I think I'll manage.'

I did the calculation in my head. Until that moment I had considered a year to be exactly fifty-two weeks, without realizing this only added up to 364 days.

'So,' said Aldo, 'now that we know the book can be used as a calendar, all we have to do is find the key page, then we can see what the number is and that'll be the week when I can meet Darshan.'

'And how are we going to find the key page?'

'Since Darshan said the book would lead me to him when the time was right, maybe it'll be one with a question about the idea that there's always a right time for things to happen.'

'There's a page like that, is there?'

'Two or three, actually.'

He started from the back of the book and skimmed through a few pages, straining his eyes in the dimming light.

'Here's one,' he said.

Does the wise leaf wait
to be taken
by Autumn?

Or does it struggle
to free itself
in the wind?

Or does it hang on
until the end,
resisting
as it falls?

'Do you think this could be the one we want?' I asked.

'Maybe. I'll show you the others and we can see which is the most appropriate. It looks like we're going to need my torch, though.'

While Aldo went over to his tent, I found the number of the page (forty-three) and noted it down. When he returned, he gave me the torch to hold as he continued flicking through the book.

'Here's another,' he said.

> *How can a fledgling be so worldly wise*
> *that, having never learned how to, it flies?*

'And there's this one as well.'

> *Does an infant suffer*
> *because she crawls?*

> *And when she tries to walk,*
> *does she fail if she falls?*

'Let's see what the numbers are,' I said.

Aldo counted the pages as I kept the torch shining on the book.

'Fourteen and twenty.' He wrote down the numbers on his notepad.

'Are there any others?'

'Just one, I think.'

He turned over a few more pages.

Does the owl worry
throughout the day
that come the night
he won't catch his prey?

'Isn't the message there more to do with trust?' I said.

'Trusting that something will happen when the time is right, you mean?'

'OK, I suppose so. What's the page number?'

'Hang on a second … Eight.'

'So you're sure there aren't any more?'

'Those were all I could remember. I might just have another quick look, though.'

He turned to the beginning of the book and began to thumb through it again, but the light from his torch was fading and he only managed to glance at a few pages before it went out.

'It doesn't matter. I'm pretty sure there are just those four,' he said.

'Which one would you choose, then?'

'Maybe we don't have to choose only one. What if I can meet Darshan in all four weeks?'

'I hadn't thought of that … Do you mind if I use your lighter to have another look at the questions?'

'And set fire to the book, you mean! Anyway, you don't need to see the questions again because I can remember them – maybe not the exact words, but enough for what we want.'

Although we agreed that the question about the fledgling was the one which best expressed the idea of there always being a right time for things to happen, we felt it didn't stand out sufficiently for us to disregard the others. It seemed that there could in fact be four different weeks when it was possible to meet Darshan.

'Did Darshan definitely say the place you could meet him wasn't in India?' I asked.

'Yes.'

'So do you think he left India when he moved out of his house in Calcutta?'

'It's a possibility. Either that or he travels abroad to visit friends or relatives.'

'But is it likely that every year he goes to another country four times in the same four weeks?'

'Maybe he travels regularly because of his job,' said Aldo.

'He could do, I suppose. What about the address? Do you think it'll be the same for each week?'

'Yes, because I'm pretty sure he said there was "another place" I'd be able to meet him; he didn't say there were "other places".'

'How are we going to find out where it is, though?'

'We'll have to have another look at the four pages and see if there's a clue in any of the questions. It might be something like I suggested before: a sort of code where the first letters of each word or line can be put together to spell out the name of a city or country.'

'What about the street name?' I said.

'Maybe one page gives that, one gives the city, one the area, and one the country.'

'And the house number?'

'That'll probably be the number of the page that the street name's on.'

'That makes sense, I suppose. So we'll have to wait till tomorrow to check that – unless you're willing to use your lighter.'

'I think I'd rather wait. I don't want to risk singeing the pages. But at least we can find out which months the four weeks are in.'

We worked out that the eighth week of the year (that is, the eighth block of seven days) fell in February, the fourteenth week was in April, the twentieth was in May, and the forty-third in October.

'By the way, which months were you in India?' I asked.

'From March till June. Why?'

'Can you remember when you met Darshan exactly?'

'Yes, because I arrived in Calcutta on the night of my father's birthday, which was the 13th of May. So it was the 14th when I went to the restaurant where Darshan found me, because I remember going there on my first day.'

'How long did you stay at his house?'

'I spent two nights there and left sometime in the evening of the third day.'

'So that would have been May the 16th.'

'Mm.'

'Then you went back a few days later and he wasn't there.'

'That's right.'

'I wonder if that was the twentieth week of the year, and that's why he'd gone away.'

'Mm, that's a point.'

Aldo worked it out in his head.

'The twentieth week was the time when I was at his house,' he said.

'Are you sure?'

'Yes – it was from the 13th of May till the 19th.'

'But if you only stayed with Darshan until May the 16th, he could have gone abroad on the 17th.'

'I don't think so, because when I went back to his house on my last day in Calcutta, the young man told me the previous tenant had left two days before, which would have been the 19th.'

'Are you sure you remember the exact date you left Calcutta?'

'Yes, because I stayed there nine nights – one for every year I'd had with my father.'

'So if Darshan was definitely in Calcutta for the twentieth week of the year, you know what that means.'

'That we can exclude page twenty from our four possible pages.'

'Can you remember what was on it?'

'Hang on a second.' Aldo took his lighter out of his pocket and used it to see the notepad. 'It was the question about the fledgling.'

'But if that one's not relevant, it's likely the others won't be either.'

'Why's that?'

'Because it seems the theme of the questions on those pages isn't part of the clue we're looking for. Anyway, to tell you the truth, I had my doubts about the idea that there was more than one week when you could meet Darshan. I'd find it a lot easier to believe he always goes to another country on the same dates if it was only once a year.'

'Maybe you're right … but I'm still curious to know if there's a hidden address on those pages.'

With great care, Aldo used his lighter to check the four pages. It only took him a few minutes to see that there was no part of an address concealed on any of them.

'So it really does look like we're back to square one again,' he said.

'Not completely. At least we've discovered we can use the book as a calendar. And I still think you could be right about the first letters of each word or line spelling out an address; I just think it'll all be on the same page.'

'And do you reckon the theme of whatever's on that page will be relevant as well?'

'It's logical to assume so,' I said.

'But what could be more relevant than the idea of things happening at the right time?'

'I don't know … There might be a question about the meeting up of long-lost friends or something.'

'I can't remember seeing one like that.'

'Maybe it's expressed in a very subtle way.'

'It's worth having a look, I suppose … But we'll have to wait till tomorrow to do that,' said Aldo, and put his lighter back in his pocket.

The only light now was the subdued glow of the half-moon. A strand of moonlight marked a pathway to us across the dark, velvety water. Its shimmering surface held my gaze. My mind wandered, and I found myself reflecting on the circumstances that had caused my path in life to coincide with Aldo's. Coming to Amorgos no longer seemed like a random decision. I wondered if there was always a more important reason for going somewhere in addition to the one you were aware of. I remembered what Aldo had said about going to India … and it occurred to me that something didn't add up …

'Didn't you say it was only when you got back from India that you realized your trip had really been about trying to feel a connection with your father?' I said.

'Yeah, that's right.'

'But then after that you told me you'd gone to Calcutta on the day of his birthday, and you'd stayed there nine nights – one for each year you'd had with him. Not to mention the restaurant you went to and the hotel you stayed at, which were both places he'd been to.'

Aldo gave a frown. 'I'm not sure where you're going with this.'

'I just figured you must have been aware of trying to feel a connection with your father while you were in India.'

He hesitated. 'I can see why it looks that way. It's hard to explain ... It was as if there were two parts of me: one was aware of what I was doing, and the other was refusing to acknowledge it – because of the resentment I was feeling, as I mentioned before. That was one of the things that got me interested in studying psychology. I wanted to understand more about the origins of conflicts like this in the mind.'

'That's something I'm trying to understand more about too ... But I guess you don't need a psychology degree to see that we often have conflicting thoughts when we're not letting ourselves do what we really want to do.'

'That's true ... though it might take a bit of practice to identify which of these thoughts are really ours and which ones are just the opinions of others.'

I began to think about some of the times when it had been hard for me to separate my own thoughts from the other voices that were trying to make themselves heard in my mind ...

Later, we talked about the different islands we had been to and the ones we hoped to visit in the future. Before returning home, Aldo wanted to go to a nearby island called Koufonisi. He still had two weeks of his holiday left and was planning to spend most of it there – which meant he would soon be leaving Amorgos. It was clear that he intended to continue his holiday alone, but even if he had asked me to go with him, I wouldn't have been able to: I only had enough money on me for another couple of days. When I asked him whether he would still leave Amorgos if we hadn't found the clue in the book, he seemed to hesitate, then said he felt confident we were getting close to finding it so it was unlikely he would have to make that decision.

12

An Open Secret?

The following morning, while I was having my breakfast on a bench in the square near the harbour, I spotted Aldo waiting at a phone box. I went over to talk to him. He told me he was going to ring his mother because it was her birthday, then he was going to take the bus to the main town up in the hills. The book of questions was sticking out of the side pocket of his trousers. He said he was intending to read through it again to see if he could find a page like the one we had described.

When I returned to the beach, I didn't sit down. I wanted to do some exploring before I left the island. I wouldn't be meeting Aldo again until much later, so I thought I would go over the hill to the other beach, then climb the next one to see if it was worth going any further. I put what I needed in my haversack and set off.

As I followed the path up the hillside, I half-heartedly tried to quell the hope of coming across the young woman I had seen the previous day. On reaching the top,

I saw that the beach was deserted. I sat on a rock for a few minutes, drinking in the vibrant blue all around me, then looked for the best route down. Although the descent was steep, I was able to pick my way through the prickly bushes and make it to the bottom without losing my footing on the scree.

After a leisurely swim in the lagoon-like sea, I spent some time reflecting on the things I had discussed with Aldo the night before, recording as much as I could remember in my notebook. An hour slipped by.

My thoughts turned to the second hill and what lay beyond it. Like the first one, it was a treeless outcrop peppered with grey-green bushes. When I walked over to it, I saw that it wasn't as steep as it looked. But the strength of the sun helped me resist the urge to race up the winding path, and I was able to enjoy the silence along the way. On the other side there wasn't a beach, just a rocky shoreline. The path continued but it didn't go down to the sea; it dipped abruptly before rising again to run along the side of the adjacent hill – a looming mass of rock with sparse vegetation clinging to its crevices. I kept going, passing several precipitous drops on my left, until I came to a point where a steep trail branched off to the right. I didn't fancy climbing to the ridge in the searing heat, and since there was no end in sight to the path I was on, I turned back.

I returned to the deserted beach drenched in sweat and plunged into the cool water. After drying off in the sun, I found an area of shade near some rocks, where I lay down and drifted off to sleep.

* * *

I woke up with a start. It had already gone five o'clock, which was the time I was supposed to be meeting Aldo. I stuffed my towel into my haversack, scrambled to put on my trainers and jumped to my feet. It wasn't a matter of urgency to be there on time, but I was eager to see if he had found the clue in the book.

When I reached the top of the hill, I tried to spot him on the beach. There was no sign of him … or his tent. My mind stalled, refusing to process the image. Then a cascade of thoughts burst in. Where had he gone? Why hadn't he told me he was leaving? What was he hiding from me? How would I get my hands on the book now? I grasped at the voice of reason: maybe he had decided to get a room for a few days. But even if he had, it wouldn't have prevented him from coming to meet me – though it could have caused him to be late, in which case he might be on his way.

By the time I got to the bottom of the hill, it was twenty to six. I clutched at the possibility that he had been there at five and then left because he had assumed I wasn't coming. About fifty metres from the spot where his tent had been was the tent of a young German couple. I asked if they had seen him. They told me they had spent most of the day in the town, and when they had returned he had gone.

It crossed my mind that Aldo might be playing a trick on me, though I had no idea what its purpose would be. It seemed more likely that he really had left. But why had he kept me in the dark about his intentions? The only explanation I could think of was that he had changed his mind about giving me the book.

Further along the beach was the tent of a young Greek man with shoulder-length hair. He told me he had seen Aldo leave in a hurry with all his stuff late in the morning.

I arrived back at my place under the tree and sat down. Had Aldo been deceiving me all along? It probably wasn't true that he had to pass the book on. No doubt it had just been a device he had used as an incentive for me to help him solve the riddle. And now that he had figured it out, as I imagined he had done that morning, he no longer needed my input.

Struggling to push these thoughts aside, I leaned back on my sleeping bag, which was rolled up loosely at the foot of the tree. There was something hard underneath it. I lifted it up and found a saucepan with a gas ring and a lighter inside – as well as a scribbled note:

My grandad's had a heart attack. Have to go to Athens to change flight and get to UK asap. Leaving on 12.00 boat. I'll be in touch about the book.

Pan and gas ring for you or anyone who wants them.

Aldo

I couldn't help wondering if Aldo had made it all up. And it was strange that he hadn't left me his address or phone number. He obviously preferred to be the one who decided when – or if – we would contact each other again.

I felt a pang of guilt over not giving any thought for his grandfather. But I was still unsure what to believe. Seeking distraction in my notebook, I began reading through my record of the experiences I had had since leaving Athens at the end of July. My recollections pushed Aldo to the back of my mind … until I got to the pages about Amorgos.

I closed the notebook and looked around. The shuttle boat was arriving to pick up its last set of passengers for the day. As it approached the jetty, which was at the opposite end of the beach to where Aldo's tent had been, several people got ready to disembark, one of whom was holding a big red towel …

Dan stepped off the boat and started walking in my direction.

'I thought I'd join you for the sunset,' he said as he sat down.

'I thought you might have brought some company – other than your towel, that is.'

'Uh? The French girls, you mean?'

'Yeah. How did it go?'

'Great. We ended up staying out all night.'

'Have you arranged anything with them for tonight?'

'Nothing definite, but they told me they'll be going to one of the tavernas in the port, so there's a good chance I'll bump into them later.'

Dan took off his trainers and made himself comfortable on his towel.

'What have you been up to today?' I asked.

'I did a fair bit of sleeping practice this morning, then I had something to eat in a café. After that I went to the town and spent most of the afternoon there.'

'It's worth a visit, then?'

'Definitely. It's like a labyrinth: lots of narrow streets connecting one little square to another.'

'You didn't see Aldo there, did you?'

'No, but I saw him earlier down in the port. His boat was late so he came across to have a word with me in the café … Did you know about his grandad?'

'Yeah, he left a note for me.'

'So you didn't see him before he left?'

'No, I just saw him in the morning when he was waiting to phone his mum. How was he?'

'You could tell he was upset, but he still found something to be positive about: if he hadn't rung his mum, he wouldn't have found out about his grandad. It still might be too late, though. He said he may have to stay in Athens for a few nights until he gets his flight sorted out.'

'What time did his boat end up leaving?'

'It must have been well after one o'clock.'

'Was he talking to you all that time?'

'Only for the last ten minutes or so. He said he'd been reading something and he hadn't noticed me. Anyway, I didn't get to the café till around half twelve.'

'Didn't you notice him?'

'No – there were a lot of people waiting for the boat. And it wasn't as if he was right in front of me; he was a fair way up the quayside.'

'Did he say anything else to you before he left?'

'Like what?'

'I don't know … like what he was going to do if he couldn't change his flight.'

'No, he didn't mention that. The only other thing I remember him saying was that there's a nice island nearby – Koufonisi, I think it's called.'

By telling the same story to Dan, Aldo had certainly made it sound more convincing, but what would really have convinced me would have been some news about the clue we had been hoping to discover in the book. As the boat had been delayed, he would have had enough time to find the key page before he left, in which case he could have given Dan a message for me. He could even have asked Dan to give the book to me, since I remembered him saying he seemed trustworthy.

'What's on your mind?' asked Dan.

'I was just thinking about Aldo. By the way, did he mention what he'd been reading while he was waiting for the boat?'

'No, but I assumed it was the little book he had in his hand when he came over to talk to me.'

'Did it have a brown leather cover with a piece of coloured string tied round it?'

'That's right – with a question mark on the front and back.'

'How do you know that?'

'Because he gave it to me to hold while he went to the toilet. At first he tried to put it in his pocket, but it wouldn't fit so he asked if he could leave it with me.'

'That's strange,' I said.

'What?'

'That the book wouldn't fit in his pocket – because that's where he had it when I saw him at the phone box.'

'Now I find it strange,' said Dan.

'What?'

'That he managed to get it into one of those pockets on his shorts.'

'He was wearing shorts?'

'Yeah. Why?'

'Because he was wearing long trousers when I saw him.'

'He must have changed for the journey, then.'

'I'm surprised he went to the trouble: he can't have had much time to play with … Anyway, did you have a look inside the book while you were holding it for him?'

'I must admit I was tempted, but it wouldn't have felt right since I imagined it was that one you mentioned before – the one you said had personal stuff in it.'

'Didn't you ask him about it when he came back from the toilet?'

'I probably would have done, but by then his boat was arriving, so we just had time to say goodbye before he took off.' Dan looked at me with a mischievous glint in his eye. 'Anyway, I thought I could always ask you.'

'As long as you don't expect me to answer.'

'Don't tell me you and Aldo are secret agents!'

'Aldo might well be, for all I know.'

'The less I know, the better, then. I wouldn't want to end up getting tortured or anything. Mind you, maybe I know too much already.'

'Like what?'

'OK, I can't be sure, but I guess it was a personalized gift – from a girlfriend maybe.'

'What makes you say that?'

'The initials on the cover.'

'What do you mean?'

'Hmm, very convincing,' said Dan.

'No, really – I don't know what you mean.'

'Didn't you have a look at the cover?'

'I saw the words in the question marks but I didn't see any initials.'

'They were in the little circles that formed the dots of the question marks. They weren't obvious, since as well as merging together, they formed the outline of the circle. But I'm pretty sure the design was a combination of an "a" and a "w".'

'Capital letters?'

'No, small ones. So does Aldo's surname begin with W?'

'I don't know – I never asked him. Anyway, the person who gave him the book had already written it before they met him, so the letters can't be Aldo's initials.'

'They could have been added later.'

'It's possible, I suppose.'

Why had Aldo never mentioned the hidden letters? During the two years that he had had the book, he must have taken note of what was on the cover. I thought of a book of mine and tried to visualize the front cover … But I could hardly remember the overall design, let alone any details. I had to admit there was a possibility that Aldo had failed to notice the 'a' and the 'w'. Yet I felt more inclined to believe that he had known all along about the letters and they did represent his initials, in which case it would confirm what I had begun to suspect: that Darshan had only ever intended the book to be for him.

I decided to tell Dan the whole story behind it. By the time I had finished, the sun was approaching the horizon.

'So what do you think?' I asked.

'About the sunset?'

'About Aldo's story! Do you believe it?'

'You mean you don't?'

'I did at first, but I'm not so sure any more.'

'Why would he make it up?' said Dan.

'To make his life seem more interesting … You can tell he's a bit of a loner.'

'Maybe so, but he doesn't strike me as the type to invent a whole story about himself.'

'OK, some of it must be true, I suppose. But I have my doubts that he had to give the book to someone else.'

'I must admit I've never heard of a book being passed on like the Olympic torch before – though it's not a bad idea, if you think about it. And I suppose in theory it could be passed on forever. I imagine that's what a lot of us want: to leave something behind that will reach people we never had the chance to meet in our lifetime.'

'But if that's what Darshan wanted, why didn't he get his book published?'

'Maybe he tried. Or maybe he wanted to trust it would find its way into the right hands without him having to do anything other than set the ball rolling. Come to think of it, that sounds like the sort of thing the man I met in Varanasi might do,' said Dan, and looked thoughtfully towards the horizon.

'Do you think he could have been Darshan? Almost everything about his description seems to match: his age, his build, the colour of his hair …'

'Didn't you say Aldo had described Darshan's hair as greyish?'

'Yes. Why?'

'Because I'm sure I told you the man I met only had a few grey bits in his hair.'

'Isn't that enough for it to be called greyish?'

'Possibly – if those particular bits happened to be very long.' Dan furrowed his brow to make it look as though he was giving the point careful consideration.

'OK, what about his height?' I asked, ignoring his attempt to wind me up. 'You never told me how tall he was.'

'He was sitting down most of the time, but as far as I can remember, he was quite tall – about the same height as me.'

'That's something else they have in common, then … And in Darshan's book there's a question about doing nothing. Didn't the man in Varanasi talk about that?'

'You really think he was Darshan?'

'All I'm saying is he could have been.'

'You don't think it would be a bit too much of a coincidence?'

'Like us two bumping into each other here, you mean?'

'OK, that *was* a bit strange, I agree,' said Dan. 'So maybe Darshan trimmed the grey bits in his hair and moved to another city. He must have changed his name as well, since I'm pretty sure the man I met wasn't called Darshan.'

'I thought you said you didn't know what his name was.'

'I don't. But I remember it was a long one – and I don't think it began with D.'

'What if it began with A – and his surname with W?' I said.

'You don't give up, do you?'

'You have to admit it's a possibility. How do we know that "Darshan" wasn't just a made-up name he told Aldo?'

Dan's expression became serious. 'There's something I think I should tell you.'

'What?'

'I'm not sure you're ready to hear it.'

'Come on – what is it?'

'OK, if you insist: "Darshan" *was* a made-up name, but the man who used it was definitely not the one I met in Varanasi.'

'How do you know?'

'Because the man who went by the name of Darshan … the man who Aldo met in Calcutta … the man who gave him the book … was … me!'

I was immobile in a maze, trying to retrace my steps.

'I thought you'd have made the connection by now,' said Dan. 'You must have seen that "Dan" is the beginning and the end of "Darshan".'

My head was spinning. I couldn't catch hold of my thoughts – until Dan started rolling around on the ground, clutching his belly and hooting like a demented owl.

'Was that supposed to be funny?' I said when he had finished his performance.

'Of course … And now there's something I think *you* should tell *me*.'

'What's that, then?'

'Why Aldo's book had to be a big secret.'

'I told you – he didn't want too many people to know about it.'

'No other reason?' said Dan, creasing his forehead in an exaggerated frown.

'What are you getting at?'

'Come on – it's pretty obvious why you wanted to keep it to yourself: no doubt I'd have cracked the code and claimed the prize while you were still trying to work out what was on the cover.'

Dan stretched out and looked up at the sky. The stars were beginning to peep through the twilight. The only sound was the lapping of the waves … until my stomach started rumbling.

'Sounds like a storm's on its way,' he said. 'Maybe I should be getting back.'

'Are you going to go for something to eat?'

'Yeah, I'll probably see if I can find Annie and Sophie in the port and have something with them.'

'The French girls, you mean?'

'Yeah.'

'Would you mind if I came along?'

'I'm not sure. You might cramp my style.'

'What style's that?'

'You know – going out with two women.'

'What if I sat on my own at the next table?'

'OK, I might consider letting you do that.'

* * *

When we reached the port, Dan spotted the two young women sitting outside at the taverna where we had been two nights before. From the way they greeted him, it was obvious they had been expecting him – as well as someone else: the table was set for four. One of them was baby-faced with blond wavy hair; the other had dark straight hair and stronger features. The one with dark hair introduced herself as Sophie.

'So we've managed to drag you away from your secret mission,' she said, and beamed a welcoming smile as she pulled out a chair for me.

'What have you been saying?' I said, turning to look at Dan as we remained standing near the table.

'Last night I told them about you and how we'd bumped into each other, so they said I should bring you along next time. But I wasn't sure if you'd be free because you seemed to be on some sort of secret mission – one that was so secret you didn't even know what it was yourself. It was all right to tell them that, wasn't it?' he said, putting on a worried look as he sat down.

'I suppose so,' I replied, sitting down opposite him. 'I'm beginning to see that the fewer secrets you try to keep, the less stressful life is.'

'Looks like you've found one of the secrets – of happiness.'

* * *

I have little recollection of what we talked about that night. The main thing I remember is how much we laughed. Dan was on top form, the jokes flowed with the wine and I left all my concerns behind. It was as if four old friends had met up again after a long time apart and effortlessly slipped back into the camaraderie they shared.

13

Parting Waves

The next day was my last one on the island. Dan would be leaving soon as well, but not with me: he had arranged to go to Koufonisi with Annie and Sophie.

In the afternoon we all met up again and had lunch together at the taverna where we had eaten the night before. By now we were treated as regular customers. The waiter offered us some walnut cake on the house. I told him it was so good I was already missing Amorgos. But the cake wasn't the only reason I was wishing I didn't have to return home: the ease with which we all got on again had dispelled any suspicions that the previous night had been no more than a wine-induced one-off, and I was feeling reluctant to part from my new-found friends.

After lunch we walked to the beach. We planned to spend the rest of the afternoon there and return on the last shuttle boat, which meant I would be at the port well in time for my seven-thirty boat to Piraeus, the main port of Athens.

I spent more time talking to Sophie, whereas Dan's attention was centred on Annie – who, with her carefree smile and sense of fun, seemed the perfect match for him. Sophie was the quieter of the two, and our conversation was punctuated with its fair share of silent moments. But it was never an uncomfortable silence, and neither of us said things just to fill it – which came as quite a surprise, considering we hardly knew each other. I concluded that the more you needed to think of what to say to someone, the higher the likelihood of that person being incompatible with you, and I promised myself I would never again initiate a conversation with anyone unless there was something I genuinely wanted to talk to them about.

The hours flew by. When the little passenger boat came chugging towards the beach, I still hadn't packed up my things – not that it would take long: I only had to roll up my towel and sleeping bag and stuff them into my rucksack. But I didn't even do that; Sophie did it for me while I fumbled to lace up my trainers. Then I dashed over to the tent of the young Greek man and thrust Aldo's gas ring and saucepan into his hands, ran back to the tree, grabbed my rucksack and set off to race to the jetty. I soon caught up with Sophie and Annie, since they were giggling so much they could hardly run in a straight line. Dan had taken my haversack and gone on ahead, and he managed to get there just in time to stop the boat from leaving without us.

Arriving out of breath and in a sweat, we jumped aboard and received a round of applause from Dan and the dozen or so other passengers we had kept waiting. Seconds later the boat pulled away from the jetty. I leaned back against my rucksack and enjoyed the rush of sea air on my face. As we began to circumvent the rocky headland, I turned round for one last look at the silent cove before it slipped out of sight.

It only took around fifteen minutes to reach the port. I still had three quarters of an hour before my boat left for Piraeus. It had already docked and embarkation was underway, but I was in no hurry to get on so we sat in a café near the quayside. The early evening sunlight was dancing on the choppy water, throwing shadows of flames up the sides of the fishing boats that were bobbing up and down in the harbour. While the others perused the menu, I tore a page out of my notebook and wrote down my address and phone number for them in case they needed to spend a night in Athens before flying home.

Dan insisted on paying for everyone as a way of thanking us for laughing at his jokes – though I did remind him that I hadn't laughed at all his jokes. I ordered walnut cake with ice cream, but by the time it arrived I was in danger of missing my boat. I wolfed it down, sprinted along the quayside and got on board just before they raised the ramp. I made my way to the top deck and exchanged farewell waves with my friends as the bellow from the ship's horn resounded through me. Within minutes the ship had pulled out of the harbour and their figures had merged into the background.

As we moved further away, the buildings took on miniature dimensions, with the blue of the shutters gradually being absorbed by the white of the walls until all that remained of the port was a pale blob amidst a shrinking mass of grey. Before long, Amorgos had receded into the past and been swallowed up by the open sea.

Next to exit the scene was the sun, bowing out in a blaze of crimson. In its wake it left a pinkish glow marking the horizon, which grew steadily fainter under the curtain of indigo that was descending on the sky.

As we weren't due to arrive in Piraeus until the following morning, I was going to need somewhere to bed down. I spotted a vacant seat sheltered from the wind and went to claim it, laying out my sleeping bag and putting my rucksack on top, then returned to the end of the ship, where I leaned against the railing to watch the inexhaustible trail of foam spewing out from below me as darkness closed in across the waves.

When I got back to my seat, another passenger's rucksack was on the one next to it. Although each seat was long enough for three people, there wasn't sufficient room for me to stretch out. I had therefore been hoping the adjoining one would remain unoccupied so I could extend my legs over the shared arm rest.

I was looking around to see if any other seats were free when I noticed someone coming up the steps from the level below. It was the young woman I had seen on the deserted beach. My heartbeat speeded up. She walked across the deck before disappearing down another flight of steps. My first instinct was to go and talk to her, though I had no idea what I would say. I remembered the resolution I had made following the moments of silence I had shared with Sophie. But maybe there was a reason why the young woman and I were on the same boat …

I ended up walking all round the ship, but there was no sign of her. Full of self-reproach for having missed my chance, I went back to where I was sitting. The person occupying the next seat had returned and was lying down, reading a magazine, which prevented me from seeing their face.

I saw a ticket on the floor.

'Excuse me, is this yours?' I said, picking it up.

The magazine was lowered, revealing a familiar face; but because of the tied-back hair and the angle from which I was looking, I didn't realize who it was at first.

'Oh, yeah – thanks,' said the young man, sitting up and taking the ticket out of my hand. 'Hey, aren't you the guy who gave me the cooking stuff?'

'Yeah, that's right. But you hadn't even taken your tent down when I left, so how did you manage to catch the boat?'

'It was only ten minutes to the port on my bike.'

We carried on chatting until we arrived at Koufonisi, the first stop, where he got off. Several other passengers made their way down the steps to disembark and a few came onto our deck to take their seats. I caught sight of the young woman again. She was carrying a big rucksack on her back, a small one in her left hand, and a tent in its holder in her right hand. Her thick wavy hair fell loosely around her shoulders. I took out my notebook to stop myself staring at her as she came closer.

'Excuse me, is this seat free?' she asked.

'Yes, someone was sitting there but they just left,' I replied, trying hard to speak in a matter-of-fact way.

'Oh, good. I was down the side of the ship on the deck below but it's very windy there. It's much better up here.' She put her things on the seat and took her sleeping bag and a hefty book out of the large rucksack, then sat down. 'Do you know what time we arrive in Piraeus?'

'Six o'clock, I think. Are you hoping to finish that before we get there?' I said, pointing to her book, *The Living Body.*

'Maybe.' She gave a warm smile, her brown eyes shimmering like rock pools in the moonlight.

I caught myself admiring her gently arching eyebrows and delicate cheekbones.

'Would you like a cheese pie?' she said, opening the small rucksack and producing a plastic bag full of food.

'I'd love one.'

While I was eating the pie, I wondered whether I should tell her I was the man on the hill she had seen from the deserted beach. She offered me a second pie as soon as I had finished the first one, so I had a bit longer to make up my mind. But I couldn't go on munching pies all the way to Piraeus.

'Where were you staying on Amorgos?' she asked.

'How did you know I was on Amorgos?'

'Because that's where the boat started from!'

'Oh yeah, of course. I was sleeping on a beach.'

'In a tent?'

'No – under a tree.'

'I don't think you're allowed to put tents on the beach, anyway,' she said.

'That didn't seem to stop some people.'

'I know. I saw two beaches where people were camping. Which one were you on?'

'I don't know what it was called, but it was a nice sandy one about half an hour's walk from the port.'

'The port we left from?'

'You mean there's more than one?'

She looked at me incredulously. 'How long were you on the island?'

'Five days – five and a half, to be precise.'

'Didn't you travel around at all?'

'Not much. I spent most of my time on the beach.'

'Don't tell me you didn't go to the monastery!'

'What monastery?'

'The famous white monastery that's built into the side of a cliff,' she said, wavering between a smile and a frown.

'Looks like I missed that.'

'At least you went to Hora, I imagine.'

'Where?'

'The main town up in the hills.'

'I'm afraid I never got round to going there, either.'

'Was that because you had a big book to read as well?'

'Only a little one, actually.' I thought about telling her what it was, but decided against it. 'So where were you staying?'

'On a campsite – the one near the port that we left from.'

'Don't tell me there are two campsites on the island as well!'

'It looks like you'll have to go again sometime,' she said with a smile.

In the course of our conversation, I found out that her name was Maria, she was Greek, she had studied physiotherapy in England and now worked in a hospital in Athens.

'By the way, did you lose your way back to your seat before?' I asked.

'I'm sorry, I don't understand what you mean.'

'I'm sure I saw you come up those steps and then go straight down those others.'

Maria gave a half-smile. 'I needed to go to the ladies, and I found some at the top of the steps close to where I was sitting. These steps are down the side, by the way – not the ones over there which you saw me come up,' she said, pointing to the steps towards the rear of the ship. 'Anyway, the toilets on this deck were being cleaned, so I returned to the other deck and walked to the end of the ship, but I didn't find any there. I looked around for someone to ask and saw an old couple. I thought they were Greek but they turned out to be Italian. They said the toilets were on the deck above and pointed up the steps behind them. I tried to tell them I couldn't use those toilets, but it was obvious they didn't understand because they just kept smiling and pointing. In the end I thanked them and went up the steps, then walked over to the other ones so I could go back down without them noticing.'

'Did you find what you were looking for after all that?'

'Yes – two decks down. But the couple from Italy still did me a favour, because if I hadn't gone up the steps, I wouldn't have seen that there were some better seats up here. And that was when I decided I would change places if anyone got off at Koufonisi.'

I sent a silent word of thanks to the elderly Italian couple.

'By the way, I've got a confession to make,' I said.

Maria frowned.

'Well … um … what I wanted to tell you is that I saw you one day on the island.'

Her frown deepened.

'I'm afraid I might have made you feel a bit uncomfortable. I was standing at the top of a hill near a beach one morning, looking for a friend, and I spotted someone in the distance. At first I thought it was my friend, but it turned out to be you.'

Maria's cheeks turned the shade of cherry blossom. 'That was you? You must have thought I was a little strange.'

'Why?'

'Because of my silly wave. But I was only trying to attract your attention. I wanted to ask you what was on the other side of the hill. I couldn't see a path and I was afraid I might be lost. I'd come a long way to make a big circle and end up at the campsite, and I didn't want to turn back. But seeing you at least told me I might be going in the right direction. So I continued on my way, and when I got down to the beach where the tents were, I asked a young couple how to get to the port.'

'And after that you walked past my tree.'

Maria looked lost in thought, as if she was rerunning the scene in her mind. 'Were you wearing bright green shorts?'

'No, but I was sitting next to someone who was.'

'That's probably why I didn't notice you: I was blinded by the shorts!'

I laughed at Maria's comment.

'Was he a friend of yours?' she asked.

'Yeah.'

'Is he still on Amorgos?'

'Yes, but he's going to Koufonisi tomorrow. Have you been there?'

'No. I was going to go last summer, then a friend asked if I wanted to go to Patmos so I went there instead. This year I thought I'd go to Amorgos and stop off at

Koufonisi on the way back. But I found so much to do on Amorgos that I ended up spending all my time there.'

'What's Patmos like?'

'It's beautiful.'

'Is it very touristy?'

'Not really, considering what's there.'

My blank expression prompted her to continue:

'Don't you know about the Monastery of St John?'

'I'm not much of an authority on monasteries.'

'Sorry, I was forgetting. Anyway, it's probably the *cave* of St John that's the main attraction.'

'I'm no expert on caves, either.'

'You mean you've never heard about the Cave of the Apocalypse, where St John wrote the Book of Revelation?'

'Oh, yeah – that seems to ring a bell. I didn't realize it was on Patmos, though.'

'Where did you think it was?'

'I just assumed it was somewhere near Jerusalem.'

'Jerusalem?!' She tried hard to contain her laughter.

'Did you visit the cave, then?'

'I did one day, but there were too many people so I didn't go inside.'

'And have you read Revelation?'

'Some of it – but I found it hard to understand.'

'It's supposed to be about the end of the world, isn't it?'

'Yes, and the beginning of a new one,' said Maria. 'Some people say it refers to the birth of a new consciousness.'

'Maybe I should read it.'

'Have you got a copy of the Bible?'
'No.'
'We'll have to get you one, then.'

* * *

I could have stayed up all night talking to Maria, and I probably would have done if she hadn't begun struggling to keep her eyes open. By then it must have been around one o'clock in the morning, so I retreated into my sleeping bag. Despite the limited legroom on the seat, I sank into the most restful sleep I had had in a long time.

14

Islands in the Sky

As the ship was docking in Piraeus, I offered to take Maria out for a meal that evening to thank her for the cheese pies. She said she was going away for a few days to visit her parents but would be happy to meet up when she came back. We exchanged phone numbers and she promised to get in touch when she returned.

From the port we took the overground electric train to the centre of Athens, where we got off at different stops. During the walk from the station to my flat, I reflected on the coincidences that had brought us together. I had previously suspected that such encounters only occurred in films and fiction, yet now I felt they could have been open to me all along but my striving to make them happen had prevented them from materializing.

I entered my apartment building and called the lift. In my pigeonhole there was a postcard from my brother, who lived in New Zealand. He had added a PS: 'Hope you liked the book.' Presumably he had sent it before the postcard, but as there wasn't anything else in my pigeonhole, it must have got delayed in the post.

On opening the door to my flat, I found a folded note on the floor. I picked it up and a little card dropped out. On the card was the name and address of a hotel. I unfolded the note:

Ciao Jake!

I've changed my flight. Leaving tomorrow (Wednesday) 8 pm. If you get back in time, phone me at my hotel (the number's on the card). I'm in room 9. If I don't see you before I go, I'll get in touch when I'm back in Bologna.

Aldo

I rang the hotel but there was no answer. I decided to unpack my rucksack, then try again. Before I had finished, there was a knock at the door. I held my breath for a second. Why would someone come round first thing in the morning? Another knock. Maybe it was something important. I went to see.

'I hope I'm not disturbing you. I heard someone come up in the lift and I thought it might be you,' said Sakis, my next-door neighbour – an elderly widower with thinning hair and a stooping gait. 'This came for you while you were away.' He handed me a parcel. 'It didn't fit in your pigeonhole so the postman left it on top of the radiator. I thought I should take it to keep it safe.'

Sakis then asked whether I had found the note my friend had left under my door. He wanted to be sure it really had been a friend of mine who had called. He said someone had rung his bell the previous day and asked if they could leave a message for me. He hadn't been sure about letting them into the building, but they had said it was important so he had opened the door. I confirmed that it had been my friend and thanked him, but our conversation didn't end there, because next he asked where I had been and if I had enjoyed my holiday. When I asked him if he had been away too, he began to tell me about his trip to Rome. Sakis was glad of the opportunity to chat, so I listened patiently as he gave me a detailed account of his holiday.

As soon as he had left, I opened the parcel. It contained the book my brother had sent. It was about the Maori people. I flicked through a few pages, then remembered I had been intending to ring Aldo's hotel again.

This time the receptionist answered. But I had forgotten that I didn't know Aldo's surname and stopped mid-sentence. She sounded hesitant and asked who I wanted to speak to exactly. I explained that Aldo was a friend of mine and it was important for me to contact him before he returned to Italy that evening. This seemed to convince her I was genuine – then she told me he had just gone out. I left a message and slammed the phone down. Why did Sakis always have to go into so much detail about everything? If he hadn't kept me standing at the door, I would be on my way to meet Aldo now.

But I knew it was unfair to be angry with Sakis. Letting him tell me about his holiday was the least I could do to repay him for the two favours he had done me.

I finished unpacking my rucksack and had a shower – leaving the bathroom door open in case the phone rang – then sought distraction in the book my brother had sent me. I lay on the bed and turned to the first page: *The original Maori name for New Zealand was 'Aotearoa', which means 'The land of the long white cloud'.*

I put the book down and looked out of the window. Beyond the rooftops hung a patch of cloud. An island in the sky. At first it didn't appear to be moving, but it was gradually breaking up. I wondered what the lifespan of a cloud was.

The phone rang. I jumped up to answer it.

'*Ciao!*'

'Hello? Is that Jake?'

'Yes. Hello.'

'It's Maria.'

'Maria! Is everything OK?'

'Yes, everything's fine. Do you always answer the phone in Italian?'

'Only today – I was expecting someone else.'

'I won't keep you long, then. I was just wondering where your flat is, because I'm leaving soon to go and see my parents and I'd like to drop by and give you something on my way to the station.'

'What is it you want to give me?' I asked after telling her my address.

'A copy of the Bible – in English.'

'How did you manage to get hold of one so quickly?'

'Someone gave it to me when I was in England.'

'Don't you want to keep it for yourself?'

'It's OK, I've got the Bible in Greek at my parents' home.'

'Well, if you're sure, thanks a lot. You don't have to bring it now, though.'

'I was thinking we could both read Revelation while I'm away, then we can talk about it when I come back.'

'Isn't it supposed to be hard to understand?'

'That's why I thought we could look at it together: we might be able to help each other figure out what it's all about.'

'Are you sure you've got time to come now?'

'Yes. I'm taking a taxi to the station, and your flat's more or less on the way. I'll be there around half past nine if that's OK.'

* * *

About five minutes before Maria was due to arrive, I went down to wait for her outside my apartment building. It must have been at least quarter to ten when the taxi pulled up. She jumped out, full of apologies, and handed me a little red Bible. I barely had time to thank her before she got back in and the taxi sped off. As soon as I was inside my flat again, I phoned Aldo's hotel in case he had rung while I had been out. But they said he hadn't returned yet.

I opened the Bible and read the first few pages of Revelation. The words 'who overcomes' appeared several times. For example: *To him who overcomes, I will give the right to eat from the tree of life* (2:7); *He who overcomes will not be hurt at all by the second death* (2:11).

What was it that needed to be overcome? What did 'the tree of life' symbolize? And what was 'the second death'?

But I wasn't able to give these questions my full attention as I was too busy waiting for the phone to ring.

* * *

At quarter to twelve Aldo finally rang. He had spent all morning sightseeing and had just got my message. His hotel was within walking distance of the big park behind the Acropolis, and since he knew the part where Socrates' prison was, we arranged to meet there at one o'clock. I asked if he had found the clue in the book, but he said we could talk about that when we met. Then I remembered his grandfather. He told me he was in a critical condition and there seemed little hope of him making a recovery.

How could I have suspected him of concocting the story about his grandfather as an excuse for leaving Amorgos? No doubt I had also been wrong in thinking he had never intended to pass on the book of questions to me.

My misjudgement was easy enough to see with hindsight, but it wasn't so easy to avoid jumping to negative conclusions when things didn't seem to be working out. I needed to have more faith in what Darshan had told Aldo: difficult situations are often there to help us in some way.

15

Socrates' Prison

I put my notebook and pen in my haversack and set off to meet Aldo, taking the quickest route through the busy streets of central Athens. I reached the park in good time. Moments later, I had traded exhaust fumes and honking horns for the fragrance of pine trees pulsating with cicadas. Slowing my pace to a stroll, I turned off the main path to follow the one leading through the trees to the site of Socrates' prison – a large cave hollowed out of a rock face with three narrow entrances blocked by iron bars.

As I approached the site, I saw someone on one of the benches facing it. It was a man with greyish hair. I came out of the trees and headed for the bench to the right of the one he was sitting on. I sat down, then cast a furtive glance in his direction. He looked around fifty years old. He was wearing a loose-fitting white shirt and dark green trousers. His appearance was similar to the image of Darshan I had formed in my mind – except for one significant feature: he wasn't Indian.

Could it be that Darshan wasn't Indian? As far as I could remember, Aldo had never actually said he was.

Once again I was beginning to have my suspicions that things were not as they seemed. But this time I would try to reserve judgement and not simply assume Aldo had misled me. I had to admit it was pure speculation that the man on the bench could be Darshan. It seemed highly unlikely that Aldo would have discovered their meeting was to take place somewhere in Athens on one of the days he happened to be here – and that he would then have arranged to meet me there at the same time.

I stole another glance at the man. His eyes were closed and he was sitting perfectly still. I checked the time. Ten to one. There was a rustle in the trees behind me. I spun round. No one was there. It had probably been a bird foraging in the undergrowth.

The man was now leaning forward and seemed to be examining something on the ground. He remained in this position for about a minute, then sat up straight again. Before I had chance to look away, he noticed I was watching him.

'Be careful where you step,' he said in Greek.

No doubt he read my puzzled expression, because he repeated the words in English. But I had wanted him to explain what he meant.

'One step without awareness could mean the end of a life,' he said, pinning me down with his piercing eyes.

'You're right. We never know when our last moment on this earth is going to be,' I replied, hoping my words would sound sufficiently profound.

He looked down at the ground near his feet. 'And neither do they.'

'Who are "they"?'

'Come and see for yourself.'

I stood up and walked over to where he was sitting.

'There,' he said, pointing to two tiny pale blue flowers amongst the stones, his round face taking on the look of an excited child who had just made a discovery.

Footsteps crunched on the gravelly path behind me. I turned round. Aldo was approaching, carrying his guitar. He was in a grey linen shirt that was almost the length of a kurta. He didn't seem surprised that I had company.

'I see you've met my friend,' he said to the man as he sat down next to him.

'Ah, so *this* is your friend.'

'Yes – the one I met on the island,' said Aldo.

'So you managed to make it here in time,' said the man to me.

'In time for what?' I asked.

'To see your friend – and meet me,' he replied with a smile, which sent a ripple of lines from the corners of his mouth up to his grey-green eyes.

I glanced across at Aldo. He was smiling to himself.

'Well, I must be going,' the man announced, and stood up. 'I imagine you two would like to talk.' He shook hands with Aldo. 'Until the next time our paths cross.' Turning to me, he said: 'Goodbye, it was nice to meet you.

Maybe I'll see you here again sometime. Don't forget to tread carefully.'

I followed his gaze in the direction of the bench where I had been sitting. A crushed flower lay where my feet had been. All I managed to say was goodbye before he disappeared into the trees.

I waited for Aldo to explain everything.

'Interesting character, isn't he?' he said.

'Yes, but why did he have to leave so quickly?'

'As he said: to give us chance to talk.'

'What about?' I asked, sitting down on the bench.

'You mean you've forgotten?'

'The book, you mean?'

'Of course.'

'But there's no need to discuss it any more, is there?' I wondered if Aldo was going to go back on his promise to give it to me. 'I'd like to know how you figured everything out, though.'

He frowned and appeared to be searching for the right words. Then I remembered that he wouldn't be able to meet Darshan until he had passed the book on, so someone must have helped him find the clue and he had therefore given the book to them – as Darshan had instructed.

'It's all right, I understand. That's just the way things turned out,' I said, trying to hide my disappointment. 'Who was it that helped you?'

'Helped me do what?'

'Find the clue.'

'What makes you think I found it?'

'How else could you have known where to find Darshan?'

Aldo's frown evaporated and he broke into a smile. 'You thought that man was Darshan?'

'OK, I know he didn't look Indian, but I can't remember you specifically saying Darshan was Indian.'

'It's true that I never asked him where he was from. I just assumed it was Calcutta. But I'm pretty sure he was Indian – though I admit he never told me he was.'

'So who was the man we were talking to?'

'Somebody I met here yesterday. He was sitting on this bench and I was on the other one, and we got chatting after I asked him something about the sign outside the prison.'

'How come he knew about me?'

'He asked if I was visiting friends, and I said I wasn't but I'd recently made friends with someone who lived here and I was hoping to meet up with them again before I left.'

'How did he know we wanted to talk about the book?'

'He didn't.'

'I thought you said that was why he'd left us alone.'

'All I said was he wanted to give us chance to talk to each other. I'd told him I was leaving today, so he knew we didn't have much time together.'

'You certainly made it sound as though he knew we were going to talk about the book.'

'Are you sure it wasn't you that made it sound like that?'

I wanted to deny this but I knew I couldn't – and was left wondering how I had become convinced that the man was Darshan despite having acknowledged the unlikelihood of such a coincidence. I reluctantly concluded that my powers of reasoning must have been suppressed by my keenness to show I had figured everything out for myself.

'Where's the rest of your stuff?' I asked.

'Back at the hotel. They let me leave it at reception. I'm going to pick it up on my way to the airport.'

The constant 'creak-creak' of the cicadas seemed to grow stronger. Then it stopped. There was barely enough breeze to disturb the boughs of the nearby pine trees. I wiped a few drops of sweat off my forehead.

'I know I said we were going to talk about the book,' said Aldo, 'but I'm afraid I haven't given it much thought since I left Amorgos. I tried to find the clue while I was waiting for the boat, but there was no question related to the idea of friends meeting up after being apart, and there was no sign of a hidden address on any of the pages. Then on the journey to Piraeus, I spent most of the time thinking about my grandad and wondering if I'd be able to change my flight. Whether or not I found Darshan didn't seem to matter any more.'

'How do you feel now?'

'At least I've got my flight sorted out, so I've done all I can for the moment … It was funny you should think that man was Darshan, though. I have to admit he did remind me of him a bit.'

'But it wouldn't be impossible for him to be here. For all we know, the "a" on the cover of the book could stand for "Athens". I'm not sure what the "w" would stand for, though.'

'What are you talking about?'

'The "a" and the "w" in the dots of the question marks. Dan said he'd noticed them after you'd given him the book to hold when you went to the toilet in the café on Amorgos.'

'So that's what he was looking at when I came out.'

Aldo unbuttoned the side pocket of his trousers, took out the book and examined the cover.

'I'd always thought that was just a wavy line for decoration,' he said. 'But now that you mention it, it does look like an "a" and a "w" joined together.'

'Can I see?'

He handed me the book. The cicadas began chirping again.

'I'm surprised we didn't see it before,' I said, looking at the design. 'It obviously means something. But I thought the clue was supposed to be inside the book.'

'So did I ... Wait a minute – Darshan said I had to study it from cover to cover to discover the clue. And he made a point of repeating "cover to cover to discover".'

'So?'

'So maybe he was trying to tell me the clue was on the front and back of the book. And, as you said before, he used the word "study" because I'd have to look carefully to see it.'

'Mm, you could be right. By the way, what's your surname?'

'It doesn't begin with W, if that's what you're thinking.'

'It was Dan's idea, actually. He thought the book had your initials on it.'

'That was logical, I suppose, since he wouldn't have known I had to pass it on.'

'He knows now, though: I ended up telling him the story of how you got it. I hope you don't mind.'

'It's all right – I had a good feeling about Dan. Anyway, it looks like he could have given us a big hand in our search for the clue.'

'Yeah, maybe … So have you got any ideas about the "a" and the "w"?'

'Not at the moment, but we've still got a few hours left.' Aldo picked up his guitar. 'Maybe I'll get some inspiration if I play a bit of music.'

I looked at the cover of the book again. The words on the front certainly made an appropriate title for a book of questions, especially when the questions were ones for which there appeared to be no fixed answers. And having bumped into Dan on Amorgos and met Maria on the boat, I had come to appreciate the words on the back …

'I think I might have found something. Have a look,' I said, passing the book to Aldo.

'Where?'

'What does it say on the front?'

'*Possibilities Abound.*'

'And on the back?'

'*The Mystery of Serendipity.*'

'And what does that spell?'

'How do you mean?'

'The first letters of each word.'

He spelt out the letters: 'P-A … T-M-O-S. Patmos!'

'That's right. The island where St John wrote the Book of Revelation.'

'Is it? I didn't know that. So you think that's where Darshan will be – on a Greek island?'

'It can't be just a coincidence that the letters spell "Patmos".'

'It's not exactly an address, though, is it?' said Aldo. 'Whereabouts on the island would I meet him?'

I considered his question. 'What about the "a" and the "w"? Maybe they represent the name of a hotel.'

'I might have thought that if one of them was an "h".'

'They could stand for the name of a café, then.'

'Wouldn't they be Greek letters in that case?'

'Not necessarily – lots of cafés on the Greek islands have English names.'

'There are plenty that don't, though … Anyway, maybe they *are* Greek letters.' Aldo glanced at the sign in front of Socrates' prison. 'Look how "Socrates" is written in Greek. Notice the second letter. It looks like a "w" in English. That's what I asked the man about when I spoke to him yesterday. I'd already guessed it was pronounced like an "o", but I was surprised when he told me it was the last letter of the Greek alphabet – I was expecting the last one to be their equivalent of "z".'

'So you think the "w" on the cover could be an omega instead?'

'Maybe – and that means the "a" would be an alpha, since they're written in more or less the same way.'

'Is it likely that Darshan knew Greek, though?'

'It's only a couple of letters. That wouldn't be too much to learn for someone who came to Greece regularly.'

'I suppose not,' I said. 'So do you think there might be a café on Patmos called "Alpha and Omega"?'

'Maybe – though it sounds more like the name of a bookshop than a café.'

'That's true … Hang on a minute.'

'What?'

'The Book of Revelation.'

'What about it?'

'I seem to remember it saying something about alpha and omega.'

'You've read it, then?'

'Only the first few pages.'

I related to Aldo the story of how I met Maria and how I ended up with her copy of the Bible. I also confessed that it was Maria who told me Revelation was written on Patmos.

'So there's definitely some mention of alpha and omega in it?' he said.

'I think so, but I'd like to check just to be sure.'

'How are you going to do that?'

'I'll have to go home and get the Bible.'

'But even if it does mention alpha and omega, how will that tell us where I can meet Darshan?'

'Because Revelation was written in St John's cave – the Cave of the Apocalypse.'

'You mean Darshan will be in the cave?!'

'Maybe, since they open it for tourists to visit.'

'So he'll just be hanging around there till I show up?'

'There's bound to be a specific time when you're supposed to meet him.'

'But there isn't even a reference to a month or day on the cover of the book, let alone a time.'

'We'll probably have to look inside it again for that. Remember we said each page represents a week of the year? Maybe one of them will have a time and a day hidden on it.'

'In the first letters of each word or line, you mean?'

'That's what I imagine.'

'But if there was one like that, I'm pretty sure I'd have noticed it when I was looking for a hidden address.'

I wondered how thoroughly Aldo had done this.

'Do you really want to go all the way back to your flat to get the Bible?' he asked.

'Yes.'

'In that case, I suppose I could look through the book again and see if I can find a page like the one you described. I guess there's a chance I could have missed it before.' He glanced at his watch. 'How long do you think you'll be?'

'About forty-five minutes. What time will you have to set off back to the hotel?'

'Around five o'clock. So we've still got over three hours.'

* * *

I managed to make it home in twenty minutes. I opened the Bible at Revelation. Scanning the first page, I found what I was looking for: *'I am the Alpha and the Omega,' says the Lord God, 'who is, and who was, and who is to come, the Almighty'* (1:8).

With the Bible in my haversack, I headed back to the park – half walking, half running as I weaved in and out of other pedestrians. There was a creeping thought at the back of my mind that Aldo was going to stage another disappearing act. I began to cross what I thought was a one-way street and didn't see a bus coming in the opposite direction. It was inches from my face as it flashed past, the blast of hot air nearly knocking me off my feet. My whole body shook as it recoiled from its brush with death. I gathered myself and continued across the street, but my heart was still racing.

Close to the park, I stopped at a snack bar to buy some water and a couple of spinach pies, then hurried along the final stretch of the way. I entered the park and followed the path through the pine trees, glad to be in the shade again after my trek through the sun-baked streets of the city.

Aldo was still on the bench. Because he was playing his guitar, I assumed he had found the clue. But he told me he had looked through all the pages and there definitely wasn't a hidden time or day on any of them.

'Did you find the part about alpha and omega?' he asked.

I took the Bible out of my haversack, turned to the beginning of Revelation and showed him the relevant verse.

'Let's have something to eat before we carry on,' I said.

We sat in silence as we ate the pies and enjoyed the cool water. The trill of the cicadas filled the air. Before long, it was hard to tell whether the sound was coming from outside or inside my head.

'So you're convinced that St John's cave is where I'm supposed to meet Darshan?' said Aldo after he had finished eating.

'That's what it looks like – though I must admit I hadn't been expecting him to choose somewhere connected with the New Testament.'

'It wouldn't surprise me that much.'

'Why not? Is he a Christian?'

'When I asked him what his religion was, he said it was anything that helped him to be a fully conscious part of all that there is. But he told me he'd found words of wisdom in texts from all the world religions, so he may well have read Revelation … It's just that if I'm going to meet him at St John's cave, there'll have to be a specific meeting time, but as I said before, there's no clue about that in the book.'

I tried hard to come up with an idea.

'Maybe there *is* a time and a day hidden in the first letters of each word or line on one of the pages, but the letters need to be rearranged in the right order,' I said.

'If you want to search for something like that, you'd better get on with it. And while you're at it, I'll have a look at Revelation.'

I took out my notebook and pen, then opened the book of questions. The page was one I had seen before, on which there were the two questions about the falling leaf. It wasn't possible to form a day and a time from the first letters of each line, and after noting down the first letters of each word, it soon became clear that they couldn't be combined to spell out anything significant either. A quick look at the opposite page was enough for me to be able to disregard that one as well.

I tried my luck again.

Does a drop of water
in a mountain stream
carry a dream
of reaching the sea,
rushing ahead,
impatient at being
so far away,
not knowing
it is already part
of what it will be?

It only took a few seconds to see that there wasn't a time and a day concealed in the words. The same went for the two questions on the opposite page:

A river's direction is decided
from source to sea;
but does this mean
it isn't free?

As it follows its flow
by letting itself go,
is there any other way
it would rather be?

After opening the book at random several more times without success, I turned back to the beginning and started to go through the pages in order. In some cases I was able to discount the page immediately (due to the absence of a 'y' amongst the letters I was considering). In other cases I was able to do so following a quick check on the number of words and lines, having worked out the maximum and minimum number of letters that could be used to spell out a time and a day. But sometimes I had to jot down the letters and try to rearrange them, which was very time-consuming, and I began to doubt that the information we needed would be concealed in this way.

'I've found another mention of alpha and omega,' said Aldo. 'Here, on the last page.'

'You're on the last one already?!'

'I thought I'd just take a quick look.'

He handed me the Bible. The relevant verse was about halfway through the final chapter of Revelation: *I am the Alpha and the Omega, the First and the Last, the Beginning and the End* (22:13).

'That's another coincidence,' I said. 'There's an alpha and an omega on the front and back of Darshan's book, and there's a reference to "the Alpha and the Omega" on the first and last pages of Revelation.'

'It looks like we could be on the right track, then. But we still need a reference to a time and a day.'

I remembered the questions about the falling leaf, and how, when I had first seen them, they had got me wondering about the reason behind the designs on the pages.

'What about the leaves on the pages? Didn't we agree they were significant?'

'Yes, but it didn't help us much,' said Aldo.

'I'm sure Darshan wouldn't have gone to the trouble to draw 365 leaves in the book just to add some decoration. Remember, that's what you thought the alpha and omega were at first.'

'What are you suggesting, then?'

'I don't know exactly, but at least we can safely assume that each page in the book represents a week of the year.'

'And that the clue to when I'm supposed to meet Darshan isn't on any of them!'

'That's what it looks like. So the only other place it could be is on the cover.'

'In which case the leaves on the pages *won't* be significant.'

'Maybe everything's connected in some way,' I said. 'Let's look again at what's on the cover: we've got the words inside the question marks and we've got the two letters, which we think are an alpha and an omega.'

'Uh-huh.'

'And what do we know about alpha and omega?'

'That they're the first and last letters of the Greek alphabet.'

'That's right: the first and the last ... Hang on a minute – what did it say in Revelation?'

I had another look at the verse on the final page and read out the words: *I am the Alpha and the Omega, the First and the Last, the Beginning and the End* (22:13).

'So the alpha and omega design on the cover could represent the beginning and the end of something,' said Aldo.

'That's what I'm thinking.'

The significance of the leaves suddenly dawned on me. 'I don't believe it could be that simple!'

'What?'

'We have the beginning and the end of something on the front of the book, and the beginning and the end of something on the back. And what do all the pages in between represent?'

'A year. Of course! So you're saying I'm supposed to meet Darshan at the turn of the year?'

'That's what it looks like.'

'New Year's Eve or New Year's Day, though?'

'Both – together.'

'How do you mean?'

'Don't forget we still need a time for the meeting – a time that will be at the beginning *and* the end of a year. On the first day *and* the last.'

'Midnight, you mean?'

'It must be,' I said.

'It certainly fits the equation. But St John's cave is hardly likely to be open at that time.'

'That won't stop Darshan from waiting outside.'

'I guess not.'

'So what do you think? Have we solved the riddle?'

'I don't know. I just find it a bit hard to believe Darshan will be on a Greek island in the middle of winter.'

'Maybe he has friends there and goes to visit them for New Year.'

'Maybe,' said Aldo. 'Wait a minute – what was that other idea you had? Didn't you say you thought there could be a time and a day hidden in the first letters of each word or line on one of the pages, but the letters would need to be put in the right order?'

'Yes, but I didn't have much luck with finding anything.'

'You didn't check all the pages, though, did you?'

'No – and I wasn't intending to, either.'

'But that's the only other idea we've got. So if we see there's no clue like that on any of the pages, it'll definitely help to convince me that the turn of the year is when I'm supposed to meet Darshan.'

I found the page I had got up to before, and, with the book between us on the bench, we checked the remaining ones. We didn't find what we were looking for.

'So what do you think now?' I asked.

'That I'll be going to Patmos for New Year. There's just one thing I have to do first.'

Aldo picked up the book, wrapped the string around the cover and handed it to me.

'Don't you want to keep it till you come to Greece again?' I said.

'Didn't you say you usually go to England at Christmas?'

'Yes, but I can make sure I get back for New Year's Eve.'

'Even if you do, there still might not be time to meet before I go to Patmos, because if there isn't a boat that morning, I may have to go two or three days earlier.'

'That's true ... What if we've got it wrong, though, and Darshan isn't there?'

'Then I might have to ask you to lend me it when I get back to Athens.'

'Of course. But if Darshan *is* there, I can hang on to it, can't I?'

'Yes – until you decide to give it to someone else.'

'When will I have to do that?'

'Whenever you like – there's no time limit. I suppose it'll depend on whether or not you want to meet Darshan.'

'Whether *I* want to meet him?'

'Didn't I tell you?' said Aldo, feigning surprise. 'He said whoever has the book next can come and meet him as well if they like – as long as they give it away first.'

'And the same applies to the person who has it after me?'

'That's right.'

'How will they know where to find him? Am I supposed to tell them?'

'Just tell them they need to study the book from cover to cover.'

* * *

Before leaving, Aldo gave me his address and phone number and asked me to get in touch when I knew my plans for the Christmas holidays, as I had said he could stay at my flat if I was in Athens when he came in the New Year. We stood up and shook hands, then he walked off through the trees.

I sat on the bench again and thought about the book. Although I had already seen all the questions, I had only been looking at them for the purpose of discovering a hidden clue, and in many cases I hadn't focused on their content. So now I was curious to see whether they could help me when I was puzzling over something.

I turned to the first page and admired the calligraphy and the intricacy of the designs. It didn't seem right for me to be in possession of such a work of art, crafted so painstakingly by a person who was unaware of my existence. If I had created the book of questions myself,

I would never have been able to do what Darshan had done: give it away and be left with nothing to show for it – not even the recognition it deserved.

How was it possible to be so creative and generous without seeking anything in return?

I moved my thumb over the edges of the pages and stopped near the end.

Is a tree proud
when its leaves sprout?

Does an ant boast
about carrying its load?

Does the water
at the top of a waterfall
look down
on the water below?

I looked at the opposite page.

Is there a greater honour
than to be present
in the unfolding
of the universe?

Can you be moved
by the Artist's hand
and become part
of this masterpiece?

16

Taking Time to See

On Thursday morning I went to pick up my timetable and the books I needed for the new academic year. The good news was that I wouldn't be starting until six o'clock on Monday (the school where I worked closed at ten in the evening) and my classes would be ones I had taught before. It wasn't going to be easy to get a bunch of Greek teenagers worked up about the English language after three months of summer holidays, but it wouldn't be so bad with students I already knew.

When I returned to my flat, I tried to read some more pages of Revelation. I wanted to be ready to discuss it with Maria when she came back from visiting her parents. But I was distracted by thoughts of taking a bus along the coast to escape the stifling heat of the city. It wasn't long before I succumbed, and I ended up spending the rest of the day at the beach.

That evening I got a phone call from Dan. He said he was coming to Athens with Annie and Sophie on Monday morning and asked if my offer to put them up still stood. I was so happy to hear from them that I didn't give much thought to where they were going to sleep. Apart from my single bed, all I had was a little sofa bed.

Now that I had guests arriving on Monday, I would have to do my lesson planning before then. But there was still plenty of time, and the sweltering temperatures showed no sign of abating, so I spent most of Friday at the beach as well.

On Saturday morning Maria phoned and we arranged to meet the following day. She said she hoped I had done my 'homework' because she had found lots of verses in Revelation that she wanted to talk about. I had just put the phone down when it rang again. It was Nicky, the owner of the school, calling to ask if I could teach an extra class on Monday as one of my colleagues had flu. I wasn't keen to do it, but I found it hard to refuse, partly because the teacher, Sophocles, was a friend as well as a colleague. So I agreed to go in at four o'clock on Monday – although I did wonder how he could be so sure he wouldn't have recovered by then.

Now I would have to get the coursebook from Sophocles. I phoned to tell him I was going to call round and asked if he needed anything, though I was hoping he would say he didn't: as well as reading Revelation, I wanted to get my lesson preparation out of the way so I would be free to spend all day with Maria on Sunday, and I didn't have much time to spare. He said he only needed some bread and there was a bakery close to his flat. But there was no bus stop nearby, so I had to walk – through congested city streets in the midday heat.

I entered the apartment building and found the lift was out of order. I had to climb six flights of stairs, thereby losing even more time. But I forgot my impatience when Sophocles opened the door and I saw his ghostly face and stubbly chin and the beads of sweat on his shaven head. He told me he could hardly get out of bed, and even if he improved over the weekend, he doubted he would be well enough to go to work on Monday. He gave me the book and thanked me for agreeing to do his lesson, adding that he would be glad to return the favour one day.

'I don't suppose you could return the favour now, could you?' I asked.

He turned a shade paler. 'Now?'

'Do you think you could lend me that – just for a few days?' I said, pointing to the fold-up camp bed leaning against the wall behind him. 'I've got some friends coming and I've no idea where they're all going to sleep.'

He wiped the sweat from his brow. 'No problem. And you can keep it if you like. I was meaning to throw it out but I never got round to it.'

'Is it broken or something?'

'No, but I hardly ever use it and it takes up too much space. So I'm more than happy for you to have it.'

'Thanks a lot.' I picked up the bed. 'It's not as heavy as it looks. I thought it was going to be a bit tricky to carry it down the stairs.'

'Why don't you take the lift?'

'It's not working.'

'Maybe someone didn't close the door properly and it got stuck on one of the floors.'

As I descended the stairs, with the camp bed in my hands and the book balanced on top of it, I paused on each floor to check the lift. Everything appeared to be in order – until I got to the first floor and saw that the door was ajar.

I left the building and crossed to the other side of the street, where there was more shade ... and a bakery. Leaving the bed outside, I nipped in to buy a loaf, then went back to Sophocles' flat, thankful that the lift was now working. He was grateful that I had remembered his bread, though I doubt he would have appreciated having to get out of bed again.

When I returned home, I began thinking about what I was going to do with Sophocles' class – a group of sixteen-year-olds who had attended the school the previous year. They were very fond of him, so I wanted the lesson to be interesting enough to make them forget their disappointment at not being welcomed back after the holidays by their usual teacher.

I opened the coursebook at Unit 1. *Impressed by first impressions?* was the title. I looked at the introductory questions: *How important are first impressions? Are first impressions always accurate?*

The people I had met on holiday came to mind. I thought of Aldo and how I had mistakenly believed that his initial evasiveness about the book of questions was an attempt to draw me into a psychological game of some sort – and I remembered how easily I had allowed these doubts to resurface following his unannounced departure from Amorgos; I thought of Dan and how I had wrongly assumed that his tendency not to take things seriously meant he had no desire to consider them deeply; I thought of Maria and how I had misread her wave from the deserted beach.

I wondered whether Aldo, Dan and Maria had formed an accurate impression of me. But what did I mean by 'an accurate impression'? I tried to see myself as each of them would have seen me. Although I believed I had behaved naturally in each case, I had probably not revealed the same aspects of my character to all of them.

Did this mean I was several people rolled into one? Or was I just playing different roles depending on who I was with? If so, who was the director of these performances? And even if the performance was always the same, would it be realistic to expect the same reaction from each member of the audience?

I remembered I was supposed to be planning an English lesson, not indulging in a session of self-analysis. But at least I had seen that the subject of first impressions could provoke plenty of discussion.

By the time I had prepared all my lessons, the heat was making me drowsy. I abandoned the idea of reading Revelation from start to finish and just skimmed through it, stopping whenever I came across a part that caught my interest.

17

St George

On Sunday morning Maria called round, as we had arranged – though not exactly as we had arranged: she was twenty minutes late. I had been pacing up and down for half an hour before the doorbell rang. I could have taken the lift but it felt quicker running down the stairs. On reaching the ground floor, I managed to compose myself and strolled out of the building. But she didn't even notice me because she was looking in the window of a gift shop across the street. I crossed the road and walked up to her, telling myself to act naturally and not say anything stupid.

She was wearing a T-shirt, light cotton trousers and trainers, while I was in a long-sleeved shirt, jeans and an old pair of sandals.

'You're going to get hot in those clothes,' she said as she looked me up and down, her tied-back hair adding depth to her lively brown eyes. 'And I'm not sure how far you'll be able to walk in those sandals.'

'We're just going somewhere in the centre, aren't we?'

'What made you think that?'

'I imagined that's what you'd want to do. Anyway, we'll have to find a place to sit down if we're going to talk about Revelation.'

She wasn't carrying anything apart from the colourful leather pouch hanging on a strap over her shoulder.

'Haven't you brought your Bible with you?' I said.

'I'm afraid I left it at my parents' house. I was late setting off for the station and I forgot about it in the rush. But you've got the one I gave you, haven't you?'

'Yes – in here,' I replied, lifting up my haversack. 'Did you make a note of the parts you wanted to talk about?'

'I did, but I put the piece of paper inside the Bible. I might be able to remember some of them if I look at yours, though.'

I wasn't keen on the idea of keeping myself amused while Maria read Revelation.

'We can leave it till another day if you prefer,' I said.

'Maybe that would be better.'

'It'd be better for me as well, actually. I didn't get chance to read it very carefully.'

'OK, that's decided, then – and it means we can do more walking.'

'Where were you thinking of going?'

'I'll show you.'

I followed her the short distance to the end of the block.

'There,' she said, pointing down a side street towards Lykavittos Hill.

I looked up at St George's – the little white church perched on the top, marking the highest point in Athens.

'Don't tell me you want to go all the way to the church!'

'If you're fit enough,' she said with a playful smile.

'In that case, maybe I do need to change.'

I went back to my flat to put on my trainers and some lighter clothes. And since I wasn't going to need my copy of the Bible now, I left my haversack there. Then we set off in the direction of Lykavittos. As we made our way through the quiet backstreets, we hardly exchanged a word, mainly because Maria was always a few steps ahead of me.

'We don't have to rush, do we?' I said.

'I'm not rushing,' she replied, looking over her shoulder. 'I usually walk like this. It opens the lungs and stimulates the circulation. Try it and see.'

'I'm not as young as you.'

'My grandfather's ninety and he doesn't have any trouble keeping up with me. Anyway, how old do you think I am?'

'Twenty-five?'

'Thanks – I'm nearly thirty.'

We continued in silence and soon reached a little square, from where a flight of steps ascended between the whitewashed apartment blocks to the foot of the hill. I was tempted to make conversation, but I was also trying to apply what I had learned from spending time with Sophie on Amorgos. We went up the steps, pausing to inhale the scent from a jasmine plant poking through a garden fence, then crossed the road encircling the hill and started to climb the stony path that wound its way through the pine trees covering the hillside.

'Maybe we should have a rest,' I said as the path became steeper.

'If you stop now, you'll lose your rhythm. But if you keep going, your lungs will expand and you'll be able to breathe more easily.'

I carried on walking at the same pace, and after a few minutes I no longer felt breathless.

'You were right,' I said. 'What happened?'

'You activated a greater area of your lungs, that's all.'

About three quarters of the way up, we came to a little plateau where there was a bench in the shade of a pine tree. We sat down and took in the view. Standing head and shoulders above the mass of concrete buildings that spread out below us was the rock of the Acropolis, crowned by the perfectly aligned columns of the Parthenon. Solar panels on rooftops glinted in the midday sun and the Aegean Sea shimmered in the distance. To our left and right, blue-grey mountains formed the horizon.

I turned to look at Maria. 'Didn't you say Revelation was supposed to be about the birth of a new consciousness?'

'That's what I heard. Why?'

'Because I was wondering what that might mean. Then this view of the city gave me an idea.'

She looked at me and waited for me to continue.

'From here we can see all the streets at the same time, but the people down there can only see what's directly in front of them. Imagine we spot a bus travelling on a main road and a car racing down a side street that joins it. Halfway down the street, the car driver has to stop because there's a van unloading. He's too impatient to wait, so he turns round and exits the street, then takes a series of turns to join it further along. He's going even faster now to make up for lost time, and when he gets to the junction he pulls out without looking and crashes into the bus.'

Maria gave a half-smile as she awaited my conclusion.

'Because we have a better view of everything, we can see that the driver gets delayed for a good reason,' I continued. 'And this is the kind of view we need if we want to have a better understanding of what's happening around us.'

'But how can we get this view if we're down there?'

'I guess we have to try and visualize it, and not just see things in terms of what seems to be good or bad for us at a particular moment,' I said, omitting to mention that I hadn't adopted this attitude the previous day when I had gone to Sophocles' home. 'And if we can see things from a higher perspective and base our actions on what will benefit the whole, we'll benefit ourselves, too, since we're all part of the whole,' I added, thinking of the camp bed I had ended up getting from Sophocles.

'In which case our aims are ultimately selfish.'

I gathered my thoughts. 'When I say we'll benefit ourselves, I don't necessarily mean in a material way.

It's more about realizing our potential as human beings. I wouldn't say that's a selfish aim, since someone who reaches that level will obviously have a positive effect on everyone around them.'

'It doesn't seem to happen very often, though.'

'Maybe it does, it's just not the sort of thing that makes the news – partly because anyone who's like that will be the last person to make a fuss about it,' I said, thinking of Darshan.

I tried to read the expression on Maria's face. She looked preoccupied. Perhaps it wasn't the right time for a deep discussion.

'What are you thinking about?' I asked.

'I'm just wondering how we can make sure we always live according to the higher perspective. I mean, how do we know when we're supposed to accept an obstacle that's blocking our path and how do we know when we're supposed to try and find a way round it?'

'Maybe that's what we're here on Earth to figure out – by trial and error as we go along.'

Maria thought for several seconds. 'Perhaps it's just a question of listening to our inner voice.'

'Which one? I've got quite a few.'

She waited a moment before answering. 'The one that reminds us who we are when we've wandered off our path; the one that warns us before we do anything which could harm ourselves or another living being; the one that reassures us when our world seems to be falling apart.'

We lapsed into silence, enjoying the light breeze on our bodies as the sun beat down on the streets below. We were at the point where the pine trees gave way to the rocky brow of the hill. For the rest of our ascent we would be exposed to the midday heat. I was content to stay on the bench, where we had some shade, but Maria was keen to keep going …

As we followed the path that zigzagged its way up to St George's, I only just managed to keep pace with her. On reaching the church, we stepped inside to take refuge from the sun in the sanctuary of the cool stone walls. There was no one else around; nevertheless, we spoke in hushed tones as we remarked on the colourful icons which covered the vaulted ceiling and met our gaze from all sides.

In front of us was the icon of St George: the gallant rider on the white horse, pinning down the dragon with the tip of his lance wedged inside its gaping jaws. What struck me was the serene expression on his face. Although it was fitting for a saint, in this case the saint happened to be a warrior up against a ferocious beast. I had therefore been expecting to see some sign of struggle in his countenance. I mentioned this to Maria.

'Maybe that's how he overcame the dragon,' she said.

'By staying calm, you mean?'

'That's right.'

'And with a little help from his lance as well.'

'Which he was able to hold firmly because of his steady hand.'

I studied the icon for a few moments.

'So you admire what St George did?' I said.

'Yes.'

'Even though he killed another living being.'

'Who said anything about him killing the dragon?'

'Come on – everyone knows the story of St George slaying the dragon.'

'I'm not thinking of the story,' said Maria. 'I'm just looking at the image in front of me. If the point of the icon was to show that he killed the dragon, wouldn't he be standing victoriously over its dead body?'

'Maybe – I'd never thought of that. So what do you think the point of it is?'

'To show that he knew how to get the dragon under control – so he wouldn't be burnt by its fire. But I imagine there's also a symbolic meaning.' She thought for a moment. 'Do you think the dragon could represent the fiery passions that will consume us if we don't master them?'

'That's an interesting idea.'

'And maybe that's the real message of the icon: we have to master these passions, not kill them. Then we can use this energy in a constructive way. But we won't have much energy left at all if we're always fighting with ourselves – which is why it's best to be calm in the face of the enemy.'

'We can't all be saints, though.'

'Maybe not. But we can learn to have some control over ourselves, even if it's just by taking a deep breath when we're feeling angry.'

In the ensuing silence, I felt Maria's presence growing stronger.

'Look how everything is finely balanced,' she said. 'The rider on the horse, the horse rearing up, the lance keeping the dragon down – as if to make us aware that with the slightest lapse of concentration it could gain the upper hand.'

We remained in front of the icon a little longer, then went outside onto the paved terrace and walked towards the low stone wall which enclosed it, squinting in the sunlight until we were able to appreciate the panoramic view. Although Maria advised against it, I stepped up onto the parapet. As I turned around to take in every aspect of the scene – sprawling city, silent mountains, distant sea and endless sky – I felt that no part of it could pull me in and throw me off balance as long as I kept my awareness centred ... on the vantage point of St George.

18

A Lesson to Remember

That night, as I lay in bed, I relived the walk I had taken with Maria and replayed snippets of our conversation in my mind. How much of what I had said was a true reflection of my own opinions, and how much had been shaped by the discussions I had had with Aldo and the words I had read in Darshan's book? Though I felt some new ideas had begun to take root inside me, I doubted I could have changed so much in such a short time. It seemed more likely that I had merely been echoing the thoughts of those whose approach to life I hoped to emulate.

It was all very well to talk about seeing things from a higher perspective and acting for the good of the whole, yet I had failed to do this on several occasions during the last few days. I had the urge to phone Maria and confess that I wasn't the person I had made myself out to be. But it was past midnight and she would probably be asleep. I decided to save my confession until the next time we met, which would most likely be after Dan, Sophie and Annie had left.

I let my mind wander back to the brief time I had spent with the three of them on Amorgos. Would there be the same feeling now that they were at the end of their holidays and preparing to return to their normal routines? At least that was what Sophie and Annie would be doing. As for Dan, I had no idea what his plans were. He had told me that he had come to Greece on a one-way ticket and intended to stay until he felt ready 'to go and do nothing' somewhere else. I would be happy to have his company for a few days, though I wasn't sure how I would feel if he needed putting up for longer – mainly because I wanted to be free to spend as much time as I could with Maria.

* * *

On Monday morning I got up early to clean my flat. I had been intending to do it over the weekend but had kept putting it off. Now it was my last chance to sweep the floor and make the kitchen and bathroom look presentable before my guests arrived. I also needed to do some dusting in the living room. But I hardly had time to finish the more pressing jobs before the doorbell rang. Grabbing a cloth, I ran it over the top of the bookcase. A layer of dust had gathered on the books as well, so I gave them a quick wipe, knocking a few over in the process. One of these was Darshan's book of questions. I took it off the shelf, rushed into the bedroom and shoved it in the drawer of the bedside cabinet before going to press the buzzer to open the door downstairs.

The reason I put it out of sight was that if Dan were to see it, he would deduce that the riddle had been solved. He might then be curious to know where and when Aldo was going to meet Darshan. But I assumed Aldo didn't want anyone else to know this. And neither did I, since, all being well, I would be meeting Darshan at the same place the following year.

I opened the door to my flat and saw that the lift was on its way up. It stopped on the floor below. Then I heard footsteps on the stairs – the footsteps of only one person, not three.

'Where are Sophie and Annie?' I asked as Dan – sporting a straw hat, rusty suntan and several days of stubble – reached the top of the stairs.

'You might have at least said hello before you started asking questions,' he said as he came inside.

'I'm just surprised you're on your own.'

'So am I.' He dumped his rucksack in the hallway.

'What do you mean?'

'One minute they were right behind me, and the next they weren't.'

He followed me into the living room and plonked himself down on the sofa. I sat in the armchair in the corner and looked at him with bated breath.

'Any chance of a cup of tea?' he said, taking off his hat.

'I was just going to offer you one. But aren't you going to tell me what happened?'

'I already have done: we got separated.'

There was a knock at the door.

'You've no idea who that could be, then?' I said.

'I was only telling the truth. I couldn't hold the lift door open because I was putting my rucksack down inside. And Annie and Sophie didn't manage to grab it before it shut because they were taking their rucksacks off. Then as soon as it closed, someone called the lift from another floor and it set off.'

I opened the door. Sophie and Annie were standing there smiling. They both had golden tans to complement their summer clothes. I wasn't sure whether to greet them with a hug, a kiss or a handshake. While I was trying to make up my mind, one after the other they gave me a kiss on each cheek and came inside. They joined Dan on the sofa, then began teasing him about his poor display of chivalry.

I was disappointed to hear that the girls would be flying home the following morning. Dan wouldn't be staying long either: Annie had invited him to visit her in Lyon and he was intending to take the first available flight. As soon as he had finished his cup of tea, he went off to find a travel agency. When he returned, he announced that he had booked a flight for Friday and said he hoped it would be all right to stay with me until the end of the week. I jokingly replied that it was a bit late to ask now, then said it wouldn't be a problem as long as he didn't lose my spare key.

We all went to a local taverna for lunch. Just as it had been when the four of us had spent time together on

Amorgos, there was a party-like atmosphere – as if we were celebrating something without knowing what it was exactly. When I had to leave to go to work, I was kicking myself for having agreed to take Sophocles' class.

As I headed towards the city centre, I could only think about what I was missing out on – then ended up missing my bus. I wasn't sure whether to wait for the next one or take a taxi. I had sometimes waited twenty minutes for a bus, whereas other times one had come straight away. But it was often so full that I couldn't get on.

I edged my way onto the street, looking out for my bus and a taxi at the same time.

'Don't forget to tread carefully.'

I turned round. It was the stranger I had met at Socrates' prison.

He looked me in the eye. 'One step without awareness ...'

'... could mean the end of a life – I know.' I stepped onto the pavement. 'I hadn't realized how far I was from the kerb.'

'It's better to be late than not get there at all.'

'It's not so good to be late for work, though.'

'It might be sometimes.'

'How do you mean?'

A bus was approaching. It was only half full.

'Sorry, I have to go,' I said as the bus pulled up.

'Goodbye then.' He smiled and shook my hand.

Once on board, I began to wonder if this encounter was the real reason for going to the school earlier. It wouldn't have happened if I had left two hours later. But what was the significance of our brief exchange?

My thoughts soon turned to the lessons I was going to teach, particularly the one with Sophocles' students. I never felt completely relaxed when I had to face a new class – especially one that would prefer to be with another teacher. And with it being my first day back after the holidays, I might need a while to get into the swing of things again. So I would have preferred Sophocles' class to be my last one of the day.

The bus turned right instead of continuing straight on. I was on the one I normally took to go to the house of a student to whom I gave private lessons. The next stop was nowhere in sight. When it eventually came into view, we were held up at some traffic lights before the doors finally opened and I leapt off. Running back to the main street, I cursed my luck at having bumped into the stranger. If he hadn't distracted me by shaking my hand, I would have been able to pay more attention to which bus I was getting on.

My bus was bound to have gone past by now, so I flagged down a taxi. There were already two people in the back, but I knew that taxis in Athens sometimes took extra passengers if they were going in the same direction. The driver wound down the window, I told him where I wanted to go and he gave a perfunctory nod. I had hardly settled into my seat when we turned off the main road. He said he was going to drop off the other passengers –

two elderly ladies with shopping bags – and assured me it wouldn't take long.

By the time I got to the school, I was more than ten minutes late. I ran up the steps into the building. Nicky was at the desk in the reception area, sorting through some photocopies. Her mousy hair was a shade lighter after a summer of Greek sun, and her lipstick brought a touch of colour to the first day of term. She looked up over her glasses and a flash of recognition brightened her face.

'I've just been calling you,' she said. 'I thought you'd forgotten about Sophocles' class. His students will be glad to see you, that's for sure.'

'Why's that?'

'Because you've saved them from a test. I had to find something to keep them occupied, so I told them I was going to give them a test to see how much they'd remembered over the summer. As you can imagine, my idea didn't go down very well. But it was either that or send them home.'

Nicky was right: the students were pleased to see me. They were happy to do anything rather than take a test, and the lesson proved to be the best one of the day.

* * *

On my way home that night, I thought about the comment the stranger had made before I had got on the bus. Had it just been a throwaway remark, or had he somehow known that being late would work in my favour? Either way, it had gone right over my head, and I had ended up behaving like the car driver in the example I had given to Maria when I had been talking about seeing things from a higher perspective. But there was no way I could have known that arriving late would be of benefit to me. How could I have been expected to see things from a higher perspective in that situation?

I remembered what Maria had said about listening to the inner voice. If I had been able to do this, maybe I would have managed to remain calm and trust that everything was happening for a good reason. But in order to listen to the inner voice, it was necessary to be calm in the first place, and this wasn't easy when things appeared to be going against you … Perhaps there was something in the book of questions that could help me deal with such situations.

I arrived back at my flat to find that my guests had gone out without me. They hadn't even left a note to say where they were. My disappointment was in danger of turning to anger, but I told myself to stay calm and not react negatively, and went to sit on my bed.

I wondered if Maria was free. She sometimes worked evenings at the hospital, and if the next day happened to be one of those days, she would be able to stay up late. I began to dial her number. But was it right to call Maria just because I was at a loose end? And what if Dan and the girls had only gone for a walk around the block and were on their way back? I put the phone down.

After staring at the wall for several minutes, I went into the kitchen to have something to eat. Then I returned to the bedroom and slumped down on the bed. It was nearly eleven o'clock. I didn't want to think badly of my guests, but it was hard not to.

As I grappled with my thoughts, it occurred to me that I was being given an opportunity to see things from a higher perspective. Maybe Dan needed to be alone with Annie and Sophie for some reason … Or maybe it was I who needed to be alone. Hadn't I been intending to look in the book of questions? I took it out of the drawer of the bedside cabinet. But before I could open it, there was a light knock on the door. A key turned in the lock. I shoved the book back in the drawer. Through the bedroom doorway I saw Dan enter the flat.

'I hope you weren't thinking of going to bed,' he said as he came into the room.

'I'm just having a sit-down.'

'Aren't you going to ask me where Annie and Sophie are?'

'I imagine you left them on the ground floor again.'

'Somewhere a bit nicer, actually: a café near the Acropolis.'

'Didn't you want to stay longer?'

'A lot longer – I've just come back to get you.'

'All the way from the Acropolis?'

'Yeah – in a taxi.'

'Why didn't you leave a note or call me from a phone box?'

'We didn't leave a note because we haven't been back to the flat since you left us this afternoon. But we did phone you – about five times. The first time I rang, there was no answer. Then whenever I tried again, it was engaged. That's why I let myself in: I thought you might still be talking.'

'Only to myself. I haven't been on the phone at all. Maybe you made a mistake when you dialled the number.'

'The same mistake five times?'

It was only then that I noticed I hadn't replaced the receiver properly. I felt ashamed for having initially misjudged my new friends. Why couldn't I have refrained from jumping to conclusions? The next time I found myself in a similar situation, I would make sure I handled it better.

* * *

Lying in bed that night, with Dan sound asleep on the camp bed a few feet away and Sophie and Annie sharing the sofa bed in the living room, I reflected on how normal it all seemed despite my having known them for such a short time. I felt more at home with them than with some people I had known a lot longer. It was as if the situation had given me the chance to practise being the person I wanted to be, without feeling restricted by anyone's expectations based on my past behaviour. Maybe this was what Dan had had in mind when he had been making a case for playing different roles.

19

Questions to Be Asked

In the morning Dan and I said goodbye to Sophie and Annie. Then I said goodbye to Dan. He was going to spend a couple of nights on Aegina, a nearby island. By now I had got used to having him around and was disappointed to hear he would be going off again. But I didn't tell him this; I just said I would see him on Thursday when I returned from work.

After doing my lesson preparation, I had some time to spare before going to the school. It was a good chance to look in the book of questions for something related to the one I had been puzzling over the previous day: 'How can I achieve the right state of mind to see things from a higher perspective in situations which seem to be going against me?'

I sat on the balcony and held the question in my mind, then opened the book at random.

Do we sometimes refuse to see
what we need to do
is simple
since we suspect it would give us
no sense of achievement?

It wasn't the type of question I had been hoping for. Maybe the opposite page was the one I was supposed to look at.

Can you be the master
and servant
of the moment?

This seemed relevant to what I had been thinking about, though I felt it related more to the state of mind I needed to achieve than to the way I could achieve it.

I looked back at the other page. Although Darshan had said the purpose of asking the questions wasn't to answer them but to see what feelings they evoked, I couldn't help answering no to this one. Why would anyone choose to make their life difficult? Most people would be more than happy to find a simple solution to a problem. And there was definitely a sense of achievement to be derived from this. I recalled the satisfaction Aldo and I had felt on solving the riddle of how to find Darshan. But then I remembered how long it had taken us to get to that point, and how – despite the setbacks we had experienced along the way – we had enjoyed the feeling of getting closer to the answer. Perhaps it was true that we wouldn't have felt the same satisfaction had we found it straight away. Could this mean, then, that we had initially failed to see the simple solution because, subconsciously, we had been seeking the feeling of achievement which would come from succeeding in a difficult challenge?

I put the book down and looked out from the balcony. Though my flat was on the fifth floor, the view was restricted by the apartment blocks on the opposite side of the street. Apart from these buildings and the rooftops of those behind them, the only part of the city that was visible was the top of Lykavittos Hill, where St George's church sat amongst the clouds in the distance.

I recalled the calmness I had felt when I had been there with Maria. I closed my eyes and saw us standing under the icon of the saint, enveloped in the cool silence of the empty church. How strange it was that whenever I revisited the memory of an experience, I had the sensation of seeing myself in the scene as though I was looking down on it from above. Could this 'higher perspective' also be reached in the moment, or was it only possible in retrospect?

* * *

While I was at the school on Thursday, I was told that my last lesson of the day (an individual one with an adult) had been cancelled. This meant I would be finishing at half past eight, so I would be able to meet Dan earlier than we had arranged. I phoned my flat on the off chance he would be there, but there was no answer.

When I arrived home that evening, Dan's rucksack was back in the flat but Dan wasn't. Presumably he was intending to return by half past ten – unless he had forgotten that was the time we were supposed to be meeting. Rather than sit around doing nothing, I thought I would have a closer look at some of the pages in the book of questions with which I wasn't yet familiar. Since receiving it from Aldo, I had resisted the temptation to do this because I wanted to use it in the way Darshan had recommended. But surely there wouldn't be any harm in browsing through it from time to time?

I was overlooking the fact that my reaction to a question would not be spontaneous if it was one I had already read carefully. But what if there were few occasions when I needed to ask the book something? I might end up passing it on without having got to know its content. I convinced myself that it wouldn't matter if I had studied a question before, since my reaction to it would probably be different each time I read it.

I opened the drawer of the bedside cabinet. The book had gone. Dan must have moved it as a joke. I went into the living room to look on the bookcase, but it wasn't there. I had never really been angry with Dan, despite his various attempts to wind me up. But it was no joke to go snooping through someone's personal belongings.

I went into the bedroom again and looked under the bed, then in the chest of drawers, then the wardrobe. I even searched the kitchen cupboards before concluding that he had taken the book with him and had been intending to put it back before I returned. Borrowing it without asking was bad enough, but there was also the chance he could damage it. And I would never be able to forgive him if he lost it.

A knot was tightening in my chest. Maria's voice echoed faintly in my head, telling me to take a deep breath. The knot grew tighter. Her voice came again. A whisper from the shadows. I went back into the bedroom, sat on the bed and tried to take a deep breath. My thoughts cut it short. I tried again. This time I managed a complete inhalation, but it didn't seem to have much effect on my mood.

After several more fruitless attempts I phoned Maria.

'Are you OK?' she said.

'Why?'

'You sound stressed.'

'I'm just a bit angry with someone – and I wanted to ask you about something you said when we were in St George's church. Didn't you mention taking a deep breath as a way to control your anger?'

'I don't remember saying that specifically, but I may well have done, since deep breathing is what I get my patients to do a lot of the time.'

'Not because they're feeling angry, though.'

'It's usually because their bodies are tense – but if they were feeling angry, I'd recommend the same thing.'

'So it works?'

'It does for me,' said Maria.

'Even when you're furious about something?'

'I don't usually get to that point if I can help it.'

'You mean you just take a few deep breaths and straight away you feel calm again?'

'There's a little more to it than that.'

'Like what?'

'The main thing to remember is that it has to be a fully conscious breath. That way, your attention will be diverted to what's happening inside your body, so you'll be more detached from what's going on around you.'

'What do you mean by "a fully conscious breath"?'

'You have to feel the air – really feel it – entering your body through your nose and gradually filling all the parts of your lungs. If you like, you can visualize your lungs as a tree without leaves, and imagine the air passing first through the trunk, then the thick branches, and then the thinner ones until it reaches the twigs. It's a good idea to hold it for a few seconds and then breathe out through your mouth – blowing the air out rather than exhaling in the usual way. Make sure you do this slowly, though.'

'Why is it better to blow the air out?'

'Because this helps you breathe in a more controlled way, as well as helping you to focus your mind on the process of breathing. And since the action of breathing out increases the blood flow to the heart, the longer the exhalation, the more blood will be supplied to it, which means it won't have to beat so quickly to meet the demands of the body. So your heart rate will slow down and you'll feel calmer.'

I heard the door open. Dan was back. I thanked Maria for her advice and said I would call her again later.

I went into the living room. Dan was sitting on the sofa with the book beside him and a solemn look on his face. By now I was wise to his play-acting. I picked up the book to check there were no scuffs on it, then sat down in the armchair and waited for him to speak. But he remained silent, staring at the floor.

'I can't believe you went through my things and took my book without asking.'

He raised his eyes. 'If you'll just calm down a minute, I'll explain what happened.'

I tried to take a fully conscious breath, but without much success.

'Well?' I said.

'When I got back from Aegina I was feeling tired, so I took a taxi to the flat and had a lie-down. After about fifteen minutes I was woken up by the phone ringing.'

'What time was that?'

'It must have been around half six.'

'That was me. I phoned from the school to let you know I was going to be home early. Why didn't you answer?'

'How was I to know it was you? You didn't even know I was here. And anyhow, I'm not in the habit of answering the phone when I'm in someone else's house ... Anyway, I nodded off again and was in the middle of a deep sleep when it rang a second time.'

'That wasn't me. I only rang once.'

'I know, because I found out who it was in the end ...
About half an hour later, the phone woke me up again.
I still didn't answer it, but I didn't go back to sleep this
time because I had to get up to go to the travel agency and
pick up my ticket for Lyon.

'As I was getting ready to leave, I thought it might
have been Annie calling – maybe to tell me there'd been
a change of plan about meeting me at the airport. Since
I still had over an hour before the travel agent's closed,
I decided to hang on a bit in case she tried again. I only
needed about twenty minutes to get to the travel agency,
so I waited till half eight. Then just as I was leaving,
the phone rang for the fourth time. It was Aldo.'

'Aldo?'

'At first it didn't register who he was, then he mentioned
Amorgos and I realized who I was talking to. When I said
you wouldn't be back till half past ten, he asked if I could
do him a favour and check something in a book he'd
given you. I told him I was on my way out, but he said it
was important.

'He explained that he was ringing from the hospital
in England and said his grandad was keen to hear
something from the book he'd brought back from India
– the one he'd given me to hold in the café on Amorgos.
There was a particular part he thought his grandad
would like, but he couldn't remember it word for word.
He assured me it wouldn't take long to find it, so I ran
into the living room to get the book off the bookcase –

since that's where I assumed it would be. When I saw it wasn't there, I thought it might be in the bedside cabinet. I ran back into the bedroom and opened the drawer, but it didn't seem to be there, either.

'I told Aldo I couldn't find the book but I wouldn't be out long and I'd carry on looking when I returned. He said he'd be at the hospital till half past nine Greek time, which was when the visiting hours ended, so I told him to give me the number and said I'd get back to him.

'By now it was twenty-five to nine. I had to go, but I knew that when I returned from the travel agency, I'd only have a few minutes to find the book, phone Aldo, find the page and dictate the words to him before he had to leave the hospital. I thought if I could find the book now, I'd be able to take it with me and call him from a phone box after I'd got my ticket. The drawer of the bedside cabinet was still open, and I noticed I hadn't pulled it all the way out before. I pulled it out completely and found the book – right at the back behind a load of papers!

'I ran to the travel agent's and managed to get there before they closed, then ran to the nearest phone box and rang the hospital. When I got through to Aldo, I told him I had the book and asked what page he wanted me to find, but he said it didn't matter now because his grandad had died.'

I didn't know what to say. I could sense Dan's eyes on me but I kept mine on the book, which I still had in my hand.

'I'm sure Aldo would have been able to remember some other pages,' I said eventually.

'But he obviously thought it was important for his grandad to hear what was on that particular one. Maybe the words would have helped him die more peacefully.'

'I'm not so sure about that. I can't imagine anyone wanting to be given a question to puzzle over in their final moments.'

'But I remember you saying the questions were supposed to help you see things more clearly.'

'That's what Aldo told me. But it's not always immediately clear what the meaning behind them is.'

'So you think he'd have wanted to confuse his grandad?' said Dan.

'Of course not. I'm just saying it might have been hard for him to choose something appropriate – you've seen what the questions are like.'

'What makes you think that?'

'You mean you haven't read any?'

'No, I haven't.'

'Really?' I said, casting him a doubtful look.

'Why would I lie to you?'

'I don't know. I just can't imagine you haven't had a look in the book.'

'It's pretty obvious you don't trust me. But if that's the way you feel, why did you let me stay at your flat in the first place?'

'There's no need to get angry. It's not that I don't trust you.'

'So why was the book tucked away in the drawer?'

'I just thought it would be safe there.'

'Safe from me, you mean? I hope you realize that if you hadn't hidden it, I'd have been able to read Aldo the page he wanted.'

'Even if the book had been on the bookcase, you still might not have had time to find the page and read it to Aldo without making yourself late. So you could even say I did you a favour by hiding it.'

Dan shook his head despairingly.

'But wherever the book had been, you would definitely have had time to find it *and* find the page and read it to Aldo if you hadn't waited so long to answer the phone.'

'So now I'm supposed to feel guilty about not answering someone else's telephone?'

A long silence followed, during which we didn't make any eye contact.

'OK, I suppose I can see why you didn't answer the phone straight away,' I said. 'And I believe you when you say you haven't looked in the book. But weren't you curious to see the questions?'

'If you must know, at one point I was about to open it, but then I decided not to.'

'Why?'

'Because I'd have driven myself crazy trying to guess which page Aldo had wanted to read to his grandad.'

I knew that if Dan had been able to find the book more quickly, there was a good chance he would have had time to find the page and read it to Aldo and still get to the travel agency before it closed. Even though Aldo was not likely to have known the number of the page, he would probably have remembered roughly where it was in the book. And no doubt he would have already written down as many words as he could remember so that when he phoned it would just be a matter of filling in the gaps.

'Look, if anyone should be feeling bad, it's me,' I said. 'None of this would have happened if I'd left the book on the bookcase.'

'Were you afraid I'd nick it or something?'

'Course not. I knew you wouldn't do that.'

'Why did you hide it, then?'

'I didn't want you to see it, that's all.'

'I don't think I follow you.'

I hesitated. 'If you'd seen that Aldo had given it to me, you'd have known we'd solved the riddle of how to find Darshan.'

'Who's Darshan?'

'The man who wrote the book. I told you that before.'

'Oh yeah, I remember now. So where's the problem?'

'Wouldn't you have been curious to know where Aldo's going to meet him?'

'Mm, that's a point,' said Dan, and looked at me expectantly.

I hadn't given much thought to what I was going to say next.

'That's the part I can't tell you,' I said.

'Because you don't trust me.'

'That's not the reason.'

'That's what it looks like to me.'

'What would *you* do in my position, then?'

'I'd tell me the meeting place and invite me along as well.'

'How could I do that? *I'm* not even invited.'

'In that case, I'll invite you,' said Dan, breaking into a smirk.

'What's so funny?'

'This whole conversation – in fact it's ridiculous. Did you really think I'd want to gatecrash Aldo's meeting with Darshan?'

'You might have mentioned it to someone else, and they may have wanted to.'

Dan rolled his eyes. I tried to come up with a better reason for having hidden the book, but I couldn't.

'I'll go and make some tea – if that's all right,' he said, and went into the kitchen.

Something I had said to Dan on Amorgos came to mind: the fewer secrets you try to keep, the less stressful life is.

When he came back in with the tea, the shadow had lifted from his face.

'So you wouldn't be interested in meeting Darshan?' I said as he handed me my mug.

'I might be.' He sat down on the sofa. 'But I wouldn't want to go anywhere I'm not wanted. I haven't done that since primary school – not that I know of, anyway.'

'What happened at primary school?'

'One of the boys in my class was having a Christmas party and it seemed everyone had been invited except me. So I was extra friendly to him and told him I'd be having my birthday party soon and was intending to invite him to it. In the end he brought me an invitation. But I spent most of the party feeling that I shouldn't be there. The worst part was when I won at musical chairs – even though I tried not to.'

'How old were you?'

'I must have been ten. But I learnt my lesson. Whenever I feel tempted to go somewhere I haven't been invited, it's usually enough for me to remember that party. Even at the time, I knew it wasn't right to pressurize that lad into inviting me. The main thing I learned, though, was that it wasn't right for me, either.'

'Look, I'm sorry for misjudging you. I just thought it'd be better not to tell anyone where Aldo's going to meet Darshan. I don't want to be responsible for anything that might disrupt their meeting. I know how much it means to Aldo.'

'Fair enough. Anyway, there's no point in telling someone something they don't need to know.'

We finished our tea in silence, then went for a walk to Monastiraki – the area of cafés and tavernas in the shadow of the Acropolis. We automatically headed for the café we had been to with Sophie and Annie. All the tables were occupied when we arrived, but we spotted some people leaving and ended up getting one with a direct view of the Parthenon – its illuminated columns standing out against the night sky, with the waning moon hovering nearby.

Dan appeared to bear no ill will towards me and was happy to tell me about his stay on Aegina when I asked him to, but we spent more time watching the steady stream of passers-by than talking to each other. I told myself he was probably preoccupied with thoughts about Annie and what he was going to do when he got to Lyon.

We parted on good terms the next morning, though neither of us mentioned the possibility of meeting up again in the future.

* * *

In the days that followed, I phoned Aldo several times to see if he had returned from England. When I eventually got hold of him, I offered my condolences over the death of his grandfather and explained why Dan had had difficulty finding the book, hoping he would understand my reasons for putting it out of sight. He asked whether Dan had quizzed me about the solution to the riddle, and when I told him he hadn't, he said: 'So you needn't have hidden it, then.'

20

The Flame of Tomorrow

The Christmas holidays had finally arrived. Since phoning Aldo in September, I had only spoken to him on two further occasions. One of them was when I called to tell him I wouldn't be going to England for Christmas after all, as my parents were going to New Zealand to visit my brother, and I would therefore be able to put him up in Athens both before and after his trip to Patmos. The other time was when he phoned to say he had booked his flight to Athens for the end of December.

My limited contact with Aldo was still more than I had had with Dan: I hadn't heard from him at all.

As for Maria, I had continued to see her whenever she was free – which, due to her work schedule, wasn't as often as I would have liked. When anyone asked about us, I said we were just friends, but I had begun to think this was misleading since it could imply that I considered a friendship to be somehow 'less' than a romantic relationship. Though I had held this view for most of my life, I now believed it wasn't the case, and that being in love had no lasting value if it wasn't based on the kind of respect and support shared between true friends – each of whose wish for the other to follow their chosen path in life was even stronger than their desire to be together.

Maria, too, was wary of romantic relationships. She had told me that the excitement of feeling attracted to someone often made her overlook certain aspects of their character with which she didn't feel totally at ease, and by the time she became aware of this, the relationship had become so established that it was difficult for her to end it. The longer it continued, the further removed it became from the one she had envisioned – or, to use her words, she felt her dream being 'slowly smothered by someone else's'.

* * *

In the afternoon of December 29th, Aldo phoned from the airport to let me know he had arrived. I wondered what it was going to be like to see him again. Previously, the main focus of our conversations had been the book of questions and our attempts to solve the riddle, but now that we appeared to have done this, we might not have so much to say to each other.

There was definitely one thing I was hoping to talk to him about, and that was the page he had wanted to read to his grandfather. I had been working hard to convince myself that enough time would have passed for him to be able to speak about his grandfather's death. It might even bring him a sense of release: perhaps he had been bottling up his feelings and needed coaxing into expressing them.

But I knew that the main reason I wanted to broach the subject of the mystery page was to see if I had succeeded in guessing which one it was. I hadn't been able to resist looking for it, and there was a certain page I had in mind.

My attention wandered to the specks of dust suspended in the sunlight filtering in through the French windows. I remembered the description that Dan had given of the room in the house in Varanasi where he had had his first experience of 'doing nothing'. A question from Darshan's book came back to me:

> *If you didn't find it so hard*
> *to do nothing,*
> *would you have done anything*
> *you lived to regret?*

It was the second question I had read when I had first opened the book. At the time, I hadn't given it much thought, but now I wished I had taken heed of its message. Had I done so, I probably wouldn't have gone to the trouble of hiding the book from Dan – and then Aldo would have been able to grant what proved to be his grandfather's dying wish. But at least I could act on the message now by making sure I didn't say anything that might upset him.

The doorbell rang. A few minutes later Aldo was sitting on the sofa. His slim build was padded out with a fleecy bomber jacket and his complexion was paler without the summer sun, but his eyes had lost none of their shine.

'So your boat leaves tomorrow night?' I said.

'Yeah – at ten o'clock.'

'What time will you get to Patmos?'

'Around eight in the morning.'

'Where are you going to stay? Most of the places will be closed.'

'There'll be at least one open – and that's all I need.'

'What if Darshan's not there? You won't mind spending New Year's Eve on your own?'

'Why not? It's just another day … Anyway, how about you? What are you going to do?'

'I'll probably do something with Maria – the girl I met on the boat back from Amorgos.'

'The one who told you about Revelation?'

'That's right.'

'Does she know about her contribution to our solving the riddle?'

'Yes. But don't worry – you can definitely trust her. I'm sure she hasn't mentioned the meeting place to anyone else.'

'I don't suppose it would matter even if she had. I don't think there are many people who would think of going there on New Year's Eve.'

'How do you think Darshan would react if someone else did turn up?'

'Knowing Darshan, he'd probably welcome them.'

'How would you feel?'

'I suppose it would depend who they were and what they wanted. But to be honest, I wouldn't appreciate having our meeting interrupted.'

'That's why I tried to keep the book hidden from Dan.'

'I know. I'm sorry if it seemed that I was criticizing you when we spoke on the phone back in September. I wasn't in the best of moods at the time.'

'It's all right, I understand. By the way, what was the … what was the reason you didn't make a copy of the questions?'

'I wanted to see if I could let go of the book completely – as Darshan had said I should do with the camera I gave to my friend.'

'And have you managed to?'

'I think so. But I knew I was going to get another chance to look at it when I came here, so I guess I've only been practising letting go of it these last few months. By the way, do you mind if I just check something in it?'

'Feel free. It's there on the bookcase. Shall I make some tea while you're doing that?'

'I'd prefer coffee if you've got some.'

I went into the kitchen to make the coffee. If I could be patient enough, Aldo might reveal the page he had wanted to read to his grandfather without my having to ask him about it. When I returned to the living room, he was out on the balcony, watching the activity on the street below. He had left the book open, face downwards, on the little round table near the sofa. I put down the cups of coffee and picked it up.

> *Can you see beyond*
> *this ebb and flow*
> *and steer your ship*
> *into the unknown,*
> *then let it drift*
> *on a different tide,*
> *leaving old foes behind*
> *to be remembered as guides*
> *to what you will find?*

*

> *Why not let go*
> *of what you think you need,*
> *and see what flower*
> *will grow from this seed?*

Neither page was the one I had had in mind. I put the book back as I had found it, fetched some milk from the kitchen, then joined Aldo on the balcony.

The cross-section of the apartment block on the opposite side of the street resembled a gigantic doll's house, each room home to a separate world of silent activity – some illuminated from within, others from outside by the street lamps that had just come on.

'It's strange to think of all those people living so close together without knowing what's going on in each other's lives,' I said.

'Mm … I suppose you could say the same about society.'

'That's true … The coffee's done, by the way.'

Aldo followed me back inside, took off his jacket and made himself comfortable on the sofa.

'Help yourself to milk,' I said. 'Do you fancy a bit of apple pie?'

'That'd be nice,' he replied, picking up the bottle of milk.

I went to the kitchen to get the pie. When I returned, Aldo was reading the book again. I peered over his shoulder to see which page he was on and tried to set down the plate of apple pie on the little table at the same time. I pushed the milk with the edge of the plate to make some space, but, with one eye on the book, I pushed it too far and it fell off. The plastic bottle made a thud when it landed. Aldo looked up with a start. Milk was pouring out all over the floor.

'You didn't put the top back on properly,' I said as I bent down to grab the bottle.

'Sorry. Let me give you a hand.'

'It doesn't matter – I'll do it.'

I went to get a cloth from the kitchen. After mopping up the mess, I sat down to drink my coffee.

'I'm afraid it's a bad habit of mine,' said Aldo.

'What is?'

'Not putting tops on properly. But it's not always completely bad: I probably wouldn't be sitting here with a ticket to Patmos if I hadn't done the same thing with a bottle of water.'

I gave a frown and waited for him to explain.

'If Dan hadn't seen the hidden letters on the cover of the book, we might never have guessed St John's cave was the place I was supposed to meet Darshan. But the only reason I gave Dan the book to hold in the café on Amorgos was because it wouldn't fit in my pocket. And that was because I was wearing my shorts, which only had small pockets. The reason I was wearing shorts was because I'd changed out of my long trousers. And that was because of a bottle of water I hadn't closed properly …

'After I'd bought my ticket to Piraeus, I rushed back to the beach and started packing up my stuff as fast as I could. I was crawling around inside my tent, grabbing things and stuffing them into my rucksack, when I realized my trousers were all wet. I'd knocked over a bottle of water, and since I hadn't screwed the top on fully, water had gone everywhere.

'But it's not unusual for things to work out like that, according to Darshan. I remember him saying it's often a seemingly insignificant incident that ends up leading to an important change in life.'

'You can trace the origins of almost any big event back to a trivial one if you try hard enough, though.'

'That's the whole point: no event is trivial. Everything you do is a link in the chain.'

I recalled how, on Amorgos, not putting on my trainers had led me to postpone my walk up the hill and sit down to talk to Aldo instead. Whether this would ultimately lead to a significant change in my life remained to be seen, but I had to admit that my subsequent contact with him had already enriched my life sufficiently for me to be able to count my lack of foresight that day as a blessing.

* * *

That evening we went for a walk in the old part of the city, taking a succession of random turnings down backstreets graced with neoclassical buildings and ending up in Monastiraki Square. Crowds of locals and tourists were milling around, the drone of their myriad voices playing second fiddle to the lively notes from a busker's bouzouki. The nearby tavernas were overflowing. Most of them had outside tables equipped with heaters. Whiffs of grilled meat pervaded the air.

We made our way across the square and headed down a side street. After a few more turnings we came to a bar. We went up a wooden staircase into a room with subdued lighting and found a table by the window. The place was almost full, and the rock music playing in the background was barely audible over the animated chatter of the young clientele.

'There's something I've been meaning to tell you – about the day my grandad died,' said Aldo after the waitress had taken our order.

I waited for him to continue.

'We knew he might not have long to live, but my gran was refusing to give up hope. When he started drifting in and out of consciousness, she asked me if I could tell him something about my trip to India to hold his attention. I wasn't sure whether we should just let him go peacefully or try to keep him with us for as long as possible, but I wanted to give some hope to my gran – and to myself – so I began to tell him the story of how I met Darshan.

'It wasn't clear how much he was taking in, but when I got to the end, he tried to say something through his oxygen mask. My gran took it off for a moment, and that's when he asked if he could hear some of the questions from the book. I couldn't remember all the words from the ones I really wanted him to hear, so I just scribbled down any that came to mind. After I'd read those to him, I said there were some others he might like, but I would have to get in touch with the person who had the book. Then I went to phone you – and Dan answered.'

'That was the first time you phoned?'

'Yeah. Why?'

'Dan said the phone had rung lots of times.'

'Well, I only rang once … Anyway, when I went back into the room, my grandad seemed disappointed that I wasn't able to read any more of the book to him, so I told him I was hoping the person who had it was going to phone later. This seemed to keep his interest going and prevent him from drifting off. After a few moments he asked if the person I was trying to contact was my father. I wasn't sure how to answer, and because I didn't want to upset him, I said it was.

'As it got closer to the end of visiting time, I told him that if he wanted to hear something more from the book, he'd have to wait until I came to see him the next day. But he said: "It's all right, I'll see your dad before then." Not long after, he took his last breath.'

A wave of sadness came over Aldo's face. He composed himself and gave a wistful smile, then carried on:

'My gran said she thought my grandad had mentioned my father because of the book of questions I'd spoken about. She told me that when my dad was a kid he was always asking questions, and he asked so many that my grandad once told him he should write a book – a book of questions.'

The waitress returned with a small carafe of raki and two tiny glasses.

'So what do you make of that?' I asked as I poured our drinks.

'Of what?'

'Your father and his book of questions.'

'Nothing, really. I just mentioned it because it was a strange coincidence.'

'So you don't think he ever wrote his book?'

'My mum never knew anything about it if he did. When I told her what my gran had told me, she said it was the first she'd heard of my father and a book of questions. It must have just been a joke he'd shared with my grandad.'

'Unless …'

'Unless what?' Aldo took a sip of raki.

'Unless it happens to be the book that Darshan gave you.'

'How could you explain that?'

'I don't know, but had you ever heard of a book of questions before you met Darshan?'

'No.'

'Neither had I. But someone had. And that "someone" just happened to be your father – who went to Calcutta.'

'You're not trying to suggest he met Darshan there?'

'It's not beyond the realms of possibility.'

'And then I just happened to meet him there too?'

'Didn't you meet him in the same restaurant your father had been to – the one he'd made a note of in his guidebook, which was in Darshan's neighbourhood?'

'Yeah, that's right.'

'So maybe it was a place Darshan often went to.'

'But the manager told me he'd never seen him before.'

'That doesn't mean Darshan had never been there. It could have been somewhere he used to go in the past. Don't forget you went to Calcutta almost twenty years after your father did. It was hardly likely to be the same manager.'

'We can't be sure of that.'

I took a couple of sips of raki, observing Aldo as I did so. It seemed he was beginning to entertain the possibility that his father had met Darshan.

'Are you sure Darshan said he wrote the book himself?' I asked.

'Yes. I remember him saying it was his last one – and his first.'

'What if he wasn't telling the truth?'

'I couldn't imagine Darshan lying to anyone. Anyway, even if we let ourselves believe my father could have written it, there's still a lot that would need explaining.'

'Such as?'

'How he managed to do that perfect calligraphy as well as all the designs on the pages in a few weeks – while travelling round India at the same time.'

'He might have written it before he went.'

'In which case my mum would have known about it.'

'Unless he kept it secret.'

'Since he was honest enough to tell her about his ex-girlfriend, I don't see why he wouldn't have told her about a harmless book. Anyway, why would it contain clues to help me find Darshan? How could that be connected with my father?'

'OK, maybe you're right.'

I thought I detected a shade of disappointment on Aldo's face – as if he had been hoping I wouldn't concede so easily. I topped up our glasses and looked out of the window. On the opposite side of the street, two stray dogs were sleeping huddled together in the doorway of a shop, lulled by the music of an accordion player who had braved the cold to bring some warmth to the passers-by in return for a few coins.

I looked back at Aldo. He was lost in thought.

'Anyway, you'll be able to ask Darshan all this when you meet him,' I said.

'You mean I should ask him if he'd been lying and the book had really been written by my father? What would he think?'

'He might think you were a genius for working it out.'

'I reckon it's more likely I'd end up losing any chance I had of gaining his respect.'

Aldo picked up his glass and drained it. I regarded him closely, watching for a sign of doubt creeping into his mind. Then I became aware of what I was doing: fooling myself as well as him. I didn't seriously think his father could have written the book of questions. I had only persisted with the idea because I had sensed he didn't want to admit that he believed it was possible. But I had ended up almost believing it myself.

A prickly silence was growing between us. I steered the conversation towards more mundane topics and didn't refer to the book again for the rest of the evening.

* * *

When I got up the following morning and went into the living room, Aldo had made himself a cup of coffee and was studying the book of questions.

'Don't you want anything to eat?' I said.

'No thanks. I don't usually eat much when I've got something on my mind.'

'What are you thinking about?'

'Those words I wanted my grandad to hear. I can't decide whether they would have been appropriate or not. At first I was sad that I hadn't been able to read them to him, but now I'm starting to think it might have been for the best. There again, maybe I'm just trying to convince myself so I can stop regretting what happened … Why don't you have a look and tell me what you think?'

I took the open book from him and sat in the armchair. Both pages had been among those I had considered when trying to guess the one in question, but since I had been unable to choose between them, I had eventually settled on a different one.

'Which page?' I asked.

'Both.'

'I thought it was only one page you'd wanted to read to your grandad.'

'What made you think that?'

'That's what Dan said.'

'He must have misheard me. I'm pretty sure I didn't tell him that.'

I turned my attention back to the words:

Have you ever watched the moon
moving
through the branches
in silence
with each step you take?

THE FLAME OF TOMORROW

Have you seen the moonlight
reaching
across the sea
to touch you
as you walk by the shore?

Did you know
wherever you go
there's a light
by your side?

*

Have you ever felt the sun
shining
inside you
as you wake in the present
and forgive all your past?

Have you seen the sunlight
dancing
on the waves
that lap more gently
as the day grows old?

Did you know
in your soul
burns the flame
of tomorrow?

Although I felt these pages to be more suitable than the one I had chosen, I wanted to find something unsuitable about them in order to ease Aldo's sense of regret – as well as my own, regarding the part I had played in preventing him from reading them to his grandfather. But I couldn't see anything in the words that wouldn't have been appropriate.

'What makes you think it might not have been a good idea for your grandad to hear these questions?'

'Maybe they'd have made him sad by reminding him of what he was going to miss about life. He loved being close to nature, and there was nothing he enjoyed more than going for walks by the sea. But there's also the possibility the words would have comforted him, since they seem to echo his own thoughts about nature.'

'It sounds like he could have written them himself,' I said without thinking.

Aldo raised his eyebrows. 'First you thought it was my father who wrote the book, and now you think it was my grandfather. Next you'll be saying it was my mother!'

'You never know. Maybe she wrote it in the loft and gave it to your father as a present before he went to India.'

Aldo appeared to be considering what I had said.

'Come on – it was supposed to be a joke.'

'I know, but the more I think about the question of who wrote the book, the harder it is to know what to believe.'

'That's partly my fault for suggesting your father could have written it.'

'Maybe – but I have to admit I'd already had that thought myself. I knew it was probably just wishful thinking, so I wanted to see if you'd come up with the idea too. But at the same time, I *didn't* want to believe the book had been written by my father, because if it had, I'd want to keep it to remember him by; but if it turned out that the idea of passing it on had also been his, it would mean I'd be going against his wishes by hanging on to it. And I wouldn't feel too good about asking you to give it back to me – especially after spending so long trying to let go of it. But I reckon the hardest part would be having to accept that Darshan had deceived me.'

* * *

That evening, after Aldo had left for Piraeus to take his boat to Patmos, I rang Maria to talk about our plans for New Year's Eve. But she told me she would be working at the hospital because the person who had been scheduled to do so had been taken ill. I put the phone down and began thinking about who else I could arrange something with. I called Sophocles, my colleague from the school, but there was no answer. I was on the point of phoning another friend, then changed my mind. I went into the living room and sat down. Why was I so desperate to have something to do on New Year's Eve? It was just another day, as Aldo had said.

I picked up the book of questions and opened it at random.

If your heart is subject to the seasons,
and your mind to the reasons
of the masses,
how will you find your way
to meet the day
before it passes?

I made the decision to spend New Year's Eve alone. I would make a plan to make no plans, and see what happened. And if nothing happened, I would make the most of nothing.

21

Seeds of Uncertainty

In the afternoon of New Year's Day, Aldo phoned to tell me he had met Darshan the previous night. Before I could ask him anything, he said: 'You were right: my father did meet Darshan – and he was the one who inspired the book. I'll tell you all about it when I see you. I'm planning to stay four more days, so I should be back on Wednesday morning. I'll phone you when I arrive.'

* * *

On Tuesday I went for a walk in the park behind the Acropolis. I made my way to the hill near Socrates' prison and climbed the wide stone steps which formed a path through the olive trees that graced the rocky hillside. Towards the top of the hill the trees thinned out, leaving an open area around the oblong stone structure that stood there. It appeared to be an ancient monument of some kind, but I had never taken the time to look at it closely as I usually had another reason for coming to the park: to see if I would run into the stranger I had met in September – whom I hadn't seen since our encounter at the bus stop.

I walked past the monument and paused to acknowledge the view. The rugged terrain fell away sharply and sloped towards the park's perimeter to meet the encroaching concrete of the city, which stretched out as far as the serene blue sea in the distance. To my left I had a clear view of the Parthenon, with Lykavittos Hill rising in the background. I turned round and looked beyond the treetops in the opposite direction, where a footpath meandered through uneven slopes of marble-like rock dotted with clumps of green and the odd cypress. But there was no sign of the stranger.

I cut across the brow of the hill and joined a narrow path leading down through a huddle of pine trees towards Socrates' prison. Silence had replaced the summer chorus of cicadas, though the sunlight filtering through the foliage was enough to evoke its echo in my mind.

When the site of the prison came into view, there was someone sitting on one of the benches in front of it: a young man with short dark hair in a fleecy bomber jacket, leaning over a guitar. My eyes were overruled by my head. It was impossible for Aldo to be here. I edged closer until I was within earshot of the music. It was the tune he had been playing when I had first met him on Amorgos. But this time it did nothing to enchant me.

I stepped off the path and moved behind some bushes to ensure I would be out of sight. As I stood there like the trees, with the sound of my breathing drowning out the breeze, I took the decision to play along with him. He was due to 'return' from Patmos the following morning and stay at my flat for his last night in Greece. I would wait for his phone call and carry on as normal. If I bided my time and asked the right questions, I should be able to expose his deceit without having to accuse him of anything.

But what if he wasn't intending to contact me again before leaving? I would lose the chance to find out what was going on. Was I willing to take this risk?

A middle-aged man with greyish hair was approaching the site of the prison. It was the stranger I had been hoping to bump into. He sat down next to Aldo on the bench and they began a conversation. I strained my ears to hear what they were saying, but their words were a distant murmur.

After a few minutes they stood up. Without waiting to see which direction they were going to take, I turned round and set off to run, not looking behind me until I was well out of the park – at which point I slowed down and glanced over my shoulder. They were nowhere in sight, but in case they were coming my way, I speeded up again and only stopped running when I reached a busy pedestrian area, where I was able to disappear into the throng.

I arrived back at my flat charged with adrenalin and flopped down on the sofa. Whatever Aldo was up to, it seemed the stranger was in on it. Did this mean Darshan didn't exist and Aldo had fabricated the story about him? If so, who had written the book of questions? And why had Aldo given it to me? What was the purpose of this elaborate game of his?

I considered asking this last question to the book, but, having begun to doubt its authenticity, I resisted the temptation. Then I had the idea of finding a completely irrelevant page, as this would help to convince me that its content was of no real significance and I had only believed in it because I had been taken in by Aldo's story.

I took it off the bookcase and opened it at random.

Does the flower
within the seed
beneath the ground
fear the light
above the surface?

I was pleased to see that my doubts appeared to have been confirmed. How could I have been so naive to believe the book had some magical quality? It was only ink on paper.

My next question was: where had Aldo been staying in Athens since leaving my flat? Maybe he had got a room at the hotel where he had stayed before. I found the card with the address on, dialled the number and spoke to the receptionist. But there was no record of Aldo on the register.

Now all I could do was wait and see if he would ring the following morning. The rest of the day dragged, and I had a restless night punctuated with dream-like interludes, from which I would awake with a jolt, thinking I had overslept and he hadn't phoned.

22

The Underlying Lie

The phone rang around nine o'clock in the morning. I sprang out of bed, then let it ring a few more times before answering. I said hello in as casual a voice as I could muster. It was Aldo.

It can't have been more than half an hour later when he got to my flat, though it had felt a lot longer. Opening the door, I scanned his face for a sign of pretence, but I could find no flaw in his friendly smile.

'Go through and sit down, and I'll make some tea,' I said.

'I wouldn't mind a cup of coffee if you've got some.'

'Oh yeah – I forgot you're not a big tea drinker.'

I went into the kitchen and made some coffee for both of us, then joined him in the living room. He had made himself comfortable on the sofa.

'So, tell me all about it,' I said, sitting down in the armchair. 'First of all, where did you stay? Did you have any trouble finding a room?'

'There weren't many places open, but I managed to find a nice guest house in the port.'

'What was the name of it? Maybe I'll be able to stay there when I go.'

Aldo averted his gaze. 'I don't think it had a name. It was one of those little family-run places.'

'It would still have had a name.'

'If it did, I didn't notice,' he said without flinching.

'So you met Darshan at St John's cave?'

'That's right.'

'Was he surprised to see you?'

'Not particularly.'

'Did he arrive on time?'

'Yes. I'd got there early, but he appeared on the stroke of midnight.'

'Then what did you do?'

'We stayed there talking for a couple of hours.'

'Outside in the cold?!'

'It wasn't as cold as I'd expected – and he'd brought a flask of tea with him.'

'He gave some to you, then?'

'Yes.'

'I thought you didn't drink tea.'

'I don't usually, but it was a kind of Indian tea with spices.'

No doubt Aldo had prepared his answers. I would have to be patient.

'So you only saw Darshan for two hours?'

'I did that night.' He took a sip of coffee. 'But we met again the next day – then a couple more times after that.'

'So what's the connection with your father?'

'Darshan was on his way back to Calcutta on the train one day and my father was sitting opposite him …'

'How did he know it was your father?'

'He obviously didn't at the time, but he realized it had been him when he met me in Calcutta.'

'How?'

'That'll become clear as I tell the story,' said Aldo calmly. 'Anyway, my father was scribbling away on some scraps of paper, so Darshan asked him if he was a writer. He replied that the only thing he could write would be a book of questions. Darshan said it was an interesting idea, but my father just gave a half-smile, as if to say he knew he was being ironic. Before Darshan could tell him otherwise, he said he'd been trying to write a poem for his wife but wasn't getting anywhere with it. He joked that it would have to be good, because even though she was Italian, her written English was probably better than his.

'Darshan asked him what he meant by "a good poem". He said he didn't know, but he'd recently been given a book of poems and he'd been studying it to get an idea of how to write one. Darshan said the only thing he should be concerned about was being sincere. My father told him he found it hard to sound natural in a poem. So Darshan asked why he wanted to write one in the first place. He said it was to give his wife a surprise for her birthday – which was the day he was due to arrive back in England. Darshan advised him to imagine he was speaking to her in a dream. My father closed his eyes for a while, then began writing again and spent the next hour or so working on the poem. Eventually he seemed satisfied with what he'd written, and he copied it into the back of his guidebook.'

Aldo paused. 'Don't you see what that means?'

'What?'

'That the poem in the guidebook had been for my mum after all.'

'Maybe your dad just said it was because he didn't want to tell Darshan about the other woman.'

'I must admit that thought occurred to me as well. But Darshan said my father had told him he was grateful for the help he'd given him with the poem because he'd recently upset his wife by having contact with an ex-girlfriend and he'd been trying to think of something special to give her as a way of showing he was sorry.'

'Have you phoned your mum to tell her?'

'I haven't had chance.'

'You can call her from here if you like.'

Aldo hesitated. 'Thanks for the offer, but I think I'd rather tell her when I see her.'

He took another sip of coffee and I did the same, stealing a glance at him over the rim of my mug to check for any signs he was lying. Before I was able to apprehend the scene, it had slipped away and he had resumed his narrative:

'When my father found out Darshan was from Calcutta, he asked him if he could recommend a hotel and somewhere to eat. Darshan told him about two places he knew and my father noted them down in his guidebook. They spent the rest of the journey talking and discovered they shared an interest in Indian philosophy. My father was keen to know more about it, so Darshan told him about Vedanta.'

'What's that?'

'The philosophy of the Vedas.'

'Who are they?'

'The scriptures of ancient India,' said Aldo, breaking into a smile. 'According to Vedanta, man's real nature is divine – it's part of the omnipresent, unchanging consciousness that's behind the appearance of this world – and the purpose of human life is to realize this divine nature. You must have heard of the Bhagavad Gita – that's based on Vedanta.'

'Oh yeah,' I said, though I wasn't sure what the Bhagavad Gita was exactly.

'Anyway,' he continued, 'when the train arrived in Calcutta, Darshan offered to put my father up, but he said he wouldn't want to bother him and was happy to stay at a hotel. Even though Darshan said it wouldn't be any trouble, my father still declined his invitation. Darshan imagined he wanted his privacy, so he took him to the hotel he'd recommended – the same one that I stayed at. They met up again that afternoon and spent the rest of the day going round the city.'

'Didn't you say your father had gone to India in the summer holidays?'

'Yes. Why?'

'Isn't it the monsoon season then?'

'That's right.'

'So it can't have been easy going on a tour of the city.'

'Maybe not, but that's what they did, according to Darshan ... Before taking my father back to his hotel, he took him to a restaurant in his neighbourhood – the one he'd recommended and the same one where I lost my bag.'

'So did Darshan know the manager who was there when you went?'

'No – it had changed hands and he'd stopped going because the food wasn't as good as it used to be.'

'But if he knew about the food, he must have gone there after it had changed hands.'

'Maybe once or twice, I imagine. So?'

'So the manager would have seen him. But I remember you saying that when you asked him about Darshan, he said he'd never seen him before.'

'Probably for the same reason that Darshan said he didn't know *him*: the restaurant had changed hands more than five years earlier, so it's pretty unlikely the manager would have remembered him, even if he had seen him before.'

I reluctantly accepted that what Aldo had said made sense, and let him continue.

'Darshan and my father arranged to meet at the restaurant for lunch the next day. It'd been raining all morning, but it had stopped before the time they were going to meet. As Darshan approached the restaurant, he saw my father sitting on a nearby wall, taking photos. Suddenly a boy ran past and snatched his bag, which he'd had next to him on the wall. My father set off to chase him across the street and managed to grab hold of the bag, but he slipped and was hit by a bus. Darshan ran into the restaurant to call an ambulance and his friend, the doctor – the same one who came to examine me – then rushed to my father, who was lying in the middle of the road. Before he lost consciousness, he said: "My son ... help him learn what I couldn't."

'The doctor arrived before the ambulance, but there was nothing he could do to save my father. When the police came, they looked inside my father's bag for his passport. All they found was a guidebook and a map of the city. Then they saw his money belt under his shirt, and that's where they found his passport.

'Darshan gave a statement to the police along with his name and address. He also gave them the phone number of his bookshop and asked them to tell my father's family they were welcome to contact him. But apparently my mum and uncle never did. He thinks the police might not have passed on the message – maybe they'd wanted to cover up some of the facts about how my father had died, since it didn't paint a very good picture of the city.

'After telling me this, Darshan asked what I thought my father hadn't been able to learn and had therefore wanted me to. I said it might have been something to do with letting go of attachments. He said: "Attachments to what?" I was thinking of my father's ex-girlfriend, so I said, "Women." But Darshan said the way he died suggested he'd been too attached to material things. I told him it was only natural that my father hadn't wanted to lose the poem, since it was something he'd created for someone he loved. Darshan said it was the feeling behind it that was of true value, and this was something no one could have stolen. So I said my father might have seen the poem as a way of proving his love for my mother. Darshan said: "If he loved her, there should have been no need for him to prove it to her."

'I asked Darshan if he was implying that my father hadn't loved my mother. He said: "I am merely saying he may not have realized that the only way to prove you love someone is to love them." He also pointed out the possibility that my father had made a copy of the poem, in which case it could have been the guidebook itself that he hadn't wanted to lose – or even the bag or the map. Whatever the case, he said, the fact remained that his desire not to lose something material had caused him to lose his life.

'Darshan explained that he wasn't criticizing my father; he was just observing the reality of his actions – and how they were related to some of the things he'd said about himself:

'When they were at the restaurant the evening before he died, he told Darshan that he was worried he might not be such a good father and he felt bad about not being able to spend so much time with me because of his job at my uncle's shop. Darshan asked him why he wasn't with me at that moment, and he said he thought the way to be a better father was to become a better person, and he believed that coming to India would help him do this. He'd heard that people in India valued different things in life, and he'd realized this was true when he'd seen the smiling faces of little children who didn't even have any shoes, let alone any toys. This had made him think I might already be too attached to possessions, and he felt responsible for that because he'd always told me to take good care of my toys and books. He said he wished he'd told me to take care of more important things. Darshan asked him what he meant by "more important things", and he said, "His dreams."

'At this point Darshan paused and asked me if I'd learned to let go of material things. I said I thought I had, and the fact I'd given the book away proved it. He said this was just the beginning: I was now aware of the importance of being able to let go of things, but I could only say I'd learned to do it until the next time I became attached to something.

'Then he asked if the book had helped me learn anything. I gave it a bit of thought and said I'd seen that questions can be useful even if they can't be answered. Darshan nodded and said that was the other thing my father hadn't been able to learn – at least not until the day before he died …

'While they were walking round Calcutta, he remembered the remark my father had made about only being able to write a book of questions. He explained to him that he hadn't meant it ironically when he'd said it was an interesting idea, since asking questions was how Socrates got people to realize the truth of what they were saying, and he believed if Socrates had written a book, it would have been a book of questions. He suggested they both write one, and said if they ever met again they could give their books to each other.

'Darshan told me that until that moment my father hadn't realized how much could be gained by sharing questions. He made a point of saying "sharing" instead of "asking", and said everyone's always keen to share their answers but sometimes sharing questions is more helpful. He told me it isn't such an original idea and psychoanalysts do it all the time, but we could just as easily do it with each other – and save money in the process.

'But Darshan said even though it was clear to him what my father had wanted me to learn, he wasn't sure whether he would carry out his wishes, since no one has the right to involve themselves in someone else's life – even with the intention of teaching them something – without sufficient signs to show it's right.'

'And what form are those signs supposed to take?'

'Molehills,' said Aldo.

'Molehills?!'

'That's how Darshan refers to coincidences. He says they're the surfacing of an underlying pattern. We never know when they're going to appear, but when they do, we know there's something present beneath the surface.'

'So coincidences give you permission to interfere in someone's life?'

'Not interfere, but play a part.'

'What's the difference?'

'How willing the other person is to let you.'

'I imagine that means you're not supposed to deceive them in any way.'

'Not for your own gain, obviously. But sometimes you might have to use a trick to help them.'

'What kind of trick?' I asked.

'It usually involves creating a situation where they'll have the chance to learn what they need to.'

'I don't think it's right to tell a lie, though.'

'That's no doubt what most people would say – but it doesn't stop them doing it.'

'So you're saying most of us are liars?'

'Not in the usual sense of the word. Darshan says we become so accustomed to our view of reality that we often tell lies without being aware of it.'

'But it's not a lie if we believe what we're saying.'

'It is if there's a part of us that knows it's not true – even if this is an unconscious part. And if that's the case, it means we're basically lying to ourselves. According to Darshan, the lies we tell others often stem from this "underlying lie", which is the root we need to dig out. But if someone's convinced that their way of seeing something is right, you're not going to change their mind by simply telling them they're wrong.'

'Why do we have to bother trying to change their mind? Why not let them see things the way they want to?'

'What if they're causing themselves to suffer?'

'It would still be their choice. I thought Darshan said we're not supposed to get involved in anyone's life unless they're willing to let us.'

'That's right, but there's a way of finding out if they're open to being lent a helping hand … What you need is a trick question.'

'How do you mean?'

'Darshan says you have to ask a question that makes them stop to think about what they're saying and why they're saying it … For example, imagine someone who believes he's the best student on his course at university – someone who feels under pressure to achieve and is giving himself stress about it. Whether or not he really is the best student is beside the point. The problem is he's too concerned about it. If you ask him how he knows he's the best, he'll probably say he just does – and there isn't much you can say in response to that.' Aldo drank some of his coffee, which was no doubt lukewarm by now. 'Can you think of a trick question to ask this person?'

'I'm still not sure what you mean exactly by a "trick question".'

'It was Darshan who gave me the example, actually, and he said you could say: "When exactly did you become the best student on the course?"'

I thought about the question for several seconds. 'So what would that person's underlying lie be?'

'Probably something like: "I need to show that I'm better than others."'

'Many people really do feel the need to do that, though.'

'Yes, but if they look inside, they'll see that they only feel that way because they've told themselves to. And they've done this out of a refusal to see the truth, according to Darshan.'

'The truth about what?'

'Who we are. Darshan says if they go deep enough, they'll find the lie that's preventing them from seeing this truth. He calls this the "original lie" – the root of all lies – which is that we're all separate from one another.'

'But we *are* all separate from each other.'

'Only on the surface – like Patmos and Amorgos: it's only the level of the sea that creates an island.'

Aldo let me contemplate his words for a few moments.

'So anyway,' he continued, 'if the person gives a knee-jerk response to your question or tries to avoid it, it's probably best to leave them alone. But if they stop to think about what you've asked, it could mean they're willing to look inside themselves.'

'Did Darshan ask *you* any trick questions?'

'Yes – I told you about the first one, when I was at his house in Calcutta and he asked if there was any reason why it might have been right for me to lose my bag.'

'Yeah, I remember that. So what was your underlying lie?'

'More or less the same as my father's: that there's usually more to gain from hanging on to something than from letting go of it. Darshan said because I'd considered his question, he knew I was willing to learn to let go of things.'

It dawned on me that Aldo might be deceiving himself as well as me with the story of Darshan and the book.

'Do you mind if I ask you a trick question?' I said.

'Go ahead,' he replied with a shrug, which seemed out of tune with the expression on his face.

'Would Darshan be here if your father was?'

'What do you mean?'

'Would this wise father figure of Darshan exist if your dad hadn't died?'

Aldo looked lost in thought for a fleeting moment. 'In my mind, you mean? Is that what you're saying?'

I nodded.

'Do you seriously believe I've been making all this up?'

'I don't really know what to believe any more. But more to the point, do you?'

'So Darshan's my imaginary friend – or father? Is that it?'

'I don't know. Is he?'

'He might be in some ways.'

'What's that supposed to mean?'

'Most of us have imaginary friends to some extent, since few of us can claim to know the true self of another – which means the image we have of someone is often different from the reality of who they are.'

'Maybe so – but at least they exist in some form or other. But in the case of Darshan, I'm wondering if there's *anything* real about him.'

'What makes you say that?'

'If I ask you a few questions, it should become clear.'

'Go on, then,' he said with a hint of irritation in his voice.

'OK … Did you really go to Patmos?'

'Yes.'

'And did you really meet Darshan there?'

'Yes.'

'So what were you doing in the park yesterday with that man we met there in the summer?'

'How do you know that?'

'I saw you.'

'Why didn't you say hello?'

'Why didn't you tell me you were in Athens?'

'I tried to.'

'When?'

Aldo took a deep breath. 'The man you saw me with is a friend of Darshan. His name's Traikos. He comes to Athens regularly, but his permanent home's on Patmos.'

'How does he know Darshan?'

'I'll get to that later – just let me speak a minute … I was originally going to take the boat back to Piraeus on Tuesday night – as I'd told you on the phone – but then I found out Darshan was leaving on Monday because he was going to India the next day. Traikos was going with him on the boat, and they said I was welcome to join them. I rang you a couple of times to tell you, but you weren't in. Traikos said I could stay at his flat in Athens if I couldn't get hold of you, so I changed my ticket and returned with them. We got to Piraeus on Tuesday morning and went to Traikos' flat for some breakfast. Then Darshan had to leave for the airport and Traikos was going to go with him. I phoned you again, but there was still no answer, so Traikos said I could leave my rucksack at his place and we could meet later in the park. Once I'd left my stuff there, there wasn't much point in trying to get in touch with you again, since you weren't expecting me till today.'

'Why didn't you tell me all this as soon as you got here?'

'Because the moment I sat down, you started bombarding me with questions. I haven't even had chance to finish my coffee!'

23

The Flow of the Unknown

'So, if the interrogation's over, I'll carry on,' said Aldo.

'Yeah, sorry. I won't interrupt again.'

'The only problem is I can't remember where I'd got up to.'

I tried to backtrack to the point where we had diverged from Aldo's account of his father's final days.

'I think you'd just mentioned the moment when Darshan suggested to your father that they should both write a book of questions.'

'Yeah, that was it – when they were walking round Calcutta … So anyway, my father said they'd have to find a way to meet up again if they ever wrote their books. He asked Darshan if there was any chance he might come to England one day, but Darshan said it'd be a good idea to choose a place neither of them had been to – one that held some unanswered questions for both of them.'

'Hang on – so Darshan's been to England, then?'

'Yes – I never got round to telling you. His family moved to London when he was thirteen. So he went to school there, and then university – to study philosophy.'

I wanted to ask Aldo some more questions about Darshan's past, but before I was able to, he resumed the story:

'Darshan said to my father that it only seemed right for them to meet somewhere between England and India. At that moment they were passing a church built with Grecian columns, so my father suggested Greece: the country where East meets West – and the homeland of Socrates. The church happened to be the church of St John, which was what made them decide on Patmos – after my father had told Darshan it was where St John wrote Revelation.

'Darshan told me that after my father's death, he got hold of a copy of the Bible and read Revelation, and was interested to find it had some similarities with the Bhagavad Gita.'

'Like what?'

'He says they both deal with the idea of overcoming our inner demons to become one with the Divine.'

I wondered if I would have come to the same conclusion about Revelation had I studied it carefully. The main reason I had intended to do this was to discuss it with Maria, but she had ended up forgetting about the idea so I had never got round to it.

I looked to my left out of the French windows. A pigeon was perched on the balcony railing. It seemed to be observing us with interest, its head cocked to one side as though it were trying to catch what we were saying. I was about to point this out to Aldo when, with a flutter of its wings, it flew off.

'So when did Darshan write his book?' I asked.

'He started it the day after my father died and completed it a few days before the anniversary of his death, writing one page every week. Then he flew to Greece. His plan was to go to Patmos, light a fire on a beach somewhere, and cast the book into it as an offering to my father's spirit.'

'You mean destroy what had taken him a year to write?!'

'I was surprised too when he said that. But he told me it was also a way of seeing whether he'd ever be able to help anyone let go of anything, since he could only teach something he'd learned to do himself.

'So he arrived in Greece, spent a couple of days in Athens, and then, the night before the anniversary of my father's death, he took a boat to Patmos. But on the journey he had a vivid dream which made him change his plan:

'He was sitting on a bench in a clearing in some woods. He had his book of questions in his hand and was waiting to meet my father. It was night-time and the full moon was rising. As the moon got higher, he was able to see the moonlight reflecting off the sea in the distance through the trees, and he realized he was on a hillside. A white owl swooped out of the darkness, dropped a leaf onto the book and settled on the end of the bench. There was something written on the leaf. Darshan picked it up and read: *These leaves I bequeath before I receive.* For a moment the owl had my father's face, then it flew off into the night.'

Aldo looked at me and waited.

'Did you say the words were "these leaves" and not "this leaf"?' I asked.

'Yes.'

'But the owl only dropped one leaf on the book.'

'That's right – it dropped it on the book.'

I spent a few moments trying to puzzle this out.

'So the "leaves" refer to the pages of the book?' I said.

'Yes. Darshan knew it meant that he was supposed give the book to me. But he wondered how he could help me learn to let go of things if he was going to give me something. It occurred to him that the words on the leaf had been "I bequeath", not "I bequeath to my son", and he thought this could mean the book should be given to others as well. Then it clicked: he would have to help me let go of the very thing he was going to give me.

'When he was on Patmos, he came across a little art shop in the port. Inside, there were some designs of leaves within leaves. They reminded him of his dream as well as a verse in the Bhagavad Gita about an eternal tree, whose leaves are said to be the songs of the Vedas. He mentioned this to the artist and found out he'd read the Bhagavad Gita. The artist referred to "the tree of life" in Revelation, and then they had a discussion about what the two books had in common.

'I imagine you've already guessed who the artist was.'

'Traikos?'

'That's right … Later that day, Darshan followed the road from the port to St John's cave, which is on a hillside on the way to the main town. As the road went higher, it took him into a wooded area. When he reached the site of the cave, he found a bench and sat down. He recognized the scene as the one from his dream, and decided that if he ended up giving the book to me, this would be where we should meet again.

'The next day he told Traikos about my father and the book of questions. Then he asked him if he'd draw some of his leaf designs in it – one for each day of the year. Traikos said it would take a long time, so he'd have to keep the book and send it to him when he'd finished – or Darshan could come and pick it up, and stay at his house as a guest.

'Darshan ended up returning to Patmos for New Year. While he'd been away, he'd come up with the two statements inside the question marks. After adding these, the dots of the question marks looked empty, so Traikos created the alpha and omega design. That's when Darshan had the idea of the turn of the year as our meeting time.'

'So for all those years after that he was just waiting for you to show up on his doorstep one day so he could give you the book?'

'Yes and no. As I mentioned before, he didn't know for sure whether it would be right to try and help me.

If our paths didn't cross, it would obviously mean he wasn't supposed to. But even if they did, he would first have to find out if I needed to learn what my father had wanted me to – though he said he'd had a pretty good idea that I would, as there aren't many people who've mastered the art of letting go. He'd also felt confident that our paths *would* cross sooner or later, because it was only natural I'd be curious about the place where my father had died.'

'But how did he know who you were when he found you in the restaurant?'

'He didn't at first, but there were several "molehills", he said. To start with, the boys running away with the bag: they reminded him of the incident with my father. And they literally ran into him – as if to jog his memory. Then, the address of the restaurant on the map inside the bag and the name of the hotel I was staying at – which were the two places he'd recommended to my father. Since neither of them were known to tourists, it meant there was a good chance I'd seen them written in my father's guidebook. On top of that, my father had told Darshan his wife was Italian and his son was called Aldo, so when I told him my name and said I was born in England but grew up in Italy, that was obviously another big clue.

'And all these signs were confirmed when he heard my surname. I had to give it to the doctor so he could call the hotel and tell them what had happened to me.'

'So if he was sure who you were, why didn't he tell you he'd known your father? Why all the secrecy?'

'What should he have done? Given me the book and told me my father had inspired it and wanted me to have it but had also wanted me to give it away to someone I hadn't met yet?'

'OK, if you put it like that. But what if you hadn't figured out how to find him? Then you'd never have found out about your father.'

'Darshan said the main point wasn't to tell me about my father, but to teach me about letting go.'

'How would he have done that if you'd felt unable to give the book away?'

'There would still have been the mystery of who he was and why he'd said I could meet him again, so I'd have seen that by hanging on to it I was losing out on something else – something unknown … something that would remain unknown until I let go of it. And thinking about this would have given me some idea of the point of letting go – which Darshan says is "to enter the flow of the unknown".'

'But what if you'd had no interest in meeting him again? You wouldn't have learned about letting go if there'd been nothing you had to let go of.'

'I never thought about that possibility – and I never asked him if he had, either. It was as if he knew I'd be curious to see him again. And he'd have known I appreciated a bit of intrigue, since he'd seen the mystery story in my bag.'

'What if you'd wanted to meet him again but hadn't been bothered about keeping the book?'

'I think he was confident that wouldn't be the case, considering how I'd tried to hang on to my camera.'

'But how was he to know you wouldn't get the solution to the riddle wrong, then give the book away and lose your chance of finding the right one?'

'I never asked him that.'

'Wasn't that what you were worried about when we were on Amorgos? It was the reason I gave you my address: so you could get hold of the book again if you needed to.'

'Yeah, you're right. But I can now see that even if I'd given it away without finding the right solution, it would still have been a lesson in letting go – in fact it would have been a more complete one.'

'But there was also the possibility you'd have spent the rest of your life trying to figure out how to find him and driven yourself nuts in the process.'

'I must admit that thought had crossed my mind. When I mentioned it to Darshan, though, he said I'd only have tormented myself about solving the riddle until I'd let go of that as well.'

'Letting go seems to be the answer to everything,' I said with thinly veiled sarcasm.

'It is – to everything you can't change, according to Darshan. But that's how you end up changing it. And that's the magic. The point wasn't just for me to learn to let go of material things, but also to let go of thinking I needed to have an answer for everything. That was the purpose of the book of questions: to teach me that.'

'I can't help feeling that all this talk about letting go is just an excuse for not caring.'

'That's the whole idea: not caring about knowing how things are going to turn out.'

'I mean not caring about another person's well-being.'

'Trying to solve a riddle doesn't exactly pose a health risk. And wouldn't you say well-being comes from not living your life with constant tension inside?'

'Definitely! So why did Darshan want to create tension for you?'

'Like cures like.'

'How do you mean?'

'He was applying the homeopathic principle. But he didn't *create* tension for me; the tendency to do that was already in my character – especially in situations where I wanted to show I was able to figure things out by myself. So if something could help me get to the root of this tendency, and I could dig out that root, then I'd have less stress in my life in general.'

'You mean as if by magic all your stress would disappear?'

'No, but I'd have been made aware of the process that creates it – in a more effective way than if I'd just read about it or been told about it. And that was what happened. You probably didn't realize, but the example

Darshan gave about the student putting himself under pressure to be the best on his course was a pretty accurate description of what I used to be like. Admitting to myself that I might need some help to find the clue in the book was my first step towards letting go of that tension. So that day on Amorgos when I asked you to give me a hand was something of a turning point for me.'

'But you can't say Darshan was directly responsible for that. He couldn't have known for sure that you'd end up asking someone to help you.'

'Maybe not, but he'd made it more likely – by saying if anyone helped me solve the riddle, they'd be the one I should pass the book on to: he knew it'd be hard for me to let go of it, but giving it to someone who'd helped me figure out how to find him would at least make it a bit easier.

'Anyway, apart from all that, it's clear that Darshan cared about my well-being, because he'd made sure he could always get in touch if necessary.'

'How?'

'On that first night in his house in Calcutta, before I'd gone to sleep, I'd taken off my money belt, taken out my passport, and shown him the names of the two people to contact in an emergency. One of these is my mother and the other is my uncle John. He'd insisted on making a copy of the page, but I'd forgotten all about it when I woke up the next morning because of the state I'd been in.'

'So if he had those addresses, why didn't he write to you?'

'The need never arose.'

'How was he to know that?'

'He said if it had been necessary, he'd have been given a sign – such as a vivid dream. But he did say he'd been interested in finding out whether I was trying to solve the riddle and if I was making any progress. He had to discover this without me knowing, though – and without trying to discover it, otherwise it would have "diluted the mystery".'

'How was he supposed to do it, then?'

'Through the mystery of serendipity ... That day when I first met Traikos outside Socrates' prison and asked him about the Greek writing on the sign, he recognized the book I had in my hand. It's pretty distinctive with its leather cover and the coloured string around it.'

'It's pretty small as well – he must have good eyesight,' I said, then remembered how observant Traikos had been when I encountered him in the park. 'Anyway, he couldn't have known it was you just because of the book ... Did you tell him your name?'

'We never got round to introducing ourselves. But he asked me where I was from. And I always have to answer that by saying I was born in England but grew up in Italy and now live in Bologna. He called Darshan the next day and gave him a description of me; and that, together with the other facts, made it pretty clear who I was.'

'But that doesn't mean Darshan knew you were close to solving the riddle – or even trying to, for that matter.'

'He knew I'd discovered how the Greek omega was written. And he knew I was familiar with the Greek islands and had a friend who lived in Greece, since I'd mentioned this to Traikos. So he knew I had plenty of help available.'

'You can't say he knew you were happy, though. You must have looked pretty down after hearing the news about your grandad. How was he to know it wasn't because you were tormenting yourself over the riddle?'

'You're assuming Traikos told Darshan what sort of mood I was in … But even if he did, the main feeling I remember having that day was relief, since I'd managed to change my flight. Anyway, you saw me the day after. How would you say my mood was?'

As far as I could recall, he hadn't seemed any different from his usual self.

'You know what,' said Aldo, 'I reckon trying to solve the riddle helped me not to dwell on my grandad so much. Now that I think about it, it was the perfect distraction.'

'OK, maybe. But that was over two years after he'd given you the book. How could he have known about your well-being during all the time up to then?'

'Because he'd given me the book! He'd explicitly said if I was ever troubling myself over something, the book would help me. And he was right.'

I leaned back in the armchair and remained silent – until another question entered my head:

'So had Darshan been waiting for you on Patmos on New Year's Eve last year and the year before?'

'Yes – even though he hadn't expected me to come so soon.'

'Does he only go there to visit Traikos, or is that where he lives now?'

'Didn't I tell you he went to the airport yesterday because he was leaving for India?'

'Maybe he was just going back for a visit.'

'It wasn't for a visit.'

'So does he still live in Calcutta?'

'No. He left in 1996 – the year I was in India and stayed at his house.'

'Where does he live now, then?'

'I can't tell you.'

'Why not?'

'Darshan asked me not to. He said the reason for that is connected with what you need to learn.'

'What makes him think he knows what I need to learn?'

'You'd better ask him yourself.'

'What did you tell him about me?' I snapped.

'Just a few things: where you live, what your job is, how we met, that we'd both been to India, and how we solved the riddle together.'

'Pretty much everything, then!'

'Don't worry. He was very interested to hear about you and said he was looking forward to renewing your acquaintance.'

'So he's expecting me to come?'

'Yes … and no,' said Aldo with a smile I couldn't fathom.

'Hang on a minute – did you say *renewing* my acquaintance?'

'That's right.'

'But I've never even met him!'

'He seems to think you have.'

'That's crazy – I definitely haven't met him before. He's just saying that to make me want to go and see him, so that I'll pass on his book and this great game of his can continue.'

'Maybe,' said Aldo, shrugging his shoulders.

'You mean you don't know?'

'Don't know what?'

'Whether I've met him.'

'All I know is that he says you have.'

'How did we meet, then?'

'I was hoping you might be able to tell me that.'

'So he hasn't told you how he knows me?'

'He said that was something he should reveal to you first – if you couldn't remember, that is.'

There was a blank space in my mind regarding my supposed meeting with Darshan.

'Is it true what you're saying, or are you just having me on?' I said.

'It's all true – though you're not the only one who finds it hard to believe you've known Darshan all along without knowing it!'

24

In Search of a Turning Point

Almost a year had passed. The beginning of a new millennium was approaching. I was looking forward to spending it on Patmos with Darshan. There was just one snag: I hadn't given the book away yet. Finding the right person wasn't as easy as I had thought it would be. Not that I had been trying too hard …

It was Christmas Eve and I was flying to England to visit my parents in York. Within minutes of take-off we were soaring above sparkling blue sea. As the plane turned in a seemingly never-ending arc, one of the nearby islands came into view: a gentle giant reclining in sunshine and shadow, waiting to greet the tiny ship sailing at a snail's pace towards it. I took full advantage of my window seat and, straining to catch a final glimpse of the city, I spotted the Parthenon: gleaming stone columns on an age-old mass of rock rising out of a sea of concrete. I wondered if Traikos would be having a walk in the park behind the Acropolis. I hadn't seen him since the day he had met Aldo outside Socrates' prison, despite all the times I had gone there in the hope I might run into him.

Once the plane had completed its ascent out of Athens, I settled into my seat and began to think about the year that had passed.

I had spoken to Aldo several times on the phone, and we had arranged to meet up in London over the Christmas period as he would be there visiting his uncle. As for Maria, I had continued to see her regularly. In August we had gone to Amorgos and shared a tent on a campsite. I recalled our last night there: floating on our backs in the sea, hand in hand under the stars, wondering if the Earth, too, looked like a twinkling speck of light to another pair of souls somewhere out there in the vastness.

But although we were effectively a couple now, we still lived separately, hanging on to our independence – and our misgivings about romantic relationships.

I had been hoping she would come to York with me for Christmas but she had arranged to spend it with her parents. So we weren't going to see much of each other over the holidays. I had already decided it was better if I went to Patmos alone, which meant Christmas was the only time we could be together. When I had asked her why she couldn't visit her parents at New Year instead, she had said she preferred to be in Athens for the millennium celebrations – and I was welcome to join her if I wanted.

Why was it that the harder I tried to make things work out, the less likely this was to happen? I took the book of questions out of my jacket pocket and opened it at random.

Can you desire without demanding,
greet without grasping,
hold without having?

Can you direct without dictating,
care without craving,
give without gaining?

Can you look without longing,
wait without wanting,
pray without prompting?

I tried to see if I could answer yes to any of the questions. In each case, it was hard to remember an instance when I had had such an attitude. It was also hard for me to imagine how it would feel to behave in this way. I read the questions again – more slowly this time and without trying to answer them ...

I looked out of the window. An ocean of cloud stretched into the distance. Before long I had drifted into a daydream: I was floating towards the soft glow of the horizon, knowing it would always be waiting to greet me since it was forever beyond my grasp ...

* * *

From the airport I took a train to King's Cross Station in central London, then caught another one to York. I was too weary to be on the lookout for someone I could give the book to, and I spent most of the journey gazing out of the window, watching the mid-winter sun dodging the clouds to throw streaks of bright green across the shadowy meadows of the English countryside.

I arrived in York at dusk. Had my parents known which train I was coming on, they would have insisted on picking me up; but when I had reached King's Cross, there had been one leaving for York straight away and I hadn't had time to phone them. I thought about surprising them, but by now they might be worried that something had happened to me. So I called them from a payphone, then went to the bus stop, which was outside the entrance to the station.

It had started to snow. I sat down on a bench under the overhang of the station roof. Sitting at the other end of it was an elderly-looking man with a shock of silver hair and grey stubble. He acknowledged me with a friendly nod.

'Are you waiting for the number one?' I asked.

'No, son.'

'Have you seen one go past?'

'Aye – plenty. Been 'ere all afternoon.'

I wasn't sure what to say next. I watched the snowflakes floating in the beam of a nearby street lamp.

'This is where I live,' he said, and made a sweep of his arm.

'Handy for the centre, then.'

He gave a chuckle. 'I sleep over there,' he said, pointing down the street towards a park near the city walls.

'Outside, you mean?'

He nodded. 'Don't get me wrong – I'm not complainin'.'

I noticed his tattered overcoat and worn-out shoes – and how his blue eyes brightened his weathered face.

'How long have you been living like this?' I asked.

'Five years. I'm sixty now.'

'You must get cold sleeping outside.'

'Sometimes. But I don't mind a bit of cold if it means bein' free. And that's 'ow I feel when I'm lyin' under the stars.'

I found it hard to believe anyone could be happy sleeping rough.

'I know what you mean about the stars. I don't think I could cope with the wet and cold, though,' I said, wondering if he was really homeless.

He kept his eyes on me. He appeared to be sizing me up.

'Do you want me to get you a cup of tea or something?' I said.

'No thanks, son – just 'ad one.'

I didn't know what else to say to him.

'I've written a book, you know – about my experience,' he said. 'It's called "Out with the Stars".'

I wasn't sure whether to take him seriously or not.

'Took me four years,' he added.

'It must be a good feeling – completing a book.'

'Aye, it is. But writin' it gives you an even better one.'

I scanned his face for a sign of insincerity.

'Number one,' he said, pointing up the street.

My bus was approaching.

'Shall I give you some money to get yourself another cup of tea later?' I said.

'That'd be grand.'

I took all the change out of my pockets, kept what I needed for my bus fare and gave him the rest.

'Well, it was nice talking to you,' I said standing up. 'Take care of yourself.'

'You too, lad.' He reached up to shake my hand. 'Merry Christmas!'

I got on the bus and found a seat by the window. The buses always waited a few minutes at the station, and as the engine ticked over, I stared absently at the falling snow, thinking about the hardships of a life on the streets. Out of the corner of my eye I saw another passenger get on. It was the homeless man. He walked straight past the driver and came to where I was sitting. I felt the eyes of the other passengers on me and caught myself hoping he wasn't going to ask for some more money.

'If I can do one, so can you,' he said, looking me in the eye. 'You just have to write the first chapter, then keep at it.'

His bright eyes lingered on me, then he turned round, left the bus and wandered off into the night. But his words stayed in my mind. What had made him say them to me? He didn't even know whether I liked writing. Maybe he had wanted to see how the other passengers would react to hearing he had written a book.

I knew it was uncharitable of me to entertain this thought, but it was easier than believing a complete stranger could have tuned in to my subconscious – since I couldn't deny that his words had touched a point of resonance. Though I had never considered writing a book, I had kept detailed records of my recent travel experiences. Should I try to put them all together? If so, which event would I start from? This got me thinking about turning points in our lives. Can we ever recognize one as it happens, or do we only become aware of them in retrospect?

I remembered there was a question related to turning points in Darshan's book. I leafed through the pages until I came to it.

If you could read
the book of your life,
would you miss out some pages
to avoid the suspense
as your story unfolded
through its twists and turns?

On the opposite page was the following question:

When did you become
who you are now?

25

Another Question Mark

My last day in York had arrived and I still hadn't found anyone to give the book to. Now I was clinging to the hope that I might cross paths with a suitable candidate on my journey back to Athens. But even if I did, there would hardly be enough time to know whether they really were the right person. And I certainly didn't want to give the book to someone who wouldn't fully appreciate it.

I had a seat reserved for the following morning on a train that would get me to London by eleven o'clock. My flight wasn't until seven in the evening, but I was going to meet Aldo at King's Cross Station and spend the afternoon with him.

While I was at my parents' house, I wanted to sort through my books and CDs to see which ones were worth taking back with me. I was in the middle of doing this when Aldo rang to say his uncle had asked him to help out in the shop while his wife went to the dentist. He would still be able to meet me, but not until twelve. If I had known earlier, I could have taken a later train and had some extra sleep before my journey. Now I would have to wait at

King's Cross for an hour, as I wouldn't have time to take the underground to another part of London and get back for twelve o'clock, and I didn't want to go far on foot since my rucksack would be weighed down with books and CDs.

* * *

The next morning my parents dropped me off at the station. I had been half hoping to see the homeless man again, but there was no sign of him, so I went straight to the platform and found a seat in the waiting room.

My thoughts soon turned to the conversation I had had with my parents about my forthcoming meeting with Darshan. My mother had advised me not to go with great expectations, as I might end up being disappointed. My father had said: 'Remember that whoever he is, he's only human.' I had told them not to worry and that I regarded it all as a kind of game. But my father had seen through my laid-back air and said: 'A big game, or just a friendly?' I had admitted it was 'quite an important game', and had then recalled the footballing days of my youth – in particular, the occasions when I had been selected for trial matches but had not played as well as I could have done. In the past he had put my underperforming down to nerves, but this time he had offered a deeper explanation: I had been focusing too much on myself instead of the game.

I reran the scenes from these matches in my mind. My eagerness to impress had made me feel I was judging myself through the eyes of others. As a consequence,

I had cut myself off from the flow of the game. In sharp contrast were the matches I had played under more relaxed conditions – ones I had enjoyed so much that I hadn't even had time to think about whether I was playing well or not.

Could it be the same with 'the game of life'?

The arrival of my train was announced. I picked up my rucksack and went onto the platform. The number of people waiting made me glad I had reserved a seat. I was able to stand back as the train drew in and they all converged on the doors. But I had forgotten I would need somewhere to put my rucksack. I rushed to join them and managed to get on just in time to claim the last space on the luggage rack near the door.

My seat was at a table with a young couple and their little boy, who was busy crushing a yogurt carton. I had booked the one near the window, but it had been taken by the father – a burly man with a constant frown – so I settled for the one next to him. Before I could sit down he had to move his bag, which he did without making eye contact.

The couple had spread their food and drink all over the table and made no move to clear away the empty biscuit packets and juice cartons that were in front of me. I took out the book of questions and opened it without thinking.

If no one could do wrong
in your eyes,
would you need to learn
to forgive?

I glanced at the opposite page.

Are you sure
the reason you don't want to change
isn't because you fear
the regret you will feel
for not changing sooner?

The questions hardly registered. My mind was engaged with more pressing ones: Weren't they going to move their rubbish? Why couldn't they be more considerate?

The boy threw the yogurt carton onto the table – and into my lap. I assessed the damage – several blobs of yogurt down my trousers – and gave him a scowl as I put the carton back on the table. The father was staring out of the window; the mother had her head buried in a magazine. I gave a heavy sigh, which failed to get their attention, then went to the toilet to wipe the marks off my trousers.

But they left the train at Doncaster, the first stop after York, and I was able to reclaim my window seat.

While the train was standing in the station, I thought about all the separate chains of events that intersect when people come together on the same journey. In my case, the sequence stretched back more than two years: breaking up with Efrosyni, going to Amorgos, meeting Aldo, helping him solve the riddle, receiving the book of questions …

As the train started to move again, I opened the book at the penultimate page.

As life fades
in the light of death,
will the meaning of your days
be manifest,
as a book's unfolding
becomes complete
when the last page
is turned?

This was the question I had thought Aldo might have wanted to read to his grandfather. I had had my doubts as to whether it was suitable for someone in their final moments, but from the conversation I had had with him about the way his father had died, I knew he believed it was better to have some time to prepare for death than to die unexpectedly, and I had therefore thought that if his grandfather had shared this view – and if he had sensed his days were numbered – the words could have helped him come to terms with his fate.

Drops of rain began to hit the window. They had reached the end of their journey – their 'last page'.

'Excuse me, these seats are ours.'

Two elderly couples were standing over my table.

'The others are free, but I've booked this one,' I said.

'I'm afraid we've reserved all these seats,' said one of the women, and showed me her ticket.

'That says "Coach E",' I said.

'That's right.'

'But this is coach F.'

'It's definitely E,' she said. 'We've just come from F. We had to get on there because we were in a hurry.'

One of the men pointed to the sign above the door, which was clearly visible from where I was sitting.

I apologized and went to the next carriage. I was relieved to see there was no one in my seat. The one across the table was occupied by a young woman. She had blond hair tied in a ponytail, was wearing glasses, and looked to be in her late twenties. Her fair complexion was highlighted by her black woollen top, which hung loosely off her shoulders.

'I've just found out I've been in the wrong seat,' I said, feeling the need to explain why I was sitting down opposite an attractive woman.

'Are you sure you've got the right one this time?'

'Yes – look,' I said, taking out my ticket.

'It's OK, I was only kidding.'

To keep the conversation going, I said the first thing that came into my head:

'Are you going to London for New Year?'

'No, I'm going to Dover to stay with my nan, but I'm breaking my journey in London so I can look round the bookshops. They have a much bigger selection than the ones in York.'

'Is that where you live – York?'

'Yes. I'm from Dover originally, but I've lived in York for the last four years.'

She glanced out of the window. I did the same, and glimpsed a cluster of bare trees huddled together in the middle of a rain-soaked field.

'So what sort of books do you like?' I asked.

'Anything that leaves me with something to think about – something I hadn't given much thought to before.'

We spent the rest of the journey talking, and by the time we got to London I had begun to feel she might be the right person for the book of questions. As we were pulling in to King's Cross, with rivulets of rain now running down the window, I suggested continuing our conversation in a nearby café. She said she had been thinking of making the same suggestion, since she didn't have an umbrella and wouldn't be going far until it stopped raining.

After getting my rucksack from the other carriage, I saw her struggling to lift hers off the luggage rack onto her slender frame.

'I don't believe you were thinking of walking round London with all that on your back!' I said. 'Let me give you a hand.'

'It's OK, thanks – it's not as heavy as it looks. It's just awkward to get on.'

As we filed along the platform with the other passengers, I remembered my arrangement with Aldo.

I stopped at a payphone and called him to put our meeting time back another hour.

We stepped out of the station into the rain, crossed the road and walked as quickly as our loads permitted until we came to a little café, where we made a beeline for the only free table – in the far corner by the window, which was steamed up from the babble of voices around us. After we had put our rucksacks down, there was barely enough space left for us. I took the seat facing the window and she squeezed into the one against the wall.

'I'm Laura, by the way,' she said, taking off her white woolly hat and wriggling out of her duffle coat.

'Oh yeah, sorry – I haven't introduced myself. I'm Jake.'

We decided what to order and discovered we had made the same choice. Then neither of us spoke. Maybe we had already said everything there was to say to each other. Laura peered through the steamy window and I looked around the café.

The wooden floor blended in with the cream-coloured walls, which were hung with black-and-white photographs. The one above Laura's head was of a lone penguin shuffling along a sloping path towards the sea. At first I had thought it was a stooping businessman carrying a briefcase, such was the photographer's skill in capturing the human-like qualities of the penguin.

The waitress came over and we asked for a pot of tea and two pieces of banana cake. She glared at our rucksacks, even though they weren't in anyone's way but our own. When she had gone, Laura shrugged her shoulders. Then she drew a smiley on the window with her finger.

'Maybe that'll cheer her up,' she said.

She cast me a playful glance, then drew a thick squiggly line above the smiley.

'That looks like a question mark,' I said.

'That's because it is one.'

'What does it mean?'

'A question, of course!'

'I mean what does the whole thing mean?'

'Why don't you guess?'

'OK. Maybe it means asking questions makes you happy – in other words, you like learning about new things.'

'That's true, actually. But it's not what I was thinking.'

'You enjoy a good mystery?'

'That's true as well, but it's not the answer either.'

'In that case, it must mean you like to keep people guessing!'

'I admit I'm enjoying this game. But that's still not the answer, I'm afraid.'

The waitress returned with our tea and cake, plonking it down on the table without so much as a half-smile.

'I think you'd better tell me what it means, or I might end up looking like her,' I said after the waitress had left.

'OK, it means there's always a question mark … hanging over … happiness.'

'For everyone?'

'I don't know – about everyone else, that is.'

Her dramatic pauses had made me think she was fooling around, but her facial expression suggested otherwise.

'So that's your face on the window?' I said.

She nodded.

'It's a pretty big smile, though.'

'Because that's what it's like when I'm happy – until the spell gets broken.'

'How do you mean?'

'It's like when I read a good novel,' she said. 'I step into the shoes of the main character and leave myself behind. While I'm reading it, I feel like a different person – and the world feels different too, as if everyone around me has also changed. But after I finish it, I soon see that everything's pretty much as it was before – including myself.'

'I know what you mean about losing yourself in a book, but I think if it really is a good one, you won't be the same after reading it.'

'In what way?'

'It could change the way you think about something. Didn't you more or less say that before, when we were on the train?'

'But you'll still be the same in many other ways – which means you end up not changing that much after all.'

I wanted to disagree with her and say that a new perspective could bring about a transformation in a person's character, but I knew how little I had changed over the last year despite the insights I had gained from Darshan's book of questions.

'Are you ready for some tea?' said Laura, picking up the teapot.

'No thanks, I'll let it brew for a while. The cake's great, by the way.'

'I'm not sure I fancy any now.'

As Laura poured herself some tea, my gaze wandered back to her smiley on the window.

'But what do you mean exactly when you say there's always a question mark over your happiness?' I asked. 'Do you mean you never know if you're really happy, or you don't really know what makes you happy?'

'Aren't those basically two ways of saying the same thing?' She took a sip of tea. 'Whenever I feel happy, it isn't long before I start wondering if I'm just fooling myself, because time and again I've seen that the things I think will make me happy end up making me sad.'

'I imagine most of us have felt like that at some time or another.'

'It's a little more often than that in my case.' She paused for a moment, her half-smile flickering under a frown. 'It's like a recurring dream. Just when I think it's not going to happen again, it creeps up on me.'

'What does?'

'That feeling – of being powerless.'

'Powerless to do what?'

She didn't answer.

'Do you feel your happiness is beyond your control? Is that it?'

She gave another frown as she considered my question. 'To be honest, it's more a feeling of being powerless to make others happy.'

'That doesn't surprise me.'

She dropped her gaze.

'What I mean is that we can never know for sure what makes someone tick,' I said. 'And anyway, I don't think it's possible to actually make another person happy. We might be able to do things to please them or say things to make them feel good about themselves, but happiness is something deeper than that – it's connected with our whole attitude to life. The only way to really make someone happy would be to get inside their head and change the way they see things.'

'Like a good book can, you mean?'

'Uh?'

'Didn't you say before that a book can change the way we see things?'

'Yes. Why?'

'Because if there's someone who needs to change the way they see things in order to be happy, and a book helps them do this, then it means the book – in other words, its author – has made them happy.'

I tried to gather my thoughts. 'But you said yourself that a book is never going to change someone that much.

And I agree, because in the end it's down to you. A book can give you an idea about how to be happy, but you're the one who's got to go out and apply it in your life. So I still think we're powerless to *make* somebody happy. That doesn't mean we can't share a moment of happiness with someone, though.'

'But what makes a moment of happiness? Surely it depends on the people involved?'

'Of course.'

'So doesn't that mean they're making each other happy?'

'I reckon it's more a case of them bringing their happiness to the situation and sharing it.'

'I think you're just splitting hairs,' she said. 'But even if it's as you say, surely this sharing of their happiness is something they feel happy about?'

'I imagine so.'

'So they *are* making each other happy.'

'But if they're sharing their happiness, it means they were already happy before – so you can't say they're *making* each other happy.'

'OK, so they're making each other happier. Can we say that at least?'

'I suppose we can allow that,' I said, then wondered whether happiness could have different levels or whether it was an absolute state and increasing 'levels' were steps towards attaining this state.

'Mmm, this is yummy,' said Laura after taking a bite of her cake. 'Why didn't you tell me?'

'I think I did, actually.'

I felt a bit hypocritical for making it sound so easy to be with someone without feeling in some way responsible for their happiness. I knew how difficult this had been for me on many occasions, especially where my relationships with women were concerned. But Laura's self-doubt had prompted me to search for some words of wisdom, and I had found myself saying things I imagined Darshan would say.

'Look, I know how you feel,' I said. 'I've often wanted to make another person happy. But apart from the question of whether this is actually possible, I think I've got to ask myself if my main desire is for this person to be happy, or for me to be able to make them happy. If it's really their happiness that I want, what difference should it make if I'm not the one who provides it?'

Laura carried on eating her cake as she mulled over my words. Once again, they contrasted with the way I had felt in my previous relationships.

I looked at the photograph of the penguin. For a moment I shared the mood of the forlorn figure as it made its way along the path. I no longer believed in the idea of trying to make someone happy and wanting them to do the same for me, yet I was unable to leave it behind as I still couldn't summon the inner source of happiness at will. I lingered on the sidelines while the game continued.

'The tea's good as well, by the way,' said Laura.

I poured myself some tea, which by now was lukewarm and stewed.

'Looks like I let it brew too long,' I said. 'Maybe this is a reminder that whenever you share something with someone, you won't necessarily experience it in the same way.'

'That's exactly what worries me – whether the other person is enjoying it or not.'

'Come on, Laura – you've got to let go of things that are beyond your control: what happened with my tea, for example.'

'I could have insisted on pouring you some before.'

'I wouldn't have thanked you for a cup of weak tea. And anyway, it still wouldn't have meant I'd have drunk it any earlier. What I'm trying to say is that each person is responsible for what they get out of a situation. And if a cold cup of tea could be enough to ruin my enjoyment of this one, you'd be better off leaving me to sulk about it rather than spending your energy trying to change my mood.'

'What if it made me happy to try?'

'Then there'd be no harm in it, I suppose – as long as you were happy just to try, without worrying about whether you succeeded or not.'

Laura retreated into her thoughts. Maybe this was the right moment to mention the book of questions. But I would have to change my arrangement with Aldo again: though I still had over half an hour left with Laura,

I would need longer than that to show her the book and fill her in with the background to it.

She had wiped some of the steam off the window and was staring absently at the steady stream of passers-by. A rainbow-coloured umbrella caught my eye.

'Do you believe that when you've got a problem you can get help from the world around you?' I asked.

'What sort of problem?'

'A difficult decision, for example. Or a situation you don't know how to resolve.'

'Well, we can get advice from other people, of course – though I admit it's not always easy to get good advice.'

'I mean do you believe we can get help in more subtle ways?'

'Like what?' said Laura.

'Holding a question in your mind and seeing what life brings your way.'

'I've done that with a book before: asked a question, then opened it to see what answer it gave me.'

'Does it work?' I asked.

'Sometimes. But I know what you're going to say.'

'What?'

'That if I want to, I'll be able to find a connection with whatever I see on the page. That's what one of my friends is always telling me: that there's nothing magic about it.'

'But even looking for a connection can help you understand things better. Obviously, you can interpret what you see in a book however you want, but that's part of the process of figuring things out: the way you interpret something tells you something about yourself. And in the end, it's only yourself you're asking. The outside world can just give you pointers to go deeper inside and find the answer.'

'I guess you're right,' said Laura. 'And that could be why I sometimes get disappointed when I ask for an answer: because I'm hoping for a sign that'll show me what to do. So maybe instead I should be looking for something that prompts me to examine things more deeply.'

'The question behind the question, in other words.'

'That's a good way of putting it.'

'It is, isn't it? But it's not mine.'

'Who said it, then?'

'The person who wrote this,' I said, reaching inside my jacket.

I took out the book and handed it to Laura.

'Oh, look – a question mark, just like mine,' she said. 'I thought that was a smiley under it for a minute … Hang on – what does this say? *Possibilities Abound.*' She turned it over and read out the words on the back: '*The Mystery of Serendipity* … This is really cool. Where did you get it from?'

'It's a long story.'

'Well, I'm not going anywhere in this rain.'

'OK, I'll tell you all about it. But don't you want to have a look inside?'

'Can I?'

'Yes. And why don't you ask yourself a question first?'

Laura closed her eyes for a few moments, then opened the book. As she studied the pages, she became increasingly absorbed in thought.

'Can I see?' I asked.

She passed me the book.

Am I free
if I need you
to agree?

Do I know
if what I learn
is just to show?

Is it wise
to use my words
to criticize?

*

Can you put off
until tomorrow
what you can live without
today
to take a step
on the road to freedom?

'Which page did you look at first?' I asked.

'The one on the right.'

I wondered if the other questions were meant for me. I handed the book back to her and she leafed through a few more pages.

'These designs are lovely – like falling leaves. I love autumn,' she said.

I no longer had any doubt that Laura was the right person for the book. But how much should I tell her about it? Perhaps Aldo ought to be the one to answer that … I remembered I had to ring him again to change our meeting time.

I told Laura I had to make a quick phone call. I said she could hang on to the book while I was gone, to which she readily agreed. But what if she disappeared with it? I had spoken without thinking. Telling myself I could trust her, I left the café and ran through the rain to the nearest phone box. Someone was using it, so I ran all the way to the station. I rang the shop and Aldo answered.

'I'm glad you phoned,' he said. 'We're really busy and my aunt hasn't come back yet. She must be stuck in traffic. But even when she gets here, they still might need my help. I'm afraid it's going to be a bit difficult to meet you.'

'Don't worry, I've got good company – that girl I met on the train. I'm pretty sure I'm going to give her the book. But how much should I tell her about it? Should I just tell her about Darshan, or can I mention your father as well?'

'I don't mind. It's up to you.'

By the time I returned to the café, Laura was so engrossed in the book that she didn't notice me until I sat down. I ended up telling her all about Aldo and his father and how each of them had met Darshan. When I told her that studying the book would reveal where and when she could meet him, I made sure I stressed the words 'cover to cover to discover'. To give her some help, I said the place was on an island somewhere in Europe.

26

Chasing Shadows

On the night of December 30th, I took the boat to Patmos. It was a ten-hour journey, which meant I would be arriving around eight o'clock the next morning. I found a quiet spot in a corner behind some seats in the TV lounge and settled down for a good night's sleep. But as soon as we were on the open sea, it became clear that it wasn't going to be a smooth journey.

Unable to sleep, I went to the café to get a hot chocolate. The ship was rocking about so much that it wasn't easy to carry it without spilling any, so I sat down to drink it – joining the motley crew of bleary-eyed passengers who were scattered around the tables, sitting hunched over their drinks, clutching them vigilantly.

Before I had drunk it all, I started to feel uneasy about leaving my rucksack unattended, so I headed back to the TV lounge. A stocky man was coming down the corridor. He had dishevelled hair and a droopy moustache and looked to be in his late forties. As we were passing each other, the ship lurched to one side, causing him to lose his balance and bump into me. My polystyrene cup flew out of my hand and its contents went all over the floor. Grabbing my arm as I tottered, he apologized and offered to buy me another drink. I told him the cup had been half empty, but he insisted on taking me back to the café.

He got me another hot chocolate and bought a coffee for himself, then suggested sitting down and carried our drinks to a table. I wanted to check on my rucksack and wasn't in the mood for small talk, but I felt obliged to go with him.

Our conversation began with 'Where are you going?' (the boat would be calling at five islands altogether), but it became more interesting when I found out he was from Patmos. He asked where I was going to stay, and when I told him I hadn't booked anything, he said most of the guest houses would be closed – though he knew one that was definitely open: his own. He promised to give me a nice room at a special price, so I agreed to stay there, trusting it would be as good as he had described.

After we had finished our drinks, he told me his name was Vassilis and he would wait for me on the quayside after the boat had docked. We shook hands, then I went back to my place in the TV lounge and got straight into my sleeping bag.

The wind hadn't let up and the boat was still being buffeted from side to side. At first my body resisted the movement as my mind allowed thoughts of sinking ships to creep in and take hold, but gradually I was able to let myself move with the waves – or rather, be moved by them – and I pictured myself being carried safely to shore. Knowing I had found somewhere to stay on the island also helped to ease my mind, and I drifted into a deep sleep.

* * *

I was woken by the announcement that we would shortly be arriving at Patmos. I gathered my things together and went out on deck, bracing myself against the chill wind. A pale orange sun floated above the horizon, casting a glimmer of warmth over the grey-blue sea.

As we approached the island, I walked over to the side of the ship to get a better view. Dominating the skyline on the hilltop overlooking the port was the Monastery of St John. With its ramparts and battlements, it resembled a medieval fortress watching over the little white houses that huddled around it. Below them, a carpet of pine forest spread down the hillside to the whitewashed buildings of the port. To take in as much as possible, I waited until we had docked before making my way down the steps to disembark.

There were more passengers getting off than I had anticipated, so I ended up standing in a queue for several minutes. Stepping onto the quayside, I was met by a waft of sea air and the cries of seagulls. A handful of people were waiting to embark, among them an Orthodox priest holding a bundle of books, his unruly beard throwing a splash of grey down the front of his black cassock.

Vassilis was nowhere to be seen. Had he had second thoughts about our arrangement? Or maybe he didn't own a guest house at all and had only said so to make conversation. I tried to think positively, telling myself I would find a good room, but there was a nagging thought at the back of my mind that I was going to end up without one. There wasn't even anywhere to sit down and have a hot drink before beginning my search, since none of the cafés along the waterfront had opened yet.

I scanned my surroundings ... Should I follow the main road away from the centre and try to find a place near the sea, or would it be better to take one of the side streets leading into the built-up area behind the row of cafés? I wanted to get a room with a sea view if possible, but the further I went from the port, the less likelihood there was of finding somewhere open. I decided to risk it. There were more buildings along the shoreline to the right than to the left, so that was the direction I took.

I had only gone a short distance from the quayside when I saw a man on a scooter approaching. It was Vassilis. He pulled up beside me and greeted me in Greek:

'*Kalimera.*'

'*Kalimera,*' I replied.

He explained that he had had to go home to drop off the big bag he had been carrying on the back of his scooter, which had made it impossible for him to take me as well. I wanted to ask him why he hadn't told me he was going to do this, but I didn't.

I got on the scooter and we rode off in the direction I had been intending to take, bouncing over the cobblestones as we went. The cobbled street soon gave way to an asphalt road which led out of the central area of the port, hugging the snaking shoreline as it bent to the right and ran alongside a strip of sandy beach. The road then veered left, taking us past a promenade before it once again curved to the right to pass a row of evenly spaced, narrow wooden jetties. They all had a small fishing boat moored to the end of them except for one. A little bridge to nowhere.

After passing a marina of yachts, we came to a fork in the road and turned inland up a steadily rising hillside. At least I thought we were heading inland … We sped past an olive grove bordered by a stone wall, and then, as the road twisted to the right, it became steeper and we slowed down slightly. When we crested the hill, where there was a little white church with its distinctive domed roof, the road bent to the left before starting to descend. It was now flanked by high rocks on one side and pine trees on the other. All at once, within the frame formed by the rock face on the left and the arching branches of a tree on the right, the sea rose into view again. It required no effort to capture the image in my mind, even though it came and went in a fraction of a second as we passed through the frame and the picture expanded before my eyes.

About two thirds of the way down the hill, we turned right onto a dirt track which ended at a whitewashed building with light blue window frames, shutters and doors. We got off the scooter and Vassilis told me to wait while he went inside. A moment later he reappeared with a key in his hand.

'Come,' he said, and led me up some steps at the side of the building.

We entered a short corridor and he unlocked the first door on the left. The room was clean, bright and spacious with simple wooden furniture, a comfortable-looking bed and a large window. He opened the door to the balcony and I stepped outside. There were no buildings between the guest house and the sea. A gently sloping field stretched down to a sandy, crescent-shaped beach lined with tamarisk trees. The beach connected two rocky headlands that curved inwards, reaching out to each other in an attempt to complete the circle. The one to the left was higher and partially covered by clumps of pine trees; the one on the right was sprinkled with shrubs and crowned with a line of rocks along its ridge. In the middle of the beach was a little jetty. A solitary skiff was secured to it, rocking from side to side as the morning breeze teased the surface of the sea.

'You like?' said Vassilis.

'Yes – very nice.'

He grinned and handed me the key. 'You need something, you ask. OK?'

* * *

On the night of New Year's Eve, I left my room before eleven o'clock to give myself plenty of time to get to the Cave of the Apocalypse. I didn't want to risk arriving late for my meeting with Darshan. Aldo had said it was no more than half an hour on foot from the port to the cave, but I wasn't sure how long it would take to walk to the port.

Surrounded by the silence of the night, I climbed the slope from the guest house. There was a chill in the air and no moon in the sky. With a thick jumper under my leather jacket and a torch in my jacket pocket, I was well prepared.

The telegraph poles along the road served as lamp posts, but they were few and far between. Beyond the range of their light, bushes and rocks merged into one dark mass. When I was parallel with the first one, a shadow appeared at my side. For a second I didn't realize it was mine. It overtook me and elongated itself before gradually fading as I got further away from the light. At the next lamp post it repeated its performance. I amused myself with this game of tag until I reached the brow of the hill and became distracted by the bright lights of the port.

At the foot of the hill was the marina, where I passed stylish yachts gleaming in the glare of closely spaced street lamps. Then came the wooden jetties with the fishing boats tied to them. Here the street lamps were dimmer, further apart, and on the other side of the road, with the result that the boats were barely visible. On the hilltop in the distance stood the illuminated Monastery of St John, with the lights of Hora, the main town, spreading out beneath it. Below them, a blanket of darkness stretched all the way down to Skala, the port town. Somewhere in the middle of that darkness was my destination.

As I approached the centre of Skala, I passed an old taverna with its door half open. The silence of the empty road had given way to the murmuring of voices and clinking of cutlery. Then a peal of laughter. Through the window I glimpsed a group of young people raising their glasses. For a moment I wished I was with them.

I walked along the deserted waterfront, where a music bar was open but nothing else, then turned right to take the road leading to Hora. Both sides were lined with little whitewashed houses, all with their shutters tightly closed. After about five minutes the road began to slope uphill, bending to the left to run alongside a row of eucalyptus trees, whose branches were stirring in the light wind that had begun to blow. As the road got steeper, houses and street lamps became less frequent.

It wasn't long before I came to a sign saying 'To the Cave of the Apocalypse' at the beginning of an old stone footpath. I turned off the road and started to make my way up the gradual incline. Bordering the footpath on the left was a stone wall, beyond which the rocky terrain sloped steadily downwards towards the port. On the other side of the path, where the shrubs and pine trees were more abundant, the land sloped sharply upwards.

About fifty metres ahead of me was a lamp fixed to a telegraph pole at a point where the path bent to the right. Beyond that there were no more lights – and the moon was nowhere in sight. I remembered Darshan's question about it following you with every step you take. But I was completely alone on this journey. I was beginning to doubt whether Darshan would be there to meet me.

When I reached the telegraph pole, I turned on my torch. With my heart beating faster, I walked into the darkness. There were now tall pine trees on both sides of me. But I didn't need my torch because strips of light were filtering through the trees from the street lamps on the main road, which ran parallel to the footpath at a higher level.

I had expected the footpath to take me all the way to the cave, but after a relatively short distance it rejoined the road, which twisted to the left and continued to rise steadily. Aldo had told me the cave was in the grounds of a little monastery that was built around it, so I had a rough idea what I was looking for.

Up ahead was a sign saying 'Cave of the Apocalypse' outside an area enclosed by a stone wall and a set of iron gates. I quickened my step. The entrance was set back from the road and illuminated by a nearby street lamp. I walked up to the gates. On the other side of them was a paved driveway bordered by a low stone wall on the left and a high one on the right. Near the low wall there were four stone benches in a row. Between the benches and the wall was a line of tall pine trees.

I rested my hand on the gates. They weren't locked. Was I supposed to wait for Darshan here? All Aldo had said was that he had met him outside the cave. He hadn't told me how close to it he had been – and I hadn't thought to ask.

I pushed open the gates and stepped inside, closing them behind me. The beginning of the driveway was partially illuminated by the street lamp. Beyond that it was pitch-black. I sat on one of the stone benches and shone my torch into the darkness. The beam didn't penetrate far. Through the trees behind me I could see the lights of the port in the distance. It was a timely reminder that I wasn't a long way from civilization, and it gave me the courage to venture up the driveway.

I forged a faint passage of light through the blackness that hung between the pine trees on my left and the wall on my right. After a hundred metres or so, I came to a small building of whitewashed stone which formed part of the monastery complex. It was set forward slightly from the other buildings, to which it was attached, and was the only one with a door. Above the door was a mosaic depicting a young man writing in a book, with an old man – presumably St John – standing next to him. I hung back as my mind raced with my heartbeat. I glanced over my shoulder. Holding my breath, I tried the door.

It was locked. Feeling more relieved than disappointed, I retraced my steps to the benches near the gates.

Sitting still made me more aware of the chill in the air. To distract myself, I looked up at the sky to see if I could pick out a constellation. A gust of wind caught the branches above my head so that they swayed in unison, as if performing an impromptu dance for my benefit. Their movements petered out, and once again I was alone with the still of the night. Perhaps they had been moving not for my amusement but for their own – mocking me and my great expectations. I recalled the dream I had had on Amorgos in which I was waiting for Darshan on a park bench and Dan turned up instead.

A loud cracking sound made me jump. Fireworks lit up the night sky above the port. Midnight had arrived, and with it a new millennium. The fireworks soared, burst and scattered, stealing the show from the stars for a brief interlude. I wondered what Maria would be doing.

Five minutes passed. Aldo had told me that Darshan had met him on the stroke of midnight. Why was he late for me? The pine trees stood impassively as I became increasingly aware of the cold. How long should I wait?

I turned my torch back on and walked the length of the driveway again. The door was still locked. I looked up at the mosaic. I imagined I was the young man writing in the book and the old man was Darshan, dictating his words to me.

I returned to the benches near the gates. As I sat there waiting, I was consumed by the gnawing thought that I was the victim of an elaborate hoax: Aldo had written the book of questions himself and made up the story about Darshan. I was some sort of guinea pig in an experiment to see how willing people were to believe unbelievable stories. How could I have been so gullible? Was he going to appear with that kindly condescending smile he sometimes gave when he wanted to show that his understanding of a situation was deeper than mine?

One thing was for sure, though: if Aldo was going to arrive, I wanted to look composed when he did. I would calmly tell him that I had been expecting him and I had my own reasons for being here ...

'Why am I here?' I said out loud. My voice echoed in my head, then fell away into emptiness. Through this gap came some words from the book of questions:

Is it a trivial matter
to share a moment
in the history of the universe?

I reflected on the moments I had shared as a direct or indirect result of my involvement with the book of questions: moments with Maria, Dan, Traikos, Laura ... and Aldo – including the times I had misjudged him and ended up feeling guilty. Was this another test to see if I could retain my composure and not jump to conclusions?

All I knew was that I didn't know what was to come. Maybe Darshan existed after all … But did it matter if he didn't?

I smiled to myself about the little drama I had just played out in my mind. Then another smile arose from deep inside – as if I was smiling with all my body. I closed my eyes and remained still as this ripple spread through me, making me forget the cold …

27

The Will of the Book

Light footsteps approached through the silence. I opened my eyes and looked to my left. From the darkness emerged a fairly tall, slim man with medium-length greyish hair. He was wearing a white kurta and a cardigan, as if he were out for stroll on a summer's evening. His face was vaguely familiar, but I couldn't place it.

'Hello Jake,' he said when he got within a few feet of me.

'Hello,' I replied, struggling to recall where we had met before. 'You must be Darshan.'

'Yes.' His thin lips formed a broad smile; his dark eyes glinted in the light from the street lamp beyond the gates. 'I hope you didn't get too cold.'

He had a Grecian nose and a firm jawline. There were no signs of ageing on his smooth olive skin apart from a few lines around the corners of his eyes.

'May I suggest we go somewhere warmer?' he said. 'My friend has gone away for a few days and kindly left his home at our disposal. It's not too far from here.'

'Is this friend of yours Traikos – the artist?'

'That's right,' said Darshan, and walked towards the gateway.

He waited for me to go out first; then, instead of coming through and closing the gates behind him, he opened them fully.

'The gates are usually left open,' he said as he came out.

'They weren't open when I arrived.'

'That's because I had closed them.'

'Why?'

'So they would have to be opened.'

I wanted to ask him what he meant exactly – and where he had been waiting and why he had been late – but he had made me feel that any further questions I asked would merely show I had failed to understand something which should have been obvious.

We followed the main road down the hill until we reached the stone footpath, then followed this for a short distance before turning off to take a narrow trail that led into the pine forest. We were now beyond the range of the street lights, though that didn't seem to bother Darshan, who strode into the darkness, whereas I couldn't see where I was going without the aid of my torch. The wind sent a ripple along the boughs of the trees lining the path as if to acknowledge our presence – or at least that of Darshan, who was always a few steps ahead of me.

We walked in silence until we arrived at a little cottage set in a garden enclosed by a stone wall. Outside the gate stood a solitary cypress tree.

'Here we are,' said Darshan, opening the gate.

We went up the gravel path to the front door. He opened it and reached inside to switch on the light in the hallway, then motioned for me to enter before him. Once Darshan had come in and closed the door, I saw the row of coat pegs behind it and started to take off my jacket, but he suggested I keep it on until the house warmed up – then took off his cardigan and hung it up.

'This way,' he said.

I followed him down a short, dimly lit corridor and into a room through a door on the right. The paved floor was partly covered by a beige rug. On the wall in front of me were several shelves packed with books. Thick beams of oak supported the ceiling. To my left there were two armchairs facing a stone fireplace. Darshan gestured for me to sit in the one on the right.

'So, it appears you have forgotten our first encounter,' he said, crouching down in front of the fireplace to light a rolled-up piece of newspaper before feeding it under the pile of twigs on which several logs had been placed.

'I'm afraid so – though I imagine it must have been sometime when I was in India.'

'It was.'

The flames from the paper took hold of the twigs and began to lick around the logs.

'But Aldo told me you'd already left Calcutta by the time I went there,' I said.

'It wasn't in Calcutta that we met.'

Darshan eased himself into the other armchair and turned to look at me. 'Do you remember the guidebook?'

'The one that belonged to Aldo's father?'

'No – though the one I am referring to also happened to be a guidebook of India.'

'Sorry, I don't know which one you're talking about.'

'If I am not mistaken, you were keen to have it in your possession – so much so that you snatched it from under the nose of another fellow.'

I remembered the incident that Dan had reminded me of when I bumped into him on Amorgos. 'You mean at the guest house on Diu?'

'That's right.'

'How do you know about that?'

'Do you remember where the bookcase was?'

'Somewhere near the reception desk, I think.'

'And can you remember who was at the reception desk?'

'Someone checking in, you mean?'

Darshan raised his eyebrows, but my mind was a blank as I tried to recall the scene.

'It appears I have aged more than a little since then,' he said with a grin.

It took several seconds for his words to register. 'You were staying at the guest house too?!'

'Let me explain … but first let me get you something to warm you up.'

Darshan left the room, returning a few minutes later with a bowl of lentil soup and a chunk of bread on a tray.

But I was more interested in what he had to say than I was in the food.

'The guest house used to belong to a dear friend of mine whom I had known since my schooldays,' he began. 'Neither of us had any brothers or sisters, which made our friendship even closer. He was also similar to me in that he had gone to England with his parents as a teenager and returned to India as an adult. He married and settled on Diu, but not long after, his wife died in childbirth. The infant was stillborn. The poor man never got over it and took his own life over three years ago. In his will he left the guest house to me, so I thought I would try my hand at running it.'

'Didn't you have a bookshop in Calcutta? That's what Aldo told me,' I said, and took a spoonful of soup.

'I left it in the capable hands of a colleague.'

'Did you have any experience of managing a hotel?'

'No. But I was ready for a change – a break from books, you could say. I had a desire to see knowledge in action, not just on paper. Running the guest house gives me the opportunity to have contact with a variety of people – and observe if there is anyone who is ready.'

'For what?'

'To learn what they need to.'

'And what would that be?' I asked between spoonfuls, which were becoming more frequent now that I had become aware of my appetite.

'What do you think?'

'I suppose it depends on the person.'

'Yes,' said Darshan. 'But we must distinguish between what they think they need to learn and what they really need to learn.'

'And who can say what that is?'

'Life always shows us what we need to learn.'

'How?'

'In countless ways.'

Darshan spoke with such authority that I felt I had no choice but to accept what he said. Then I remembered the words of my father – 'Whoever he is, he's only human' – and this gave me the courage to question his claims.

'How do you know that life always shows us what we need to learn?' I asked.

'Because that is one of the purposes of life.'

'And how do you know that?' I said, trying to sound more inquisitive than impertinent.

'Because I have learned to read the leaves.'

'The leaves?'

'The leaves from the tree of life. Each moment is a falling leaf … and in every leaf is the tree. I wonder if you have seen it.'

'Seen what?'

'The tree within the leaf.'

'I'm not sure I follow you.'

'That may help,' he said, pointing to a close-up photograph of a leaf in a wooden frame on the wall above the fireplace.

I stood up to take a closer look. It struck me how the stem was similar to the trunk of a tree, the more prominent veins resembled branches, and the finer ones looked like twigs.

'Are you talking about the whole being present in every part?' I asked.

'I am.'

'So you're asking if I'm able to recognize how every thing is connected to everything?'

'That's an apt way of putting it.'

'Well, to do that, we have to see things from a higher perspective – especially when they seem to be going against us,' I said, remembering my conversation with Maria when we had visited St George's church. 'But that's easier said than done. I often think I understand the reason for something and how it's connected with something else – then later I find out I was wrong.'

'And why do you think that is?'

'I don't know – maybe the signs aren't always clear.'

'Or maybe you can't see clearly because of the fog,' said Darshan.

'What do you mean?'

'Perhaps you would like to finish your food. Then we can talk about the fog.'

I sat down again and returned to eating my soup. After I had emptied the bowl, Darshan took it away on the tray. When he came back into the room, he took a log and some twigs out of the metal bucket beside the fireplace.

'Do you like cricket?' he asked.

'Not so much.'

He put the wood on the fire, which crackled with renewed vigour as the flames consumed the twigs and enveloped the log.

'What about football?' he said, sitting down in his armchair again.

'I used to play a lot when I was younger.'

'Do you support a team?'

'I did when I was a kid.'

'So you know the feeling of watching a match and wanting your side to win.'

'Of course.'

'Wanting it so badly that you are not too concerned about the manner in which the result is achieved.'

'I suppose so.'

'And wanting it so badly that you don't appreciate how well the opposition are playing.'

'Mm, probably.'

'That's what creates the fog,' said Darshan.

'I'm not sure I understand.'

'Your view is clouded by your desire for a certain outcome. But why not desire a different one? Or better still, don't desire any particular outcome and just enjoy the game.'

'How could I do that as a football supporter?'

'By being just that.'

'How do you mean?'

'By supporting the game instead of a team – as a neutral observer would do.'

'It'd hardly be very exciting like that!'

'So the desire for a certain outcome creates excitement?'

'Of course.'

'And tension,' said Darshan.

'I suppose that's unavoidable.'

'Exactly – you can't have one without the other. But isn't there enough already in life without having to search for excitement?'

'Not for some people.'

'Perhaps because they are not aware that they are part of the whole.'

I looked at the fire. The form of the log was becoming less distinguishable from the flames. I now felt warm enough to take off my jacket, which I put over the back of my armchair.

'But it's only natural to want things for yourself and feel excited about getting them,' I said.

'There is nothing wrong with desiring something – unless of course your desire is to cause harm. The problem lies in believing it is right for us to achieve our desires. That doesn't necessarily mean it is wrong for us to achieve them, just that we can never be sure.

'When someone says "Think positively", what do you take it to mean?'

'The same as most people, I imagine: to believe things will work out for us.'

'In other words, that they will work out the way we want them to?'

'Yes, obviously.'

'Which means we are leaving ourselves open to pain and disappointment should the opposite happen. And we are also presuming to know what would be good for us. But if instead we adopt the view that "thinking positively" means seeing whatever happens in a positive light, we will release any tension we may have about the outcome – and simply enjoy the game of life, regardless of the result.'

'That's easy enough to say, but it's not so easy to see something in a positive way if it's the opposite of what you want.'

'That depends on how well you wish to know yourself.'

'Sorry, I don't follow you.'

'Wouldn't you agree that your reaction to not getting what you want reveals more about your character than the way you react when you do get what you want?'

'Yes, I suppose so.'

'So, if you are interested in knowing yourself better, you will be able to see an unfulfilled desire in a positive light.'

'What about the most basic desire of all: the desire to live? It's not so easy to see our death in a positive light.'

'It was for Socrates,' said Darshan, looking into the fire. 'He willingly took the poison rather than trying to escape his punishment. He said he had no way of knowing that the place he was going to wasn't better than where he was. He had recognized the true nature of death as merely a transition from one state to another.'

'Maybe so. But we can't all be great philosophers.'

'But we can all realize what he did: that we don't know as much as we think we do.'

My eyes were drawn to the fire once again. The flames seemed to have a life of their own, as if they had come from somewhere else to consume the wood – even though it was clear they only existed because of it.

'So is that what I need to learn – how my desires can prevent me from seeing the signs that life is giving me?' I asked.

'I believe so. Or, to put it another way, how striving for what you want can prevent you from receiving what you need.'

'How did you know this, though?'

'A molehill told me.'

'A coincidence, you mean?'

'That's right. Do you recall that when you grabbed the guidebook, you knocked another book off the shelf?'

'Yes, now that you mention it.'

'But you don't know which book it was, I believe.'

'No,' I said, remembering that I had only been interested in getting my hands on the guidebook, and then, feeling embarrassed about the way I had beaten Dan to it, had left as quickly as I could.

'Allow me to show you.'

Darshan walked over to the bookshelves and returned with a little book, which he handed to me before sitting down again. It had a brown leather cover and was bound with orange-and-green string, which was wrapped around it. On the front there was a question mark with the words 'Possibilities Abound' inscribed inside it. On the back was another question mark, containing the phrase 'The Mystery of Serendipity'.

'That's impossible,' I said. 'I gave this to someone a few days ago.'

'Are you sure?'

'I'm positive.'

'Why don't you look inside?'

I unwound the string and opened the book at the first page. The same three questions were on it – written in dark green ink in the same style of calligraphy – as well as the leaf designs around the edge. I flicked through a few more pages.

'It's the same book, I'm sure.'

'It may look the same, but it's not the one Aldo gave you. However, it was clearly the will of this book to fall into your hands, and since it has found its way back to you, it is yours to keep if you wish.'

'Well, if you're sure. I'd be very pleased to have it. Thank you … But where has it been all this time? Didn't anyone else in the guest house show an interest in it?'

'They didn't have chance … When you replaced it on the bookcase, you just shoved it on top of the other books rather than taking the time to put it back amongst them. And you didn't notice you had pushed it too far, so that it fell down behind the shelves. I must point out that the bookcase doesn't have a back on it – that function is performed by the wall. So the book remained out of sight behind the two encyclopedias which live on the bottom shelf.'

'Hadn't anyone seen it before that?'

'No. I had only just put it on the bookcase that morning after returning from Patmos.'

'I still can't believe no one else noticed it – even if it was behind some others.'

'The fact that this is indeed hard to believe is what made me believe it was meant for you.'

'But how were you intending to meet me again so you could give it to me?'

'I had no idea – until Aldo told me he had passed the original on to you.'

'How did you know that was me? I mean, how did you know he'd given it to someone who'd stayed at your guest house?'

'Molehills, my friend … One morning at breakfast time I overheard you telling someone – I believe it was the same fellow who was at the bookcase with you – that you lived in Athens. When Aldo came here last year, he told me he had been helped to solve the riddle by somebody he had met in Greece – an Englishman called Jake who lived in Athens. He said this person had been to India the year after he had, so I asked him if he knew whether they had been to Diu. He remembered they had, because it was a place he hadn't visited and he had therefore been interested to hear about it. He gave me a description of their appearance, and when he told me their surname was Readman, I no longer had any doubt who it was since I had seen your name in the hotel register – and I wasn't going to forget such an appropriate one!'

'So did you also know I was coming here to meet you?'

'That was by no means a foregone conclusion: Aldo had told me how fond you were of my book,' said Darshan with a smile.

'But how did you know it was something I needed? Just because I knocked it off the bookshelf?'

'That was certainly a sign – especially as it landed at your feet. Then I heard from Aldo that you had found some of the questions helpful.'

'Are you sure you want *me* to have it, though? Shouldn't he be the one who gets it? It's only because of his father that it exists in the first place.'

'Aldo has his own copy. I gave it to him when we met here last year. I asked him not to tell you this, of course. It was important for you to let go of the book completely when you passed it on.'

'Why is it so important to let go of things?'

Darshan stood up and took the framed photograph of the leaf off the wall. He handed it to me, then sat down again.

'Turn it over,' he said.
There were some words on the back:

Just as a tree
sheds its leaves
to conserve its life force,
so can we
leave those ways
that no longer serve
our growth.

And like the tree,
which is nourished
by the same leaves
that return
through the earth,
we too can grow
by letting go.

28

Running for the Bus

'So how many copies of the book have you made altogether?' I asked.

'Just the two – though each one is another original version, not a copy as such.'

'When did you make them?'

'I started on them not long after arriving on Diu. Then I sent them to Traikos so he could do the designs before I went to see him on Patmos at the end of the year.'

'And he didn't mind drawing all those leaves again?'

'He's an artist, remember – and he might be rather offended that you didn't notice the new designs,' said Darshan, affecting a serious tone.

I looked at the book again. It was newer than the other one, but my surprise when Darshan had handed it to me had blinded me to this detail.

'What about anyone else who figures out the riddle and comes here to meet you? Are you going to make a copy for them too?'

'That is my intention.'

'But I don't understand why you didn't have some copies printed before you gave the original to Aldo – so you wouldn't have to start from scratch every time.'

'I enjoy the creative process. And I enjoy the challenge – of letting go. To be more precise, letting go of something I know I will never be able to reproduce exactly, thereby opening the possibility of creating something new rather than simply trying to repeat what has gone before – just as it is with each day we live, and every moment of each day.'

I began to leaf through the book. I remembered that the question about the moon moving through the branches was close to the middle, but I didn't come to it until I had almost reached the end. On the penultimate page there had been the question that compared life to a book's unfolding. This time there was the following one:

If I could dance
and forget
the dancer,
sing
and forget
the singer,
play
and forget
the player,
what would there be
between
the moment and me?

I looked at the opposite page.

*How long
does a moment last?*

I checked the last page. It was the same as the one in the original.

'So all the pages are in a different order except the first and the last,' I said.

'That's right.'

We lapsed into silence and the crackling of the fire took over.

'So, now that you are here, my friend, would you like to tell me why you came?' said Darshan.

'There were several reasons, I suppose. First of all, I was curious to meet you. To be honest, there were times when I had my doubts you existed and I thought it might all be some sort of psychology experiment that Aldo was conducting.'

'And what did you imagine its purpose to be?'

'I don't know … maybe to see how much we can be influenced by imaginary people that have been created by others.'

Darshan seemed to hesitate for a split second. 'That's an interesting thought. But I trust you are satisfied that I exist now,' he said, and broke into a smile.

I smiled back at him.

'So what were the other reasons for your coming here?' he asked.

'I also wanted to prove to myself that I could let go of the book.'

Darshan leaned forward and stirred up the fire with a poker.

'And I wanted to find out what you thought I needed to learn,' I said.

'And have you done that?' he asked without looking up.

'That's what we've been talking about, isn't it?'

'It is.' He sat back in his chair and looked at me. 'So now, tell me: what do *you* think you need to learn?'

'I agree with what we said before: I need to detach myself from my desires enough to be able to understand situations more clearly – and see them in a positive light.'

'Is there anything else?'

'Well ... I feel I've had glimpses of how everything's connected and how we can be guided by these connections and feel part of something greater than our individual selves. But they're just like ripples on the surface – with long periods of forgetting in between.'

'So you need to find a way to be a fully conscious part of all that there is?'

'Yes ... And maybe that's how I'll find the silent stream.'

'The silent stream?'

'It's an idea I had about love: that it's a flow of energy from the source of life.'

Darshan looked thoughtful. I hoped he was going to tell me he liked my metaphor. The shutters rattled as the wind sighed outside the window.

'Would you say you have learned to maintain your balance in a relationship?' he asked.

'How do you mean?'

'While you were staying at the guest house on Diu, I couldn't help noticing that your attention was disproportionately focused on the young lady who was with you – to the extent that your behaviour was dictated by her mood. You appeared unable – or unwilling – to free yourself from this attachment, with the result that your true self was being kept prisoner by your desire to keep someone.'

'How did you know that?'

'As I said before, running the guest house gives me the opportunity to study people closely … So, do you feel you have resolved the issue?'

'I think so. I'm in another relationship now, and I don't feel the tension I felt in my previous one. I've learned that wanting someone isn't the same as loving them, and I'm not afraid of losing someone any more – because you can only lose something you had in the first place, but no one can ever belong to you.'

The flames flickered in the hearth. I wondered what Maria was doing … and who she was with … and if she was thinking about me … It seemed I wasn't as relaxed in our relationship as I wanted to believe. There were still times when I experienced feelings of possessiveness, but I was denying this to myself because being possessive didn't fit the image of the person I aspired to be.

But who was this 'I' that didn't accept the person I was at the moment? Was it a higher self, or a judgemental one? If loving someone meant accepting them despite their flaws, then whoever this 'I' was, it was unable to love – which was equally hard for me to accept.

'Can you accept the part of you that doesn't accept yourself?' I said out loud, staring absently at the flames.

'That's an interesting question.'

I turned to look at Darshan. 'It was the first one I read in your book.'

'What was your reaction to it?'

'I didn't know what to make of it, to tell you the truth.'

'How about now?'

'All I know is that I feel more comfortable with the blank I draw from trying to answer it.'

'Then you have seen that a contradiction can bring balance. This is the real meeting place we reach by letting go – not the cave of St John.'

'What do you mean exactly?'

'I am referring to the meeting place between contradictory aspects of yourself: the halfway point between desiring and not desiring. This is your most important task of all: to unify these aspects. But it is not something which is meant to be done only once. It needs to be done throughout your life – whenever a desire is putting distance between you and the moment and threatening to knock you off balance.'

'How can I do it?' I asked.

'Have you ever run to catch a bus?'

'Quite a few times.'

'Tell me about one of them.'

'Actually, I ran for a tram when I was in Calcutta – with my girlfriend. I remember it was on Mahatma Gandhi Street. We saw one leaving, so we ran as fast as we could and managed to jump on – then found out it wasn't the one we wanted.'

'How did you feel when you were running to catch it?'

'We were afraid of missing it, because it was getting late and we weren't sure when the next one would be.'

'So you didn't derive much enjoyment from the situation.'

'Not really.'

'But it was an ideal opportunity to do so.'

'How?'

'If you had not presumed it was the right tram, then instead of worrying about trying to catch it, you could have enjoyed running for it in the knowledge that it might have been the wrong one after all. Running for a bus – or a tram – without caring whether you catch it or not is one of the simplest ways to reach the meeting point between desiring and not desiring … or, in other words, the feeling of desiring while letting go of desiring.'

'OK, but how can you let go if you know for sure it *is* the right one to catch?'

'How can you ever be sure?'

'It's not too difficult: you just check the number,' I said, aware that I was being facetious, yet not knowing why.

'We are not concerned with numbers here. We are concerned with reasons why it could be beneficial for you not to get whatever it is you are chasing. For instance, can you be sure that the bus you are so keen to catch won't be involved in a crash?'

'OK, maybe not … And I suppose if I do miss it, I might bump into someone while I'm waiting for the next one,' I said, remembering my encounter with Traikos at the bus stop in Athens.

'Precisely. So try to picture the scene: you are running for a bus, you remind yourself there is no way of knowing whether it is right for you to catch it or not … and you find the meeting point between desiring and not desiring.'

'As simple as that?'

'Yes. As simple as that. Now, if you can remain there long enough, you will also come to know the meeting time.'

'What's that?'

'The beginning and the end … of who you are.'

My puzzlement must have been evident.

'In that moment you will cease to feel a separate part of the whole, yet you will feel more alive than ever,' explained Darshan.

'I never imagined running for a bus could be a mystical experience,' I said, allowing a note of sarcasm to enter my voice, then immediately regretting it.

Darshan's eyes narrowed. 'What is it that makes one moment different from any other? What are you waiting for in order to have your "mystical experience"?'

'I'm sorry. I just find it hard to believe it could be so simple to experience a higher level of consciousness.'

'Everything is simple once you have learned how to do it. But that doesn't mean the learning process is simple. A lot depends on how much resistance you have inside.'

'I agree that it might be possible to let go and enjoy running for a bus, but what about situations that are more important – when the outcome of something could have a big effect on your life?'

'As I pointed out before, how do you know that the bus isn't going to crash?'

'OK, but it's not very likely. I'm talking about situations where there's a greater risk of something bad happening.'

'I am sure you will have seen that in many cases "something bad" turns out to be not so bad after all … But if you do end up in a situation which seems hopeless, finding that meeting point may be the only thing you *can* do … I believe you have already had a taste of it – earlier tonight when you were outside the cave of St John.'

'Was that why you were late – to see if I could let go?'

'Let's just say I arrived on time.'

I began to feel that the events I had experienced since meeting Aldo on Amorgos were pieces of a jigsaw suspended in time and space. The more I understood how they were connected, the more I was able to see the big picture. But the overall design kept changing as more pieces were added. And there seemed to be no limit to their number. Nor did they need to be added in chronological order: the next piece could be an event which had happened prior to the one I regarded as the first piece – as was the case when Darshan made me aware that I had knocked the book of questions off the bookcase in his guest house more than a year before meeting Aldo. Hence it would be more appropriate to refer to the first piece as the central piece, from which the jigsaw could expand into both the future and the past …

'Now, my friend, perhaps we should call it a night,' said Darshan. 'Just remember: the only thing that is certain in life is that nothing is certain – not even this. So the sooner you feel at ease with uncertainty, the better.'

I thanked him for his hospitality and we arranged to meet the following afternoon.

When I left the cottage, the wind had dropped and the crescent moon had risen. It appeared to be moving with me through the trees as I followed the trail through the pine forest. Once again I remembered Darshan's question about the moon accompanying you with every step you take, which was on one of the pages Aldo had wanted to read to his grandfather before he died. I thought of Aldo's grandfather, and a shiver darted down my spine as I sensed our connection through time – from the moment of that casual remark about writing a book of questions which he had made to Aldo's father long before Aldo and I were born … to this moment I was living in the moonlight of a new millennium.

29

Is It Wise to Desire to Be Wise?

On New Year's Day I met Darshan outside a café in the port. (This time he arrived punctually.) Once again he seemed more suitably attired for summer than winter.

'Have you been to Kastelli?' he asked.

'Where?'

'The ancient acropolis.'

'No. Where is it?'

'I'll show you.'

We set off along the main road and followed it out of the central area of the port, then turned left down a side road before climbing some steps that zigzagged through the whitewashed houses and took us to a sloping path which joined an asphalt road. A rocky hillside strewn with bushes rose to our left and descended to the port on our right. Before long the land levelled off. We turned onto a gravelly track that ran past some wooden shacks with hen coops attached. Nearby, goats stood munching grass in relative freedom, their movement restricted by the tethering of a front and back leg. The hens were too busy pecking away at the ground to notice us, but several of the goats looked up and regarded us curiously.

Beyond the shacks was a stone wall bordering some fields. At this point the track veered left to run alongside it. When we reached the wall, Darshan pointed out the ancient acropolis – standing in ruins on top of an imposing outcrop in the distance. We paused to set our destination in our sights, then continued on our way. The only sounds were the crunching of stones underfoot and the humming of the wind in my ears.

We stayed on the track until we came to a gap in the wall, then cut across a field before passing between some farm buildings and following a winding path that ascended gradually through an open area of rocky ground. The final ascent was steep, yet Darshan negotiated it with youthful agility. We passed a little white church and climbed onto the windswept ridge of the outcrop, from where the land fell away to form the craggy cliffs that marked the shoreline.

The site appeared to be no more than an assortment of stones in heaps of various sizes, most of which were partly obscured by the patches of thorny shrubs that had long since invaded the terrain, but a closer look revealed traces of walls and buildings.

'All that is built on earth will fall,' said Darshan as I surveyed the ruins. 'It's worth reminding ourselves of this from time to time.'

We sat down on the remnants of a flight of steps and took in the panoramic view of the neighbouring islands.

The royal blue of the sea and the azure of the sky faded into a whitish haze that masked the horizon; the constant crashing of the waves on the rocks below was like the distant roar of a fast-flowing river. As I looked and listened, I lost touch with my thoughts …

The clear skies and bright sunshine were reminiscent of summer, though the wind wasn't so obliging. I was therefore glad of my leather jacket. But Darshan wasn't even wearing his cardigan.

'Aren't you cold?' I asked.

'No.'

'Don't you ever feel the cold?'

'I feel it – but it doesn't make me cold.'

'How do you mean?'

'I am aware of it, but I don't become it. It's rather like meeting an angry person: you may feel their anger, but that doesn't mean you have to become angry yourself – though this is what happens in many cases.'

'But feeling the cold is a physical sensation,' I said.

'Are you sure it is purely physical?'

I recalled what had happened while I had been waiting for Darshan outside St John's cave – how my perception of the cold was overridden by the wave of well-being that washed over me when I came to terms with the situation.

'And what about anger?' said Darshan. 'Is that purely mental? You only have to look at someone when they are angry to see that isn't the case.'

'OK, I take your point. But how do you do it? How do you block out the cold?'

'By not trying to. I don't resist it, because I don't see it as something unpleasant. It is simply an aspect of life – one of the many intriguing things to experience in this world.'

I pulled up the collar of my jacket to shield my neck from the wind. I couldn't say I was intrigued by the cold.

'Can I ask you some things about your book?' I said.

'By all means.'

'Is it really true that you can ask a question, then open it at random and find some words that will help you?'

'What do you think?'

'It certainly seemed like that many times. But there was often the thought at the back of my mind that if I tried hard enough, I'd be able to find a connection between any page and what I asked – though I didn't necessarily see that as a bad thing, since I thought it could still get me thinking about things in a different way.'

Darshan appeared to be considering what I had said – either that or giving me time to do so myself.

'What I will tell you,' he began, 'is that if you can achieve the right state of mind before opening the book, you should be able to feel a connection between your question and the words you see on the page. But you won't have to try hard to do this, since feeling requires no effort.'

'What state of mind do I need to have?'

'What we discussed last night: the one between desiring and not desiring. Otherwise it will just be a case of trying to get the answer you want – which defeats the object of asking in the first place. A sincere question carries no expectations regarding the answer – not even the expectation of receiving one.'

'But how does it work? How is a randomly chosen page able to give you guidance?'

'With the right state of mind, there is no such thing as a randomly chosen page. If you can attain this state of mind, you will be in tune with everything around you, and you will be able to tap into the wisdom of the universe.'

Darshan closed his eyes. I expected him to open them after a few moments, but he didn't. I closed mine too. The distant waves seemed closer. Their presence grew stronger and stronger until they felt within reach all around me.

But it wasn't long before the sound of the waves receded. My thoughts drifted to the recent days I had spent in England. An image of the homeless man I had met in York came into my mind, carrying the echo of his parting words. I opened my eyes. Darshan was looking at me. I told him about my encounter with the man and his suggestion that I should write a book.

'Would you mind if I wrote the story of how your book came into my hands?' I said.

'Why would I mind?'

'I just thought I should ask, since it would basically be a book about your book.'

'And what is your motivation for writing this book?'

'What do you mean exactly?'

'Exactly what I say: what is your motivation?'

'I want to share the things I've learned – that's all.'

'That's all?' He looked at me intently.

'Yes,' I said, struggling to meet his gaze.

I felt as if he was scrutinizing my innermost thoughts – thoughts that not even I was aware of.

'Let me tell you a story – about another book,' he said. 'There once lived a young man who was a seeker of knowledge. He had heard that somewhere in a remote mountain area lived a wise man who had the answers to all the questions anyone could ask. So he set out to find this man and gain his wisdom. After travelling all day on foot along treacherous mountain paths, he found his home and asked him to be his teacher. The wise man was impressed by the young man's determination, so he agreed and allowed him to stay.

'Every day the young man recorded what he had learned, and over the next three years he filled a thick book with the knowledge he accumulated. At the end of the third year, he told the wise man he was ready to return to the world. The wise man advised him to stay longer, but the young man said he felt it was time for him to share his newly acquired knowledge. The wise man said he wouldn't stand in his way if his mind was made up, so the young man set off with aspirations of becoming a revered teacher. All he took with him was a leather bag containing his book, some food and water, and a box of matches.

'Several hours into his journey it began to rain. At first it was only a drizzle, but the further he went, the heavier it became. He looked for a place to shelter, and in the distance he spotted a tree by the path. There was someone lying underneath it. When he got closer, he saw that it was a frail-looking man. The man was in great pain as he had broken his leg – he had slipped and fallen whilst trying to climb a rocky hillside. The young man asked him if he lived in the mountains. He said he didn't but was on his way to find a wise man who he had heard lived in the area. He explained that he had been looking for a shortcut up the hillside because he had realized his journey was going to take longer than he had expected and he wasn't equipped for travelling very far.

'In spite of all the young man's new knowledge, he didn't know how to heal a broken leg, though he imagined the wise man would be able to. He would have to go and get him, but it would be night-time before they returned and the injured man could suffer from hypothermia if he stayed outside in the cold in his wet clothes.

'The young man searched for a better place to shelter and found a little cave hollowed out of a rock face. He helped the injured man to reach it, then went to gather some wood to make a fire. But he couldn't find any dry pieces. The only thing he could make a fire with was the paper from his book, which he had been able to keep dry inside his bag. What should he do? He couldn't leave the man without a fire, but how could he destroy three years' worth of knowledge? He would never be able to remember everything he had recorded. It also occurred to him that if the book was destroyed to save the injured man and the wise man healed his broken leg, this man would then stay with the wise man and might end up with more knowledge than he had.'

Darshan paused. 'So what do you think he did?'

'I don't know.'

'What would you have done?'

'I'd have used the book to make a fire and then gone to get the wise man.'

'Are you sure?' Darshan gave me a searching look.

'OK – that's what I like to think I'd have done, but I admit it might not have been so easy to give up the book.'

'That's exactly how the young man felt.'

'So what did he do?'

'He managed to find some pieces of wood that weren't so wet, and put them in a pile within reach of the injured man. He selected a few, then tore the last page out of his book to start a fire – he chose this one because it was still fresh in his mind. The flames soon died, so he tore out the penultimate page and tried again to get the fire going. This time he had more success, but the damp wood still didn't burn easily. He would have to leave more paper with the injured man. He couldn't bring himself to leave the whole book, so he began tearing out pages and stuffing them into his bag – and ended up removing over half the book. He left the remaining part, but didn't tell the man what it contained; he just said it was of personal value to him and he should try to use as few pages as possible. Nor did he say that the person he was going to fetch was the wise man; he told him it was a healer who lived in the mountains.

'He gave the box of matches and most of his food and water to the injured man, then set off back to the home of the wise man. It was late in the evening by the time he arrived. After he had changed into some dry clothes, they headed down the mountain with the wise man's donkey, taking it in turns to ride on it so they could catnap during the journey. They reached the cave a few hours before dawn.

'Can you guess what they found?'

'What?'

'The man was lying dead next to the remains of a little fire that had long since gone out.'

'Had he been killed by a wild animal?'

'No – he brought his death on himself.'

'How?'

'By not using the book on the fire. He was curious about its content, so he looked inside before tearing out any pages and realized it contained special knowledge – the type he was seeking. He couldn't bear to destroy it, so he tried – and failed – to keep the fire going with only the damp firewood.'

'But the young man was also to blame for what happened,' I said, 'since he should have left the whole book behind and told the man to use as much paper as he needed. And he could have told him what the book contained and that it was the wise man he was going to fetch so that the other man would have known he'd have the chance to get the same knowledge himself.'

'Indeed.' Darshan fixed his gaze on me, and for a moment I felt as if I was the young man in the story.

'How did the young man react when he saw that the other man was dead?'

'His first feeling was one of relief at seeing the rest of his book intact – followed immediately by remorse. But the wise man had noted his initial reaction and said: "You are not ready to return to the world, because you never truly left it."'

'What did he mean exactly?'

'That the young man was still ruled by his ego – trying to get knowledge from others so that he could show the world what he knew. But this kind of knowledge is second-hand. It is not "pure". Pure knowledge cannot be acquired from someone else – or lost or forgotten. It can only be gained through direct knowing.

'Self-knowledge is such knowledge, and a person who has gained this could never treat another without care or respect. And they would certainly never choose to do anything that might endanger someone's life.'

'So if you know yourself, it means you're a good person?'

'Being a good person is not the issue here,' said Darshan. 'If you truly know yourself, it means you have become a fully conscious part of the whole. You are aware of your true nature and therefore know you are neither a good person nor a bad person … Imagine you are a cloud. If you know what you are, you know you are part of the sky – an inseparable part. It follows that you would never seek to harm another cloud, since you would be harming another part of what you are. Nor would you seek to harm yourself, as you would also be harming what you are part of.

'So,' he continued, 'by all means write your book. But don't lose your way to self-knowledge through your desire to demonstrate knowledge to others – or share it, as you say. It is important to recognize the difference between wanting to share knowledge and wanting to show that you have it.

'When you are truly living what you have learned, you will no longer have the need to talk or write about it – at least not out of a desire to prove anything to anyone, since this desire only arises from the need to prove something to yourself. The day you find you are living your book will be the day you are able to let go of it.'

While I reflected on Darshan's words, the descending sun passed seamlessly through shades of orange and red before sinking into the surrounding blue.

'But if I record all this in a book, it means I'll reveal your meeting place. And then what will happen if a crowd of people turn up to see you on New Year's Eve?'

'A crowd?' said Darshan, raising his eyebrows. 'Maybe no one will read your book – that's assuming you write it, of course. And even if someone does read it, they won't necessarily want to meet me.'

'I'm just speaking hypothetically.'

'And worrying hypothetically … But if someone *was* willing to go to all that trouble to meet me, there would probably be a good reason for it – in which case I would be interested in meeting them too.'

I was starting to think it might not be such a good idea to write a book after all. I wasn't sure if I was ready to share Darshan with complete strangers.

As the light began to fade from the day, the wind became stronger. I wished it could blow away the tangle of thoughts in my head.

'I have a request to make regarding your prospective book,' said Darshan.

I waited for him to elaborate.

'I would like to request that, should you ever want to publish it, you will not attempt to do so while I am still on this earth.'

'Why not?'

'So I can continue my game of "pass the parcel" without the risk of being interrupted.'

'I thought you said you'd be interested in meeting someone who wanted to meet you.'

'One or two people would be fine. But three would be a crowd. And trying to have a conversation with a crowd isn't something that appeals to me.'

The idea of having to wait indefinitely to publish my book while at the same time not wanting that day to come brought my train of thought to a standstill.

I remained caught up in my concerns until Darshan suggested we should head back as it would soon be dark. With the light rapidly growing dimmer and the wind giving chase, we made our way down the outcrop and retraced our steps through the shadowy fields. Night was already upon us by the time we reached the side road which joined the main road to the port. We came to a halt under a solitary street lamp near the junction.

I had been hoping I would be able to meet Darshan again the following day, but he said he was leaving early in the morning to go to Ikaria, a nearby island where Traikos was giving an exhibition of his artwork. He planned to stay there for several days before going to Athens to take his flight to India. When I asked if I could see him the next time he came to Patmos, he reminded me of his arrangement to meet whoever was in possession of the book of questions. He had taken it for granted that I had passed it on, but I wanted him to know I had kept my side of the agreement, so I told him about Laura. I mentioned the possibility of her not being able to solve the riddle, which would mean he wouldn't be meeting anyone on Patmos the following year.

'In that case, I shall meet no one,' he said.

I couldn't hide my disappointment.

His face was serious, though his eyes shone with compassion. 'If our paths are meant to cross again, you can be sure they will.'

But his words were of little comfort to me as we shook hands and said goodbye.

30

The Silent Stream

The following morning I woke up with a head full of questions. Why was Darshan reluctant to meet me again on Patmos after being so willing to spend time with me on this occasion? Had he really been interested in helping me? Maybe he had just been using me for his own amusement, gaining satisfaction from seeing me fall under his spell.

And if he ran the guest house on Diu, how likely was it that he would travel all the way to Patmos every year to see if a stranger was 'ready to learn what they needed to'? It sounded more like the work of a psychologist. Could that be it? Was he in reality a psychologist carrying out a study of some kind? I had previously thought Aldo might be doing this with the aim of seeing how willing we are to believe in imaginary figures created by others, but since my idea had been based on the non-existence of Darshan, it had obviously proved to be unfounded once I had met him. Yet now it occurred to me that Darshan could still be an 'imaginary figure': a persona created by his real self for the purposes of the experiment he was conducting.

If that was the case, should I assume Aldo was his research assistant? Or had he, too, been an unwitting subject? But even if he had, that would only make two of us, and as it was only possible to recruit one subject per year, this would make for a long-drawn-out experiment … unless there were other books of questions with different meeting places encoded in them and Darshan spent his time travelling to these places to meet whoever figured out how to find him.

One thing appeared to be clear, though: if Darshan was playing a role, it was that of a guru figure. Perhaps his study was an investigation into how keen we are to seek out such people and how we can be influenced by them – and how we could lose our way by trying to copy them. I remembered his story about the wise man. I couldn't deny that it reflected my hope of meeting a person like that as well as my desire to become one myself … But what about Darshan? Was he truly wise, or did he merely aspire to be? Maybe it was true that he had run a bookshop, and years of reading had given him a wealth of 'second-hand' knowledge – plus the desire to live out some of his fantasies.

I went onto the balcony to clear my head in the sea breeze and enjoy the scenery, but my questions pursued me, clouding my view. Was Darshan a genuine man of wisdom selflessly sharing his knowledge, a researcher playing a role, or a would-be guru with delusions of grandeur? Whoever he was and whatever activity he was engaged in, had my involvement with him come to an end? And had he really gone to Ikaria? I decided to find out for myself.

It was around eleven o'clock when I set off in the direction of Traikos' cottage. The air was crisp and a blustery wind was running amok amongst the bushes by the roadside. With my long stride I soon reached the little white church at the top of the hill, which overlooked the port in the distance. A single ship was approaching, while an armada of clouds sailed across the sky to keep the sun at bay – though every now and then it managed to burst through and scatter its beams over the restless waves.

I wondered if the approaching boat was the one Darshan was supposed to be taking: maybe it had been delayed. I speeded up, and when I got to the port I looked across at the line of passengers waiting on the quayside. Darshan wasn't among them. By now the boat was docking and I was able to see its list of destinations. Ikaria wasn't one of them. I had a quick look up and down the waterfront, then went to check inside the handful of cafés that were open, but I didn't see Darshan anywhere so I continued on my way.

I turned onto the main road to Hora and began my steady climb. My mind was now racing with anticipation, and when I arrived at the point where the old stone footpath met the road, I was hardly aware of the distance I had covered. I followed the path until I came to a narrow trail that branched off into the pine forest. Even though it had been dark when I had gone to the cottage before, I felt confident that this was the way. But my stride had become less purposeful. The further I went, the more I doubted the wisdom of my actions. I hadn't even thought about what I was going to say to Darshan if he did turn out to be there.

I reached the cottage. The wind had dropped, leaving a hush in the air. The cypress near the garden gate cast its shadow over me. It stood motionless and silent. The guardian of a mystery. I opened the gate and walked up the gravel path, feeling like a trespasser. As I approached the front door, I noticed an envelope attached to it. My name was on it. I had the sensation I was being watched. I scanned the pine trees beyond the garden wall to my left and right. Not a soul in sight. It had probably just been my imagination. I pulled the envelope off the door and opened it. Inside was a piece of paper bearing some words written in dark green ink in a familiar style of calligraphy:

Are you here
to know
who I am,
or to be
what you are?

Are you here
to be
what I am,
or to know
who you are?

I quickly read the questions, then knocked on the door. I waited a few moments and tried again. My knocks were met with empty echoes. Once more I looked in the direction of the pine trees, half expecting Darshan to appear. They stood undisturbed, their boughs laden with silence.

I had to admit it seemed fitting that Darshan had left me with a couple of questions – particularly as they were related to the thoughts I had been having about him. But my doubts had only surfaced that morning, so how could he have known? Was it evidence of his wisdom, or merely a lucky guess?

I sat on the doorstep and read the questions a second time as the wind began to blow again. The garden gate creaked. I looked up. No one was there. My only company was the cypress tree, swaying with its shadow. It was perfectly content to be what it was – and I was perfectly capable of appreciating it, even though the essence of its existence was a mystery to me …

I remembered my moment of letting go outside the cave of St John, and I felt myself nearing a similar conclusion to the one that had brought me to that point: did it matter if I didn't know who Darshan really was? And besides, how could I tell whether he was wise unless I was too? But I could still benefit from his message. He had already made me aware of my misguided desire to share knowledge without having truly acquired it, and now he appeared to be encouraging me to take things a stage further and 'realize' the knowledge he had spoken of.

I folded the piece of paper to put it in my pocket. There was something written on the back:

> *The river reaches the ocean to know*
> *it must cease to be in order to flow.*

* * *

At midday on January 3rd, I checked out of my room. Vassilis offered to give me a lift to the port, but I had plenty of time and it was a sunny day so I wanted to sit on the beach for a while before going to take my boat.

I was well on my way down the winding road that led to the bay when I heard the whirring of a scooter behind me. Vassilis pulled up and handed me some food in a plastic bag. I hardly had chance to thank him before he rode off.

When I got to the beach, I took off my rucksack and sat down, then opened the plastic bag. Inside, there was a large chunk of local cheese, a loaf of bread and some home-made walnut cake. Even though it was winter, I could still feel the warmth of the sun on my face, so I wedged the bag between a rock and the stone wall behind me to keep it in the shade.

Leaning back against my rucksack, I soaked up the surroundings. A cloudless sky stretched down to meet the placid blue sea, which sparkled in the sunlight as it lapped gently along the sandy shoreline. The drooping branches of the tamarisk trees swayed lazily in the soft breeze; the only sound was the rippling of the waves. I wanted to capture the scene and preserve it in my mind so I could revisit it whenever I needed an escape from my thoughts ...

I spent the next hour or so looking through the notes I had made of my conversations with Darshan. I felt I hadn't shown him enough appreciation for all the hours he had spent with me and for the patient manner in which he had listened to me – not to mention the words of insight he had imparted. I had behaved as though I was entitled to take up as much of his time as I wanted, and when we had said goodbye, all I had been concerned about was his apparent reluctance to meet me again.

Why couldn't I have been more aware of my behaviour? I still had a long way to go on my road to self-knowledge. Would I ever become a fully conscious part of the whole – like a river becoming part of the sea?

Could I 'cease to be in order to flow'?

As the afternoon wore on, I became so absorbed in my thoughts that I ended up losing track of time and leaving the beach much later than I had intended. There was still time to get to the port before my boat left, but it would no longer be the leisurely stroll I had envisioned.

My hurried steps aroused the interest of a donkey in a nearby field. It flicked its tail and brayed when I passed by, as if encouraging me to go faster ... or telling me to slow down: I had nearly reached the top of the hill when I realized I had forgotten the bag of food that Vassilis had given me. I considered not going back for it, but there was always the chance he would come across it and think I had been ungrateful. Plus I was going to need some food for my journey. I returned to the beach to get it, then climbed the hill again as fast as I could.

When I got to the top I saw my boat arriving and broke into a run. The road wasn't very steep – it wound its way steadily downhill to join the main road that led to the port – though that didn't stop me from almost tripping over as I took a bend too quickly. Regaining my balance, I was struck by a thought: it wouldn't be the end of the world if I missed the boat. Maybe there was a reason why I wasn't supposed to take it. I remembered what Darshan had said about running for a bus, and slowed down slightly.

The tension in my chest dropped away, leaving space for my lungs to expand. In the distance the ship's flag fluttered in the breeze that was now blowing through the window of my mind. I looked beyond the harbour, reached across the waves, and touched the meeting point of sky and sea. I breathed in the brilliant blue all around … and slipped into the silent stream.

BV - #0129 - 291124 - C0 - 198/129/28 - PB - 9781917056298 - Matt Lamination